Highlander Tempted

Courageous Highland Hearts
Book Two

Jayne Castel

WINTER MIST PRESS

All characters and situations in this publication are fictitious, and any resemblance to living persons is purely coincidental.

Highlander Tempted, by Jayne Castel

Published by Winter Mist Press

ISBN: 978-0-473-61600-7 (paperback)

Edited by Tim Burton
Cover design by Winter Mist Press
Cover photography courtesy of www.shutterstock.com
Dagger vector image courtesy of www.pixabay.com

Visit Jayne's website: www.jaynecastel.com

Will she ever have her own 'Happy Ever After'? A disfigured chieftain, a match-making lady—and the friendship that turns into a once-in-a-lifetime love.

Neave Munro prides herself on her ability to solve other people's problems. After helping her elder sister and husband reconcile, she decides to assist a friend in need as well. Only, he seems reluctant to accept her help.

John Mackay lost an eye and his right hand in battle years earlier. Despite that he is still a warrior of renown, he believes no woman will want a 'maimed' husband. He watches a chieftain's beautiful daughter from afar but has no intention of ever approaching her—until Neave, a lady who has become a good friend, comes up with a plan.

But the path to true love is never smooth, and Neave's task turns out to be more difficult than she expects. And when an unwanted suitor starts to stalk her, Neave must turn to John for help.

Suddenly, the lines between friendship and love become blurred. Has Neave, in her quest to help John find love, ruined her own chance at happiness?

HIGHLANDER TEMPTED is Book Two of the Courageous Highland Hearts series. This steamy and emotional follow-up to Jayne Castel's bestselling Stolen Highland Hearts series follows the lives of four battle-hardened Highland warriors and the courageous sisters who capture their hearts.

Historical Romances by Jayne Castel

DARK AGES BRITAIN

The Kingdom of the East Angles series
Night Shadows (prequel novella)
Dark Under the Cover of Night (Book One)
Nightfall till Daybreak (Book Two)
The Deepening Night (Book Three)
The Kingdom of the East Angles: The Complete Series

The Kingdom of Mercia series
The Breaking Dawn (Book One)
Darkest before Dawn (Book Two)
Dawn of Wolves (Book Three)
The Kingdom of Mercia: The Complete Series

The Kingdom of Northumbria series
The Whispering Wind (Book One)
Wind Song (Book Two)
Lord of the North Wind (Book Three)
The Kingdom of Northumbria: The Complete Series

DARK AGES SCOTLAND

The Warrior Brothers of Skye series
Blood Feud (Book One)
Barbarian Slave (Book Two)
Battle Eagle (Book Three)
The Warrior Brothers of Skye: The Complete Series

The Pict Wars series
Warrior's Heart (Book One)
Warrior's Secret (Book Two)
Warrior's Wrath (Book Three)

The Pict Wars: The Complete Series

Novellas
Winter's Promise

MEDIEVAL SCOTLAND

The Brides of Skye series
The Beast's Bride (Book One)
The Outlaw's Bride (Book Two)
The Rogue's Bride (Book Three)
The Brides of Skye: The Complete Series

The Sisters of Kilbride series
Unforgotten (Book One)
Awoken (Book Two)
Fallen (Book Three)
Claimed (Epilogue novella)
The Sisters of Kilbride: The Complete Series

The Immortal Highland Centurions series
Maximus (Book One)
Cassian (Book Two)
Draco (Book Three)
The Laird's Return (Epilogue festive novella)
*The Immortal Highland Centurions: The Complete
Series*

Stolen Highland Hearts series
Highlander Deceived (Book One)
Highlander Entangled (Book Two)
Highlander Forbidden (Book Three)
Highlander Pledged (Book Four)

Guardians of Alba series
Nessa's Seduction (Book One)
Fyfa's Sacrifice (Book Two)
Breanna's Surrender (Book Three)

Epic Fantasy Romances by Jayne Castel

For Timbo. My husband *and* best friend.

"Rare as is true love, true friendship is rarer."
—Jean de La Fontaine

1

NEAVE'S MISSION

December 25, 1437

LAUGHTER AND MUSIC echoed off the rafters inside the great hall. Neave Munro twirled amongst the dancers, a wide smile stretching across her face.

How she loved Yuletide. It was, without doubt, her favorite time of year.

Sweat trickled between Neave's shoulder blades as she flew around the dance floor. Despite that snow covered the ground outdoors, it was hot and smoky inside the great hall this eve. The aroma of the banquet they'd recently consumed—roast venison and platters of braised vegetables—still hung in the air, blending with the scent of wood smoke, the yeasty smell of ale and mead, and the odor of too many warm bodies crammed into one space.

The music died away, and Neave flashed a grin at the other dancers. Still smiling, she made her way back toward the dais. Approaching the clan-chief's table, she took in the *Bratach Bhan*, the famous Mackay war banner that hung above her. Usually, the white and blue banner, and the array of blades and axes upon the pitted sandstone wall on either side of it, dominated the hall. But not so today.

Neave and her sisters had worked hard with the servants to ensure the great hall looked festive. Banks of candles lined the walls, and boughs of holly and ivy hung from the rafters. Wreaths decorated the long trestle tables.

"Back so soon?" John Mackay of Aberach greeted her when she slipped back onto the bench seat. He then winked. "Eilidh has more stamina than ye, it seems."

Neave snorted before her attention shifted back to the dancers. The musicians in the gallery had started another tune, and her youngest sister, Eilidh, was flitting around the floor like a butterfly, her lovely face flushed with pleasure.

"I've only missed two dances this eve, I'll have ye know," she pointed out, casting the chieftain an arch look. She enjoyed her banter with John, even if many folk within Castle Varrich likely wondered about the nature of her friendship with the laird of Achness.

On her first day here, he'd sat down next to Neave, flashed her a warm smile, and asked her about her journey north from Foulis Castle. From that moment, they'd struck up an easy rapport. Neave missed his company whenever he returned to Achness. Aye, she had her three sisters—Beth, Jean, and Eilidh—but John shared her wicked sense of humor.

"Here, lass." He pushed a cup of ale across to her. "Ye look like ye could do with this."

Indeed, she could. Neave raised the pewter tankard to her lips and took a deep draft. "And why aren't *ye* out there dancing?" she asked, wiping her mouth with the back of her hand.

The clan-chief's cousin cocked an eyebrow before raising his cup of ale in his left hand. John had been away from Varrich for the past months, re-establishing himself as chieftain of Achness now that Niel Mackay had returned to lead the clan.

Tall and lean, although broad-shouldered, John had curly black hair that framed his face and kept falling over his eye patch. His single blue eye—the hue of clear sky— gleamed as he met her gaze. It had taken Neave a while to get used to the fact that he wore a patch over his left eye, obscuring what she imagined was an empty socket from view. He'd lost both a hand and an eye in that fateful battle—Drumnacoub—a few years previous. The Mackays had prevailed that day, but their victory had come at a cost for John Mackay. John's right arm hung by his side, a wooden carved hand replacing the one he'd lost in battle years earlier. However, he tended to keep that hand hidden under the table.

In the months they'd been friends, John had never spoken of that battle, and Neave hadn't questioned him about it. Instinctively, she knew he was sensitive about the scars Drumnacoub had left upon him.

"I'm well into my cups," John announced. "I'd likely fall head-first into the hearth."

Neave rolled her eyes. That was nonsense. In the ten months she'd lived at Castle Varrich, she'd noted that Niel Mackay's cousin could hold his drink.

"Well, perhaps we should provide everyone with another duet later, as we did yester eve," she suggested. The evening before, they'd sung *Taladh Chriosda*— Christ's Child Lullaby—in front of the bonfire in Tongue, the nearby village. The song was one that always reminded Neave of her mother. She'd enjoyed the duet; John Mackay's resonant bass voice had surprised her, as had the discovery that he could sing.

"Perhaps," he replied, favoring her with a coy grin.

Neave peered at him over the rim of her cup. "Ye never told me ye had such a fine voice."

"Well, I'm not one to brag."

She favored him with an arch look. "Evidently."

"I enjoyed singing with ye, Neave," he admitted then. "It's been a while since I sang anything."

Neave nodded. She imagined he hadn't had much time for singing of late. John had been occupied with looking after things until Niel escaped from Bass Rock, the island prison where he'd been incarcerated for a decade. Those had been tumultuous years, in which he'd been forced to deal with treachery from within the clan itself.

Neave had been happy to join the villagers for their celebration of the 'Long Night'. They'd drunk mulled wine and watched the bonfire roar high into the gelid sky.

The only shadow over the evening was that one of the revelers—a big, scary-looking man across the fire—hadn't taken his eyes off her all eve. Wherever she'd gone, his intense gaze tracked her. In the end, Neave had been relieved to return to the castle.

"So," John said after a pause, before nudging her elbow with his. "Do any warriors here for Yuletide catch yer eye? I hear yer sister is eager to see ye wed."

Neave tensed before casting Beth a dark look. Oblivious to her glare, Beth was engaged in an intimate discussion with her husband. The couple gazed into each other's eyes, taking no note of their surroundings. Neave sighed. Despite that she wished Beth wouldn't go around telling folk her younger sister needed a husband, it warmed her to see her and Niel so clearly in love.

It was a happy resolution that Neave was proud to have played a part in—and this morning, Beth had shared the news with her sisters that she was with bairn.

"I'm not interested in suitors at present," Neave replied, shifting her attention back to John. That was true. She was too busy enjoying life at Castle Varrich to be on the hunt for a husband. But now that Beth was wedded, it was Neave's turn, and despite her off-hand response, she knew she'd have to look to her future soon.

But not this eve. Couldn't she just enjoy Yuletide without thinking to what lay ahead?

"What of ye, John?" she asked, suddenly keen to turn the conversation away from herself. "Ye have eight and twenty winters ... it's high time ye found yerself a wife."

His mouth quirked. "Are ye proposing to me, bold wench?"

"No, clodhead ... of course not," Neave replied with a toss of her chin. "Ye can't tell me ye don't have yer eye on a woman?"

John's smile faded, and Neave realized with a jolt that he did.

Turning to him, she met John's eye. "Who is she then?"

He brushed her question aside with a scowl. "No one."

"Is she here?"

The way his face stiffened told her all she needed to know. The object of his desire was indeed present within the great hall. Swinging around, Neave swept her gaze over the crowd once more.

However, there were a number of lasses dancing below, many of them fair. It was impossible to know which one her friend favored.

"Go on, John," she said, turning back to him. "Ye can tell me."

Still scowling, he took a gulp of ale. "If I tell ye, promise to keep it to yerself," he growled.

"I swear."

"Well ... it's Janneth Mackay."

Neave stilled. "Hugh Mackay of Loch Stach's daughter?"

He nodded, his expression turning pained. "God's teeth, Neave ... don't make me regret telling ye."

"Ye won't," she assured him before turning back to survey the dancers.

Janneth Mackay was among them.

As Neave recalled, for she'd met her at Beth and Niel's wedding months earlier, the lass was indeed lovely. Far taller than any of the Munro sisters, and as slender as a willow-reed, with hair the color of sea-foam and huge sea-blue eyes, the chieftain of Loch Stach's only daughter grinned as one of Niel Mackay's warriors swung her around.

Such a jewel would be sought after by many.

Neave swiveled back to John and leaned in, lest anyone seated nearby overhear them. "Have ye approached her?" she whispered.

Horror darkened John's gaze. "Why would I do that?"

"Because how else can ye woo her?"

"I'd rather not do that, Neave ... she won't want me."

Neave stilled, frowning. "Excuse me?"

John muttered an oath under his breath. "Aye, I *am* regretting this."

Ignoring his protest, Neave studied his face.

She'd known John a few months now, yet had never seen this side to him before. To the world, John Mackay appeared confident and totally at ease with himself.

But with women, he was not.

"What do ye mean?" she probed.

John pulled a face. "Janneth is as bonny as a summer's dawn ... why would she be interested in a man missing a hand and an eye?"

Neave's frown deepened. "Do ye really think women so shallow?"

He met her gaze. "No ... but the likes of Janneth can choose from any number of warriors. In her place, I wouldn't pick me."

Neave made an irritated noise in the back of her throat. She couldn't believe she was hearing this from him. "What a load of utter cods," she replied, her tone sharpening. "Ye have much to recommend ye, John. Ye are strong, kind, and noble-hearted. If a woman turns her back on ye for injuries ye acquired while protecting yer clan, then she isn't worth having."

John stared back at her, his gaze widening.

Embarrassed by her outburst, Neave took a fortifying sip of ale. She hadn't meant to go on so—only that she didn't like to see her friend withdraw from women out of fear of rejection.

"Thank ye, Neave," he said softly, a smile molding his lips. "I shall try to remember that."

"Good," Neave huffed, shifting her attention to where Janneth had taken her seat next to Jean. As she looked on, Hugh Mackay's daughter laughed at something Neave's sister had just said.

Neave's gaze then flicked back to Beth and Niel. The couple were now kissing. Beth perched upon her husband's lap, her arms entwined around his neck. Their happiness made warmth seep through Neave.

She hoped that, one day, she too could find a love as powerful as the one her sister and the Mackay clan-chief shared.

And as she watched them, an idea sprang to mind.

I helped Beth and Niel mend their relationship ... perhaps I can help bring John and Janneth together.

Neave pondered the notion, letting it swell and gather in detail in her mind.

Aye, she had a gift for seeing what others needed and assisting them. It gave her pleasure and a sense of accomplishment to see people happy and know that she'd helped them achieve it. And being able to help those she cared for—in a world that could be arbitrary and cruel—brought a measure of relief. Not everyone received a happy end in this life; but with a few nudges from her, John Mackay would.

Looking once more at where Janneth and Jean now chattered happily together, a smile lifted the edges of Neave's mouth.

"Ye are looking mightily pleased with yerself, lass," John said, intruding upon her thoughts. "What are ye plotting?"

He was observing her, a wary expression upon his face. John was a sharp-witted man—very little escaped him—and although she hadn't said a word about the plan that was taking shape in her mind, he clearly suspected she was up to something.

He was right. She'd make it her mission over the coming year to bring Janneth and John together. And if fortune shone upon her, she'd see them wed by next Yule.

"Nothing," Neave said lightly, holding her cup aloft in a toast. She then grinned at him. "Drink up, John ... and ready yerself ... for ye are about to ask the fair Janneth for a dance."

2

NOW IS YER CHANCE

JOHN STILLED, LOWERING his cup of ale. Then, to cover up his discomfort, he scowled. "I'm not going to do that."

Neave held his gaze, her green eyes, flecked with brown, glinting with determination. "Aye … ye are. We can't have ye pining after a lass. The best remedy for unrequited love is action."

John did take a gulp of ale then, although a fit of coughing seized him when it went down the wrong way. "I think unrequited love is a bit strong," he wheezed as Neave slapped him on the back. And it was—aye, Janneth had captured his attention, but he wasn't besotted with her. Over the past year, whenever she'd been present, he found his gaze drawn to her. The woman was indeed bonny, with a sweet nature he found appealing. However, he'd been content to admire her from afar.

Loneliness often visited him this time of year: Yuletide made him reflect on the fact that time was marching on and he remained unwed. But even that hadn't made him approach her.

"Whatever ye wish to call it, ye will only make yerself unhappy if ye don't act," Neave continued, her jaw firming in that stubborn way he'd come to recognize over the past months.

A wry smile tugged his lips then. Folk thought that Beth was the most headstrong of the four Munro sisters. But while the eldest of the sisters definitely possessed a stubborn grit that made her the perfect match for his strong-willed cousin, Neave was irrepressible.

It was usually a trait that John admired in the lass. Yet not this evening.

This eve, after consuming a huge Yuletide banquet and large quantities of ale, he was content to remain seated and watch others dance.

"Go on!" Neave wrested his cup of ale from him before giving John a playful shove. "The music is ending … the next song will begin soon. Now is yer chance!"

"Christ's teeth, woman," John muttered. "Don't ye ever relent?"

"Not until I get my way … now go on, before someone else asks her first."

Rising to his feet, John's gaze shifted to where two of Niel's men looked as if they were heading toward the bench where Janneth was seated, still deep in discussion with Jean. Breac Mackay, the young laird of Balnakeil also appeared to be gravitating in her direction.

Aye, John was about to miss out on his chance.

Muttering another oath under his breath, he made his way off the dais. As he did so, he noted that his legs were steady under him.

Satan's cods, he wasn't nearly drunk enough for this.

He hadn't been lying earlier when he'd told Neave that a woman as lovely as Janneth wouldn't likely be interested in a maimed warrior. Four and a half years had passed since he'd woken after the Battle of Drumnacoub—when the healer had told him that they'd been victorious over the treacherous Neilson Mackays and their Sutherland allies.

But it had been a Pyrrhic victory—for although they'd bested their enemies, the battle had exacted a devastating toll on the Mackays of Varrich. John had been maimed, and in the aftermath, the clan-chief, Angus-Dow Mackay, had been murdered. A skulking Sutherland bowman had struck him down while he searched for his dead kin. Of course, the aging clan-chief had been an easy target. He hadn't been well enough to fight in that battle, and had instructed his men to carry him down to the battlefield once the fighting was done.

John had never considered himself a vain man, yet his loss of a hand and an eye embarrassed him. He wore a patch over his left eye, an adornment that Neave said made him look like a pirate, and he strapped on a wooden hand to the stub of his wrist. Over the years, he'd learned to fight as well with this left hand as he'd once done with this right—it had been a hard-won struggle at first, yet he'd managed.

All the same, embarrassment swept over him, hot and prickling, as he stopped in front of Janneth, arriving just ahead of the three other men. The lass halted her conversation with Jean and raised her chin, her blue eyes widening when they settled upon him.

John's pulse kicked up a notch. Curse Neave and her foolish ideas. He was about to be rejected.

Around them, the music died away.

Clearing his throat, John favored the lass with a smile. "Would ye care to dance, Lady Janneth?"

A pause followed. It was only a heartbeat or two, yet to John, it seemed an eternity. Suddenly, it felt as if every gaze in the great hall of Castle Varrich now rested upon him.

John started to sweat. How strange it was that he could deal with death and violence without flinching, but quailed at asking a bonny lass to dance.

A gentle smile curved Janneth's pink lips. "Aye, John … of course," she replied, her voice low and melodious.

And with that, she rose gracefully to her feet, nodded to Jean, and glided toward the dance floor.

Stunned, John watched her go.

He'd been braced for a polite refusal, followed by an excuse of how her feet were sore. Instead, she seemed happy to dance with him.

"John?" Jean's voice snapped him out of his reverie. He blinked, his attention shifting to where Neave's younger sister frowned at him. "The music's started … ye'd better join her" —she nodded toward where the other men still hovered— "before someone else does."

Taking the hint, John nodded, swiveled on his heel, and followed Janneth.

He enjoyed the dance, and the next one too, for Janneth was gracious enough to accept a second invitation. Fortunately, neither of the dances required them to hold hands—the left one wasn't a problem, yet he didn't want Janneth to have to grasp his wooden claw. As usual, he wore a long-sleeved lèine that he deliberately let fall over his false hand.

He was loath to let Janneth touch it. What if she found it repulsive?

The music was lively, and John was grinning by the time he thanked Janneth and allowed Breac Mackay to cut in.

Making his way back to the dais, he also marked the wide, slightly smug, smile stretched across Neave Munro's impish face.

Not for the first time, it struck him how comely his friend was. When Neave smiled, her right cheek dimpled. She wore her chestnut-brown hair loose. It fell in heavy waves over her shoulders, the color contrasting against the crème-colored kirtle she wore. Small and slender, with a heart-shaped face that was often creased into an expression of mischief, John had caught the longing looks some of the clan-chief's men favored her with.

However, Neave seemed oblivious.

Maybe that was why they'd become fast friends. Neave was a woman without artifice. Among the four sisters, she and Eilidh, the youngest, were perhaps the bonniest, yet none of them had been brought up to regard their looks as a way to gain what they wanted. Eilidh was too shy for that, and Neave too vivacious. It made her refreshing company.

If John were honest, he'd noticed Neave the first day she'd arrived at Castle Varrich. Yet her straightforward way with him, when he'd been seated next to her later on, had let him know that she wasn't interested in being wooed.

Instead, she wanted his friendship—and John had been happy to give it.

He didn't have any living siblings. Both his younger sister and brother had died in childhood, and although he was close to his cousin Niel these days, he hadn't gotten the chance to spend much time with him before his incarceration at Bass Rock.

"Not just a gifted singer … but a fine dancer too," Neave greeted him, still smiling, when John slid onto the bench seat next to her and lowered himself down. "What other hidden talents do ye have?"

John snorted. "Och, ye do go on, Neave." He then nudged her with his elbow. "Pass me that jug of ale, lass … dancing is thirsty work."

Neave nodded, handing over the earthen jug and watching as he refilled his cup. "Well?"

John noted the hint of impatience in her voice and swallowed a smile.

"Well, what?" he said, feigning innocence.

"How did ye fare?"

John shrugged and raised the cup to his lips, taking a long draft. Indeed, dancing did give a man a thirst. "Ye saw for yerself."

"Aye, but did ye speak to her?"

John cocked an eyebrow. "Not really … the music was too loud."

Neave huffed impatiently. "That won't do … ye must make sure ye remedy that once she returns to her table."

"Neave," John warned, his voice lowering. "I appreciate ye giving me the kick in the arse I needed earlier … but enough." His gaze fused with hers. "I don't need any further assistance."

Her brows knitted together. "But—"

"Ye mean well, but ye need to let me be now. I can conduct my own affairs."

Neave's pretty mouth pursed. "And what *are* ye planning to do?"

"Nothing for the meantime," he growled. "I'm going to drink my ale and enjoy the festivities, as should ye."

John's gaze went then to where Breac Mackay was swinging Janneth around. The lass's pale blond hair billowed behind her like a flag.

"I'm surprised Breac Mackay had the nerve to cut in," Neave murmured, leaning close as if afraid someone might overhear her. "Janneth's father can't stand him. I heard Hugh talking to Niel earlier ... he's furious the clan-chief invited Breac and Iver to attend Yule with us all."

John nodded, glancing over at where Hugh Mackay sat, farther down the table. And as he'd expected, the chieftain of Loch Stach wore a scowl upon his face. "Aye," he murmured. "He looks like someone just pissed in his porridge."

"I know the Mackays of Balnakeil and Dun Ugadale turned against Angus Mackay once," Neave continued. "But that was years ago ... can't Hugh let the past lie?"

John huffed a sigh. "It doesn't matter ... ye know how we Highlanders are. We nurse our grudges like bruises."

Neave met his eye squarely then, in that direct way he'd never encountered in any other woman. "*Ye* aren't like that, John."

His mouth quirked. "Well, I'm not as old as Hugh ... maybe resentment creeps upon a man later in life."

Neave gave a soft snort. "Ye've dealt with uprisings within the clan too ... yet all that nastiness with the Neilson Mackays didn't embitter ye."

John's smile faded. "Aye, but I have nothing to do with them these days ... after Drumnacoub, we cut them off from the clan."

Considering this, Neave took a sip from her cup. "And so relations within the Mackays are well again?"

"Aye ... it seems so." Glancing back at Neave, he found her watching him intently. "But it pays never to be complacent," he added. "Niel knows he must never take loyalty for granted ... the way his father did."

The sound of a woman's laughter reached him then, and he focused on the dance floor once more. Janneth was certainly enjoying her circle dance with Breac. Seeing the joy on her face as the swarthy young chieftain twirled her around him, John reflected that *he* hadn't made her laugh like that.

His chest tightened then. Janneth was a kind-hearted woman. It was likely she'd agreed to dance with him out of sympathy. The well-being that had settled over him after dancing with the lass ebbed, leaving him feeling oddly chilled, despite that it was overly warm inside the great hall.

He might feel lonely at times these days, but at least it spared him humiliation.

3

ST. STEPHEN'S

"PERHAPS WE SHOULD have left this visit till tomorrow," Neave muttered between gritted teeth. "The wind is cold enough to freeze the very marrow of yer bones."

"These cakes will be stale tomorrow," Jean replied, stubbornness lacing her voice. "And there are plenty of empty bellies that will appreciate them."

Neave stifled a sigh. Her sister was right, of course—it was St Stephen's, the day after Yule, and it was tradition to give gifts to the poor. Only, it had been a shock to emerge from the sheltering curtain walls of Castle Varrich into the teeth of a vicious wind. It drove straight through the layers of fur and wool she'd donned before departing.

She drew up her fur-lined hood, from where it had blown back, setting her jaw against the chill. The two sisters were making their way down the icy path below the castle. It was a decent walk to their destination, Tongue village, and the sisters carried two heavy baskets of left-over honey cakes from the banquet of the day before.

After all the over-indulgence, it had been a relief initially to leave the keep and stretch her legs. But with the slick stones making the path perilous, and the keening wind, Neave wished she were seated by the fire in the women's solar, as Beth and Eilidh would be at present.

Nonetheless, those less fortunate than her would be feeling the cold today, and it seemed only right that they shared cakes with them.

Heads bent, the two sisters picked their way down the path before taking the road through fallow fields toward the village itself. The dark soil was frozen in the mid-winter, but come spring, lines of kale, turnips, and cabbages would turn the fields green. Copses of skeleton trees, their bare branches outlined against the smoke-colored sky, surrounded the village. The sisters passed by the kirk and its sheltered graveyard before heading to their first stop on the outskirts of Tongue.

Isla, a widow with four bairns under the age of seven, was grateful to see them. She lived in a squat cottage with a thatched roof in need of repair. Unfortunately, Isla had no man to tend to such matters, for her husband had been one of the many warriors who'd followed Niel Mackay to war against the Gunns over six months earlier. He'd fallen at Sandside Bay.

"Thank ye." Isla favored Jean with a tired smile as she took the stack of honey cakes Jean handed her. Neave noted the hollows under the woman's eyes. Isla was only a couple of years older than her, and yet grief, worry, and hard work had aged her of late. "The bairns will enjoy these."

Peering into the smoky recesses of the cottage, Neave caught sight of four children, their pale faces pinched with hunger and cold. A tiny lump of peat burned upon the hearth in the center of the cottage, but Neave noted it barely took the chill off the air. Life had been hard indeed for Isla since she'd lost her man.

"Ye need to put more fuel on the fire, Isla," Jean informed her. "It's too cold indoors."

The widow's gaze guttered. "I would ... but I'm down to my last brick of peat ... we need to make it last."

Jean stilled before her jaw firmed. She then handed Neave her basket so that she could dig into the purse at her belt. Withdrawing a silver penny, she pressed it into Isla's hand. "Here ... this should buy ye enough fuel to keep ye warm until the end of January."

Isla's eyes flew wide. "I can't take yer coin, Lady Jean."

"Aye, ye can … ye must … for the bairns."

Isla's throat bobbed, her gaze flicking from Jean to Neave. Watching her, Neave saw the woman's struggle. Pride warred with need. She didn't want to accept Jean's charity, and yet she knew what refusing the silver penny would mean for her children.

Long moments passed before Isla's mouth compressed. Her fingers closed about the penny, and she favored Jean with a tight nod. "Aye … for the bairns. Thank ye, Lady Jean."

Leaving the widow's cottage, the sisters ventured farther into the village. As they walked, Neave cut Jean a sidelong glance. "Careful, Jeanie," she murmured. "I know ye mean well, but not everyone appreciates ye being so heavy-handed with yer goodwill."

Jean glanced her way, frowning. "Isla required help, and I gave it," she replied, her voice tight.

"Aye, and yer kind heart does ye credit. All the same, remember that Isla and others in the same position have their pride." Neave paused then, wary of offending her sister. Jean could be prickly at times. "Just think how ye'd feel."

Jean's face tensed. Her hood had fallen back, and the wind whipped the tendrils of frizzy hair that had escaped her braid across her face. Jean's hair had a will of its own, and even when she attempted to tame it with a severe bun, strands still managed to escape. "I was only trying to aid Isla," she replied, her tone hurt now. She then cast Neave a sidelong glance. "It seems odd, ye giving me this advice."

Neave raised an eyebrow. "Why's that?"

"Well, usually, it's ye who pushes her help upon others."

"Is that so?" Neave didn't bother to hide the irritation in her voice.

"Aye … Beth didn't ask for yer assistance … and neither has John Mackay."

Neave frowned at these blunt words—she now regretted telling her younger sister about her plan to bring John and Janneth together. She'd promised John she wouldn't tell anyone about his interest in Hugh Mackay's daughter—but her sisters didn't really count … did they?

"Ye like to stick yer nose in other folk's lives," Jean plowed on, "so why shouldn't I?"

"I'm not 'sticking my nose' in. I merely 'help' them get the happiness they deserve."

"Really? If I recall, yer *meddling* nearly chased Laila away when Da first showed interest in her."

Neave clenched her jaw. She hated it when one of her sisters brought that subject up. It was true: she hadn't taken kindly to her father seeking a new wife—even though he'd mourned their mother deeply after her passing. She might have said one or two things initially to Laila to put her off, and now cringed to remember it. Her behavior wasn't something she was proud of, especially as she adored her stepmother these days and was glad her father had married her.

However, at the time, she'd been jealous that George Munro wished to start another family, with another wife. It had felt as if he were leaving his old family behind, as if he had no time for his daughters anymore. But after a tearful argument with her father—the weeping had been on her part, of course—Neave had stopped fighting change.

Silence fell between the two sisters then, before Neave drew in a deep, steadying breath. "I'm not proud of how I treated Laila in the beginning," she admitted finally. "But I learned from it." Her gaze narrowed once more as she pinned Jean with what she liked to call her 'older sister stare'. It was a look that Beth had perfected over the years: the glare that warned a younger sibling to mind her tongue. "Perhaps ye feel ye are in no need of such lessons."

In response, her sister snorted.

Nonetheless, Jean took her advice, and when they delivered the rest of the cakes, she refrained from pushing coin on folk. The last of their stops was at the cottage of an elderly widower. Auld Eoghan was bent and frail, his rheumy eyes peering out from a spider web of wrinkles when he opened the door to the sisters. "Who's this then?" he asked, squinting.

"Good day, Eoghan," Jean greeted him with a smile. "It's Jean Munro. My sister Neave and I have brought ye some Yuletide treats."

The old man smiled back, revealing more gum than tooth. Glancing past him into the interior of the dimly-lit dwelling, Neave noted that the hearth barely gave off a glow. Eoghan was bundled up with furs as if he were outdoors.

"Aye, some honey cakes," Jean replied.

"Ye are a sweet lass," Eoghan said, his bony hands taking the cakes. Shuffling back from the door, he placed them on a bench under the shuttered window. "Do ye want to come in ... I can warm ye both a cup of mead?"

"Aye, that sounds wonderful," Neave spoke up. In truth, her fingers, toes, and the tip of her nose were all numb from cold. She desperately needed to get out of the biting wind.

Indoors, the sisters perched on low stools while Eoghan heated some mead in an iron pot over the glowing coals.

"Can I help, Eoghan?" Jean asked, fidgeting on her seat as she watched the elderly man fumble with the cups.

"No, lass ... I can manage."

"B—" Jean began, only to be cut off by a sharp jab to her ribs by Neave's elbow. Cutting her sister a warning look, Neave stifled a sigh of exasperation. Jean just couldn't help herself from interfering.

Frowning, Jean held her tongue for a short while. However, when Eoghan leaned over the fire and started to ladle the warm mead into cups, she cleared her throat. "Would ye like me to put some more peat on the fire?"

"I've run out, lass," Eoghan replied with an apologetic shrug. "I meant to fetch some from the peat dealer this morning, but my bones are too stiff to make the trip."

"We shall make it for ye," Jean said eagerly.

"Jean—" Neave began, but her sister cut her off with a quelling look. "Ye just give me the coin, and I shall fetch it after my cup of mead," she finished, her tone firm.

Eoghan's lined face creased into a slight frown. "Are ye sure, lass? I don't want to put ye to any trouble."

Jean favored him with a warm smile. "It isn't any trouble at all."

"See," Jean announced as the sisters made their way up the frozen street toward the home of Ian Mackie, Tongue's peat merchant. "Auld Eoghan appreciates my help."

Neave's lips thinned. Jean was in a particularly headstrong mood today, and she didn't feel inclined to argue with her again. As such, she merely shrugged. She was looking forward to returning to the keep and warming herself by a roaring fire. John was still resident at Varrich, although not for much longer. Neave planned to have a private chat with him before he departed for Achness the following morning. They needed to put a plan in place for how he'd woo Janneth. She'd been a trifle frustrated the day before when he hadn't asked her to dance again.

Neave's brow furrowed. *He won't win the lass if he doesn't make an effort with her.*

They were halfway up the street, near the central market square now, when they passed Tongue's forge. The sharp tang of hot iron drifted out into the morning air, a distinctive smell that not even the chill wind could erase. It seemed that the smith was hard at work.

As if summoned, a big man ducked out of the doorway, a bucket in hand, before heading to the stone trough against the exterior wall of the forge.

Neave's heart kicked against her ribs. She recognized him.

The smith was the individual who'd stared so blatantly at her two days earlier. She'd hoped he'd been a visitor to the village for the Long Night festivities, but with a sinking heart, she realized that he lived here.

Glancing up, the blacksmith looked their way. His storm-grey eyes widened when he saw the sisters approach. His gaze skimmed over Jean and rested upon Neave.

Her belly clenched at the naked interest that flared in his eyes. "Good morning," he greeted them. The smith had a rough, drawling voice, and Neave didn't care for his brazen stare.

"Good morning," Jean chimed, oblivious to her sister's discomfort, or the smith's bold gaze. "Don't tell me ye are working on St Stephen's?"

The smith shrugged. He was about to reply when a tall, dark-haired man also ducked outside.

John Mackay flashed the Munro sisters an affable smile. "I'm to blame for putting Roy to work today," he admitted. "My favorite dirk has a nick in the blade."

A relieved sigh gusted out of Neave at the sight of John. For some reason, she always felt secure whenever he was nearby. On the night before Yule, when they'd sung before the bonfire, she'd been relieved the warrior was at her side. If he hadn't been, the blacksmith might have transitioned from staring to approaching her.

The smith cast John a frown, clearly irritated the man had interrupted them. "Aye," he rumbled. "It's almost done."

"There's no rush," John assured him. He then shifted his attention back to Neave and Jean. "Ye've emptied yer baskets, I take it?"

"Aye," Jean replied. "Although we're just making a trip to the peat merchant's … auld Eoghan's run out of fuel for his fire."

John nodded. "Do ye need any help?"

"No … Ian Mackie will have a cart we can use," Jean assured him with a warm smile. Like all the Munro sisters, she'd become fond of the clan-chief's big-hearted cousin. His duties as chieftain had drawn him back to

Achness, but they'd all gotten to know him during the months he'd resided at Castle Varrich.

"All the same, I'll accompany ye," John replied before turning to the smith. "I'll be back shortly, Roy."

The smith shrugged once more. "Suit yerself." Then, casting Neave another lingering look, the big man ducked back inside his forge.

"He's a grumpy one," Jean noted as the three of them continued on their way.

John gave a laugh. "Aye, but Roy Morrison is a talented smith all the same."

Neave stiffened. *Roy Morrison.*

She remembered Beth telling her about how, months earlier, an individual by that name had suggested the Mackays attack Dounreay in order to draw the Gunns into battle. The tale had bothered her. Morrison hadn't asked for anything in return, but she still didn't trust him. He'd wanted Niel Mackay to slaughter the Gunns, had wanted revenge against their clan-chief, and she wondered about his motive.

"So, he was the one who urged Niel to strike at Dounreay?" she asked, anxious to confirm that this was indeed the man Beth had spoken of.

John's expression sobered. "Aye."

"Did Niel ever discover *why* he hated the Gunns so much?" she asked.

John shook his head. "He did ask him again, I believe ... but Roy was evasive. I'd say, whatever it was, the grudge is personal. Perhaps he once worked for the Gunns and was replaced ... however, with his level of skill, I find that hard to believe."

Neave frowned. There were other reasons why a smith might be sent from Castle Gunn. Unease tickled the nape of her neck, and for an instant, she considered confiding in both John and Jean of how the smith had stared at her upon the Long Night's festivities. However, she checked herself.

Men gawked at women all the time; she didn't want to make a fuss over nothing.

4

GAMES OF ARD-RI

"YE ARE QUIET this morning, Neave," John noted. "Is something amiss?"

The pair of them stood a few yards back from where Jean was talking with the peat merchant. From the unyielding tone of Jean's voice, it sounded as if the lass was bartering with Ian Mackie.

Neave shook her head before favoring him with a smile. The bright expression contrasted with the worry that had clouded her hazel-green eyes earlier. "It's just this cold," she said with a dramatic shiver before pulling her fur mantle close. She then glanced up at where the clouds still hung grimly overhead, her nose wrinkling. "If only the sun would show its face."

"It's just the beginning of the cold," John warned her. "More snow is on its way ... hopefully, I'll reach Achness before it arrives." His brow furrowed then. He didn't wish to be delayed. His steward, Murdoch, would be looking after things in his absence, yet now that John had made Achness his permanent residence again, he'd noted work that needed to be done there. The crop rotation in the lower fields had to be discussed with the cottars, for they'd had a poor harvest the previous summer, and the eastern walls were in need of repair. His lands also sat near the Sutherland border, and there had been complaints of sheep rustling that had to be looked into.

Neave cut him a sidelong look. "Have ye spoken with Janneth yet?"

Her abrupt change of subject didn't come as a surprise, and neither did the glint in her eye. Neave Munro was like a hound on the scent once she set her sights on something. Not for the first time—now that his belly wasn't filled with rich food, and his guard lowered by too much strong drink—John definitely regretted revealing his interest in Hugh Mackay's daughter.

He could tell that Neave had taken his situation to heart. She was resolved to play match-maker between him and Janneth, something that made John's scalp itch.

In truth, he'd been happy to admire Janneth from afar. Aye, he was well past the age now when most men were wedded, but that wasn't enough to make him actively pursue the beauty.

"No," he admitted softly, adding enough edge to his voice to hold a warning. He glanced away, noting that Jean and the peat merchant appeared to have reached an agreement. As he looked on, she pressed a coin into the man's palm. "There hasn't been time."

"Well, we must make time this afternoon," Neave replied.

He shifted his attention back to his friend before frowning. "I've got a few things to discuss with Niel before my departure tomorrow, and I'm sure Janneth doesn't—"

"Of course Janneth will have time for ye," Neave interrupted him. She flashed John a playful smile. The irrepressible woman then winked. "Just leave it to me, Mackay ... I hear Janneth likes a challenging game of Ard-ri, and I know just the opponent for her."

"Why do I let myself be talked into these things?" John muttered to himself as he left the clan-chief's solar and made his way downstairs to the great hall. For some reason, he found it impossible to deny Neave Munro, even when she was bent on interfering in his life.

After the noon meal, he and Niel had spent most of the afternoon discussing how John planned to use the land the clan-chief had recently gifted him. As a show of gratitude for John's loyalty over the years, Niel had bestowed him the lands of Lochnaver.

It was a generous gift, one that John had never expected.

In reality, John had hoped to linger in the solar with Niel and discuss his growing concerns about the Sutherlands—but Neave had organized for him to play a game of Ard-ri with Janneth in the great hall, and so here he was.

Entering the hall, he saw that—apart from the servants who were setting up trestle tables for supper, which was just over an hour away—the large space was empty.

Save for two women seated at a small table by one of the two enormous hearths either end of the hall.

John made his way toward them, his boots crunching upon dry rushes.

As he neared the table, he saw they'd already set up the Ard-ri board. Ard-ri—High King—was a game he'd been playing since he was a wee lad. Nostalgia pulled at his chest as he recalled perching on his father's knee and listening to him explain the rules.

It was a game of strategy, played upon a grid. One player was the attacker, with eight pieces at their disposal, while the other was the defender, using four pieces to protect their king.

"That's a fine board," he greeted Neave and Janneth with a smile. Indeed, the pieces were all carved from white and blue stone, and the king piece at the center of the board even sat upon a throne.

Janneth favored him with a demure smile. "Aye, it's Da's ... he never travels anywhere without it."

"Here, John." Neave rose from her seat. "I've been keeping this warm for ye."

Janneth's smile faded. "Ye aren't leaving, are ye, Neave?"

Tension coiled in John's belly at the sudden caution he saw in Janneth's eyes. The woman didn't wish to be left alone with him.

Neave, who was in the process of moving away from the table, halted, her gaze darting between the two of them.

John silently cursed her. This was what came from meddling.

"Of course I shall stay," Neave said lightly, although when John looked her way, he saw her gaze wasn't sparkling as it had been earlier. Aye, the lass thought she knew best, but perhaps she should have spoken honestly with Janneth before maneuvering the pair of them into this awkward situation.

Without another word, Neave pulled up a stool while John settled himself in the chair she'd vacated.

Now that he'd glimpsed the reserve in Janneth's eyes, there was little point in making light banter. They might as well get on with the game.

"Neave, can ye take two counters—one white, one blue—and hide them behind yer back?" he asked.

John would have done it if he'd been able to grasp a counter in his right hand.

Nodding, Neave stood up, moved to the table, and did as bid.

John then met Janneth's eye. "Left or right, Lady Janneth."

"Right," she replied softly. Her discomfort seemed to be easing now that Neave remained present, but John's wound tighter. When he was around women, he didn't like drawing attention to the fact he had only one hand— but it was too late already.

Neave extended her right hand and turned it over, revealing the white.

John nodded. "Ye will be defending."

"Aye, and it looks as if ye will be the marauding Viking drakkars," Janneth answered.

And so it began.

Despite his discomfort, John enjoyed playing Janneth. He'd played Neave many a time, although she often lost concentration, which enabled him to beat her. But Janneth Mackay was a surprise. A sweet temperament and gentle tongue hid a strategic mind.

Her goal was to ensure the king moved out from the center to the edge of the board without being taken—and if she managed it, the game was hers—while it was his mission to prevent her. As always, John's strategy was to build a blockade around the king so he could no longer move, but Janneth was wily. She deftly moved her defenders so that gaps remained in his blockade, all the while inching toward the edge of the board.

To his embarrassment, the lass easily won their first game.

"By blood and bone, John," Neave commented from the sidelines, while Janneth set up the board once more in a cross formation so they could play again. "She thrashed ye."

"Aye, thank ye for pointing that out." John kept his tone easy-going, although, in truth, it was a slap in the face to be bested so easily.

And by a woman.

His father had once told him that women lacked the strategic thinking required for Ard-ri. He wished Sìomon Mackay had played with Janneth; he'd have revised his opinion if he had.

"Ye play extremely well," John observed as he waited for Janneth to choose whether she'd attack or defend in the next game, as was the winner's prerogative. "Did yer father teach ye?"

Janneth huffed a laugh, before favoring him with a wry smile. "Da is a good player," she admitted before picking up the king to indicate she would defend once more. "However, it was my uncle who taught me." Her gaze shadowed then. "He died last winter."

John favored her with a sympathetic look before his gaze scanned the board. The attacker moved first, and he wanted to ensure he gained an advantage early on. "Ye sound as if ye were very close to him?"

"I was."

Reaching out, John moved his first piece. He then sat back, watching his opponent's lovely face as her gaze settled upon the board. He made the mistake of glancing Neave's way then, and her quick smile made the uneasiness that had settled in his gut upon sitting down to play Ard-ri knot tighter.

Neave clearly thought bringing him and Janneth together like this was a good idea, yet he wasn't so sure. This whole situation was awkward.

"I've never visited Loch Stach," John said after a pause. "Although I've heard it's bonny."

Janneth nodded, yet she refrained from answering until she'd moved her first defender. "Aye, it is," she replied, her gaze flicking up to him once more. "Stach Tower sits on the shores of a large fresh-water loch," she murmured. "Its waters are always dark in color—pewter grey when it's stormy, and deep-blue when the sun shines. Like Varrich, we are surrounded by mountains, although they loom closer. Ben Stach rises steeply from the loch's southwestern shore, casting a shadow over Stach Tower, and Arkle lies directly to the north. They are both bonny mountains ... although Arkle is my favorite. It's made of a glistening white rock, which makes it sparkle in the sunlight."

Listening to her description, John relaxed a little. He thought then that he'd like to one day see Arkle for himself.

"It sounds a fine spot," he replied before moving another piece. He glanced up then to see his opponent watching him with a veiled look.

"It is," Janneth replied. "But if I didn't know better, I'd think ye were trying to distract me."

"I should have warned ye; he does that," Neave quipped from the sidelines. Shifting his attention once more to his friend, John saw that she was grinning. "It's a tactic he employs regularly with me."

John snorted. "I don't need to distract ye, Neave. Ye have the attention-span of a gnat."

Neave rolled her eyes at that, although they both knew the truth of it. He *had* been trying to distract his opponent from the game, something both women present had marked.

Glancing back at Janneth, John saw that the lass was now smiling. Her tension had eased, and when her gaze met his, her blue eyes twinkled with good humor.

John grinned back at her, his own discomfort settling. Warmth pooled under his ribcage as his gaze drank in Janneth Mackay's fair face. Perhaps Neave's meddling wasn't going to end in his humiliation, after all. Maybe she'd been right to suggest he and Janneth played Ard-ri together this afternoon.

Holding her eye, John inclined his head. "Go on, Janneth … it's yer turn."

"John is a charming man, is he not?"

Janneth glanced Neave's way, her expression shuttered. "Aye … I like his dry sense of humor." She paused then before her mouth lifted into a smile. "However, he could do with tightening up his play of Ard-ri."

The two women wandered along one of the paths that lined the terraced vegetable garden outside the castle's southern curtain wall, their boots crunching on fresh snow. Many of the beds were bare this time of year, and it was a gelid afternoon, yet Neave had been keen to show Janneth her 'sanctuary' before night fell. The days were far too short at present, and already, evening's shadow crept over the damp walls.

There was a stark beauty to the garden when it was frosted with ice and snow. Even in the depths of winter, Neave ventured out here daily. It was indeed her refuge, the place where she could be alone with her thoughts. There were times when the noise and activity of a busy keep overwhelmed her, when she craved the peace of this garden.

Neave cast her an arch look. "Don't tell me ye *let* him win that last game."

Janneth's grin told her that she had.

Huffing a laugh, Neave pulled her fur mantle about her, leading the way past where rows of winter cabbages peeked up through a crust of snow. "All the same ... he's one of the good ones," she continued, drawing the conversation back to the laird of Achness's qualities. "And brave too ... John's defense of Castle Varrich prevented the Nielson Mackays from seizing power."

Janneth didn't answer. When Neave swiveled around to see if she'd heard her, she saw the woman had stopped and was looking at where the last rays of daylight highlighted the top of the garden's snow-topped western wall.

Neave's lips parted, and she was about to repeat her comment when Janneth spoke. "Da has told me the tale many a time," she murmured. "Of how John Mackay rallied the forces of Strathnaver to stand against our traitorous clansmen and their Sutherland allies." She turned to Neave, meeting her eye. "We have much to thank him for." Their gazes held for a heartbeat before Janneth inclined her head, favoring Neave with a smile. "Ye aren't match-making, are ye, Neave?"

"Of course not," Neave replied, dismissing the question with an airy wave, even as her pulse sped up. The knowing glint in Janneth's eye warned her that she'd been, perhaps, a little heavy-handed in her praise of John.

Maybe she should tread more carefully, or she risked being more of a hindrance than a help to this union.

5

I'VE MISSED YE

"JOHN HAS ARRIVED."

Smiling, Neave glanced up from where she was digging out weeds. She planned to plant out onions in this bed, once the soil had warmed a little. Her gaze alighted upon where her elder sister stood.

Then her belly gave a strange flutter.

Two months had passed since Yule, and she hadn't seen the laird of Achness in that time. Although she'd known Niel had invited him to a clan meeting, the news that John Mackay was now within Castle Varrich's walls pleased her.

"Well," she said, pushing down the odd sensation. "I look forward to hearing his news." She straightened up then, stretching her cramped back. Sometimes, she got so carried away in the garden that time passed without her taking much notice. Gardening allowed her to lose herself in repetitive activity—it gave her busy mind a rest.

She'd lost track of the hour this afternoon too, for when she looked up, she saw the sun was sinking toward the west.

"Niel and I are going to take a cup of wine with John in the chieftain's solar, once he's washed and changed," Beth continued, a half-smile curving her full lips. "Did ye wish to join us?"

Once again, Neave's belly did a dive.

What was amiss with her this afternoon? She'd thought she'd eaten a decent noon meal, but perhaps she was hungry.

"Aye," she said, feigning nonchalance, "although I'd better go to my chamber and wash the dirt off myself first." She pushed herself to her feet and removed her gardening gloves. As she did so, she noted Beth was still smiling. Her sister appeared in the full-bloom of health these days—pregnancy suited her. She was showing now, a soft bulge under her kirtle. However, the light in her hazel eyes told Neave that her sister had marked her reaction to the news of John's arrival—almost as if she'd been looking out for it.

"How go things between John and Janneth?" Beth asked.

Neave loosed a sigh. "I have no idea," she admitted. "John hasn't mentioned anything in his last letters." Placing her gloves in her gardening basket, she picked it up and made her way with her sister down the narrow path between the terraces of beds she was preparing for the first of the spring plantings. "I do hope he's corresponded with her over the winter."

"I don't know why ye are so keen to find John a wife," Beth replied with a shake of her head. "When he'd be perfect for *ye*."

Neave resisted the urge to roll her eyes. This wasn't the first time Beth had brought this subject up. It appeared to mystify her that an unwed man and woman could be friends without there being something else between them.

But that was the case between Neave and John. He was like the brother she'd never had, and he treated her like a younger sister. Apart from her father, Neave had never had such an easy rapport with a male.

"I've already explained. John and I don't see each other that way," Neave replied, pushing her irritation aside as the pair of them made their way out of the walled terrace garden. "Anyway, it's Janneth he wants ... and I intend to help him win her."

Beth huffed. "John Mackay isn't a shy man. If he truly wants a lass, he'll pursue her."

Neave cast her sister a quelling look. "Appearances can deceive ... John's *situation* doesn't make finding a wife easy." She clamped her mouth shut then. She hadn't discussed John like this with any of her sisters, and despite her close relationship with Beth, it felt uncomfortable to do so now—as if she was breaching his confidence.

Beth's brow furrowed. "Because of his injuries?"

Neave remained stubbornly silent.

"Surely, most women can look past that?" Beth continued, her tone softening. "Niel once told me that John was embarrassed about his missing eye and hand ... and that was why he remains unwed ... but I must admit I just thought it was because he hadn't yet met the right woman."

"Aye, well ... John is adept at hiding how he truly feels," Neave replied, casting her sister a meaningful look. "As are many men."

Catching Neave's meaning, Beth nodded. All was well these days between the Mackay clan-chief and his wife, but Niel and Beth had locked horns for the first months of their marriage. Niel had only recently escaped from ten years of captivity on Bass Rock, and had struggled to readjust to life amongst his clan once more. But as the weeks wore on, it had become clear he was unable to let Beth in. In the end, she'd discovered that, although her warrior husband could face down a claidheamh-mòr-swinging enemy without flinching, he'd been afraid of his own heart.

Of course, Neave was quietly smug about the part she'd played in helping them. She'd gone to Niel and told him her sister was desperately in love with him and he needed to do something about it. Beth had been furious at her interference, and Neave had been sorry to upset her so. But in the end, her act had been the catalyst that brought them together.

"John is lonely," Neave said then, her voice barely above a whisper. They were making their way up the path to the gates now. Around them stretched a wide blue sky, and the carven edges of Ben Hope and Ben Loyal glowed in the afternoon sun. There was still a bite to the air, yet the sun finally had some force to it, signaling that winter was easing its grip and spring was almost upon them. "He hides it well, but I glimpse it sometimes ... I just want to help him."

"Ye look out for all those ye care for, Neave." Beth stepped close, wrapping an arm around her shoulders and squeezing. "Sometimes, I think ... *too* much so."

Neave stiffened in her sister's embrace. "What do ye mean by that?"

"The fate of others isn't always within yer control," Beth replied, her tone still gentle. "In fact, I'd say it rarely is."

Neave snorted. "That's a cynical thing to say."

"Maybe ... but while ye run yerself ragged trying to ensure the rest of us are taken care of ... what of ye?"

Neave cut her sister a glance, cocking an eyebrow. "Excuse me?"

"Time is passing, dear sister. When are ye going to look to yer own happiness? Instead of working to bring John and Janneth together, ye should be encouraging suitors of yer own."

Neave rolled her eyes. "There's plenty of time for that ... I'm not a spinster yet."

The warmth of the solar enveloped Neave as she stepped inside. It was chill in the hallway, and the hearth in her bed-chamber had gone out. As such, she sought out heat. This time of year, it could be warmer outdoors than within the damp stone walls of Castle Varrich. At least in the garden, she'd had the sun warming her back.

However, the instant she stepped within the clan-chief's solar, she forgot the roaring fire. Instead, her gaze went to the tall man who'd just unfolded himself from one of the chairs by the hearth.

"John!" Checking the urge to rush across the solar and crush him in a hug, Neave forced herself to move sedately toward him.

Despite that they'd had one of the coldest winters she could remember, the laird of Achness looked well. His single cerulean eye twinkled, and his dark, curly hair fell across his patched eye in a manner that made Neave itch to reach out and brush it back.

However, she checked the impulse.

"Neave," he greeted her, his voice a warm rumble. "It has been too long."

They halted a few feet apart, smiling at each other. Awkwardness prickled over Neave then. She suddenly wasn't sure what to do. Curse her, what was the matter with her today?

This was John, her friend. She didn't need to be nervous or embarrassed in his presence, and yet she had to admit she felt oddly gauche.

"Aye." Neave cleared her throat then. "I've … missed ye."

Goose-wit, why had she told him that? She could feel the heat rising up her neck. Mother Mary, she didn't want to blush. This was Beth's fault for questioning her about her friendship with John. It made her feel self-conscious about how she interacted with him.

However, John's gaze was guileless as his smile widened. "I missed ye too, Neave."

Neave found herself smiling back. "How long are ye staying?"

"Hopefully, for a few days at least, John?" A low male voice intruded.

Neave swiveled to see the clan-chief was pouring them all goblets of what appeared to be bramble wine. She'd been so intent on John she hadn't even noted Niel's presence. Beth sat a few feet from her husband, upon the window seat.

Neave tensed when she saw the shrewd way her sister was looking at her.

The sisters' gazes locked for a brief moment, and then Neave frowned. *This is yer fault.*

To her annoyance, Beth merely flashed her a wide smile. "Aye, John … surely yer steward can look after things at Achness for a short while?" Beth asked innocently.

"Aye, Murtagh does an able job," John replied, his mouth quirking. "He serves me well … as he did my father. But, we've had a few issues of late" —John glanced Niel's way, his expression sobering— "with the Sutherlands. I don't like to be away from Achness for too long."

"Aye, those bastards are growing bold," Niel muttered. "The sheep and cattle rustling on yer lands is no coincidence. Robert Sutherland still nurses a grievance against ye, John."

The clan-chief handed them all out goblets of wine, before gesturing for John and Neave to take the high-backed chairs in front of the fire while he settled himself on the window seat with his wife.

Neave took a sip of rich wine, before asking, "For Drumnacoub?"

"Aye," Niel replied, stretching his long legs out in front of him and crossing them at the ankle. "Like me, Sutherland has a long memory."

Neave took another sip of wine and let its warmth pool in her belly. She then marked the glint in the Mackay clan-chief's eye.

Of course, Niel had held onto his own resentment and hatred for a long while. But ever since resolving things with Beth, he'd lost the need for vengeance that had once burned within him. These days, he no longer seethed with impatience, yet the man still had a latent intensity, a charisma, that drew the eye. She had to admit Niel Mackay was one of the most striking men she'd ever laid eyes on; although, if she were honest, he'd always intimidated her a little. It had taken all her courage to confront him about Beth the year before.

"Sutherland would have been disappointed indeed to discover I didn't die of my wounds," John said, swirling the wine in his pewter goblet. "And even more vexed still when ye returned to rule the Mackays."

"Aye, well, may he choke on it," Niel replied, lifting his goblet high in a mock salute.

"And don't forget that Sutherland promised his two daughters to the Nielson Mackays if they went up against us," John added. "I hear both lasses eventually wedded men far beneath their rank ... something that would have also displeased their father."

Niel flashed him a grin, his cobalt-blue eyes glinting. "Aye ... no doubt, Sutherland blames ye for that too."

John snorted. "We'll be able to discuss what to do about Robert Sutherland when the others arrive," he replied.

"Have ye invited all yer chieftains, Laird?" Neave asked. The question appeared casual, although what she really wanted to know was whether Hugh Mackay of Loch Stach would be attending. He usually brought his daughter with him whenever he visited Castle Varrich—and it would give John and Janneth another chance to spend time together.

"Indeed," Niel replied. "I gather them all to me a couple of times a year, at least ... and there are a few things I wish to discuss at this meeting."

"Such as the Gunns?" Beth asked.

Niel gave his wife a sidelong glance before shaking his head. "There's not much to say about them at present. The Gunns have gone quiet over winter."

"What of William Gunn?" Neave asked, curiosity getting the better of her. "Will ye keep him prisoner forever?"

Both Niel and John looked her way then, the latter observing her over the rim of his goblet, his gaze slightly narrowed. Did she imagine it, or was that censure she'd just glimpsed in John's eye? Indeed, it had been an impertinent question, but it had slipped off her tongue before she'd had time to check herself.

For the second time since entering the solar, heat flushed across Neave's chest and crept up her neck. Perhaps she had spent too long outdoors under the sun today; the wine had gone straight to her head.

Sensing the tension that had settled over the solar, Beth cleared her throat. "Aye, well, after the Battle for Ruaig Shansaid, the Gunns won't likely be bothering us for a while."

"That doesn't stop Tavish Gunn from pestering me with missives," Niel growled, his brow furrowing. "Another letter arrived from Castle Gunn yesterday … requesting that we release his brother."

John cocked an eyebrow. "*Requesting?*" His gaze met Niel's. "I suppose that's a welcome change."

Niel pulled a face. "Aye, but it has the same end. Gunn will remain my prisoner."

Judging from the flintiness that glinted in his eyes, the clan-chief didn't intend to soften his stance. "Tavish Gunn will give up eventually," Niel continued, keeping his attention upon John. "And in the meantime, holding his brother hostage ensures he behaves himself."

"Aye," John replied with a nod. "We don't need both the Gunns *and* the Sutherlands to contend with at present."

The two men continued to converse about relations between their neighbors, and this time Neave let them talk without interruption. Instead, she leaned back into her chair and savored the bramble wine. Meanwhile, Beth picked up her current sewing project—a shift for the coming bairn. It was a companionable scene, accompanied by the crackle of the hearth.

Neave glanced then at the window. The shutters were open, although there was no chill intruding, for Niel had recently had a glass window pane installed—the first Neave had ever seen. The glass was costly and had come all the way from Flanders, yet it allowed the shutters to stay open longer so that daylight could illuminate the solar.

After a while, Niel turned to Beth and asked her about her visit to the healer that day. Tess had apparently assured her that the pregnancy was progressing well. While the clan-chief and his wife spoke together, Neave seized her chance to talk with John. Leaning forward, she smiled. "Castle Varrich isn't the same without ye,

John." She wasn't flattering him—it was the truth. At mealtimes, her gaze would often stray to the space at the table in the great hall where John used to sit. She'd missed their banter and his good-natured teasing.

John smiled back. "I'll admit it's taken me a while to get used to residing at Achness again after living here for so long," he replied, "although I'm finding my feet now."

Neave leaned closer, lowering her voice when she asked, "So ... have ye written to Janneth over the winter?"

John's smile faded. "Perhaps."

"It's unlike ye to be coy," Neave replied, a little vexed by his answer. "So, ye are keeping secrets from me now?"

His mouth lifted at the corners, although his gaze remained shuttered. "No, but I'd rather woo Janneth my own way, Neave," he said, holding her eye. "At my *own* pace."

6

AN ARDENT ADMIRER

"GOOD MORN, LADY Neave."

The rumble of a male voice made Neave turn. She'd just passed under the stone arch leading out of the bailey and was heading right toward her garden, wicker basket tucked under one arm. It was a mild morning, and with the arrival of the Mackay chieftains, the keep was noisier and more chaotic than usual. She'd spent the morning with Janneth. The two women had chatted over their embroidery hoops in the women's solar, and although Neave had burned to know if John had been in contact over the winter, she'd held her tongue.

Janneth hadn't said a word about the chieftain of Achness. Instead, the women had discussed the harsh winter, the growing tension between the Mackays and the Sutherlands, and Beth's pregnancy. Speaking of everything *except* John frustrated Neave, and she'd been relieved when Jean and Eilidh joined them. She'd then excused herself, gathered her basket, and headed toward her sanctuary.

Neave looked forward to losing herself in her garden until it was time for the noon meal. But when her gaze alighted upon a big, dark-haired man, she stilled.

Roy Morrison flashed her a wide smile. "I was hoping to see ye up here."

Neave tensed at his familiarity.

Mustering her wits, she forced a smile and remembered her manners. "Good morning."

"It has been a long while since I've seen ye down in Tongue," Morrison said once more, his iron-grey stare pinning her to the spot. "Why is that?"

Neave's pulse quickened. Since Yule, she'd made an effort to give the village's forge a wide berth. It unnerved her to think that Morrison had marked her absence.

"I've been busy," she replied, still keeping a smile upon her lips. She then motioned to her gardening basket. "There is much to be done this time of year."

His gaze continue to bore into Neave, and he took a few steps toward her, closing the gap between them. "A keen gardener, are ye, lass?"

Neave swallowed. "Aye." She then cleared her throat. "What brings ye up to the castle, Morrison?" She then noted that the smith carried what looked like leather-wrapped blades under one arm.

His head inclined. "Please, call me Roy." When she didn't reply, his mouth curved into another smile. "The Mackay has ordered some new blades ... so I thought I'd deliver them to him in person." Morrison moved closer still then, crowding her. "It's a pleasure to see ye, Lady Neave," he murmured. "As bonny as the first flower of spring, ye are."

Neave's heart started to kick against her ribs. The words were pretty, and if another man had said them, she might have taken the comment as a compliment. But something in the smith's voice made her hackles rise.

His gaze was even bolder than she remembered—it felt as if it were stripping her naked.

They were alone out here; Morrison could take liberties. She wanted to turn and flee to her garden, but she was on her own this morning. And if the smith followed her, she'd be cornered.

"Excuse me," she murmured. "I must return to the keep ... I've forgotten something."

Neave then darted around his broad body.

"Not just yet, lass. I haven't finished with ye." She felt the brush of Morrison's hand as he made a grab for her, yet she was faster.

An instant later, Neave dived toward the gates and the bailey beyond.

John was standing with the farrier, one hand on his gelding's rump as the two men chatted together, when Neave rushed back under the stone arch leading into the bailey.

Her pixie-face was flushed, her hazel-green eyes startled.

Stilling, John watched her head toward the steps leading up to the keep. She was walking so fast she was almost running, her small form bristling with tension.

An instant later, Tongue's blacksmith entered the bailey, a wrapped bundle of blades under one arm.

John frowned, his attention flicking back to where Neave was now taking the steps, two at a time. "Neave!" he called out. "Is something amiss?"

"No," she sang out. "I just forgot something."

However, despite her assurance, John caught the panicked edge to her voice. Neave had been in a light mood when he'd seen her cross the bailey a short while earlier, on her way to her garden. What had unsettled her so?

Brow still furrowed, John glanced back to where Roy Morrison was walking toward him. The man's expression was inscrutable, although John caught the gleam in his eye.

"Greetings, John," the smith called out. "I've got some blades for the Mackay ... where can I find him?"

"He's meeting with tenants this morning." John stepped away from his horse, leaving the farrier to resume shoeing the beast. "I can check those for him and take them to the armory."

Roy Morrison frowned at this; clearly, he expected to be sent up to the clan-chief's solar.

"Come on." John gestured for him to lay the blades out on the leather cloth upon the cobbles. "Let's have a look."

With a grunt, the smith did as bid. Hunkering down, he spread out the collection of broad-swords he'd made for the clan-chief.

At just a glance, John could see that they were beautifully wrought, the long, double-edged steel blades gleaming in the morning sun. Bending down, he picked one up with his left hand, examining it. A pang went through him as he held the weapon aloft. Ever since losing his right hand, he could no longer wield one of these in battle: a claidheamh-mòr needed to be gripped two-handed. These days, John fought using a lighter English-style longsword.

"A fine blade," John murmured, testing its weight. "Ye've outdone yerself ... as usual." He then turned to the blacksmith, his tone cooling as he continued. "What did ye just say to Lady Neave?"

Morrison flashed him a grin. "I merely greeted her."

"It looks as if ye did more than that, Roy."

The smith shrugged. "Can I help it, if the lass startles easily?"

John's mouth thinned. Neave Munro wasn't the nervous type. Roy Morrison had clearly crossed the line in some way.

"In that case, I suggest ye leave her be in the future," John replied cooly.

Their gazes locked then, and John swore he saw something dark move in the man's storm-grey eyes. An instant later, Morrison's gaze shuttered, and John thought he must have been mistaken.

A pause followed before the blacksmith replied, "Aye ... as ye wish."

Later that morning, John sought Neave out in her garden. After Morrison had departed the keep, returning to his forge in Tongue, she'd ventured outside once more.

John had spied her leaving, and he waited a short while before following the pebbly path outside the curtain wall that led to the south-facing terrace garden. It had been a while since he'd visited the garden,

although he'd heard that it had thrived ever since Neave
Munro had come to live here.

Formerly, Niel's mother, Lady Estelle, had taken care
of the garden, but after her death, it had become
overgrown. However, as he stepped through the narrow
entrance, his gaze sweeping over the neatly-kept terraces
of beds, he marveled at how verdant it was looking these
days. Neave had already started planting seedlings, of
the hardier brassicas, despite that winter's bite hadn't yet
eased.

Halfway down the garden, he spied Neave, bent over
as she weeded around rows of cabbages.

"What a magical place this is," John commented as he
approached. "I can see why ye like spending time in
here."

Neave glanced up, her eyes flying wide, her body
going rigid. An instant later, she relaxed when she saw it
was him. Favoring him with a tight smile, she put a hand
to her chest. "Sorry, John," she murmured. "I was
leagues away. Ye gave me a fright."

"I didn't mean to startle ye," he replied, drawing
closer. Noting the tension on her face, he frowned. "I
don't know what Morrison said to ye earlier … but he'll
leave ye be from now on."

Neave straightened up, her lips parting. "Ye spoke to
him?"

"Aye."

Her throat bobbed. "He's taken a liking to me … I first
noted it at Yuletide, and I've been trying to avoid him
ever since." She paused then, shrugging her slender
shoulders. "I suppose there's nothing wrong with a man
admiring a lass … but he looks at me as if I'm prey."

John moved closer, his gaze never leaving hers. "Why
didn't ye say anything before? Ye know ye can always
come to me for help."

She gave a nervous laugh before raising a gloved hand
and brushing a lock of chestnut-brown hair off her brow.
The gesture left a smear of dirt. "And say what … the
blacksmith keeps favoring me with lusty looks? I'd have
looked a goose."

"Never." John's mouth quirked then. "Ye've got dirt on yer face ... can I wipe it off?"

She nodded.

Raising his left hand, John rubbed the smudge away with his thumb. He was aware then of just how near the pair of them were standing—far closer than they ever had previously. He caught the scent of lavender. It was a perfume he always associated with her.

Without realizing what he was doing, John inhaled the scent deep into his lungs. The day before, Neave had admitted that she'd missed him. Her candid comment had pleased him, for he too had felt her absence over the past two months. Neave Munro brought sunshine into his life.

The moment drew out, and John blinked. Neave stood quietly, staring up at him with a slightly quizzical expression upon her elfin face. She was likely wondering why he hadn't moved away.

"There ye go," he said, embarrassed at being swayed by the scent of lavender, mixed with the sweet perfume of her skin. "It's gone now."

"Thank ye, John," she replied, her mouth—a lush cupid's-bow—curving into a smile.

"Neave!"

Stepping back, John turned to see Eilidh rush into the garden. Her heart-shaped face was flushed, her oak-colored eyes bright. She was carrying a small bundle. "Something has arrived for ye by messenger."

"For me?" Neave removed her gardening gloves and dropped them at her feet. "From whom?"

"I don't know." Eilidh skidded to a halt and, gaze shining, thrust the bundle at her elder sister. "Go on ... open it!"

A groove formed between Neave's eyebrows as she turned over the leather-wrapped package, secured with twine. "Perhaps it's from Da ... or Laila."

John recalled that Neave's stepmother had recently given birth to a baby boy, and the Munro clan-chief was understandably overjoyed. "Did yer stepmother say she was going to send ye anything?" he asked, intrigued.

Neave shook her head. "But I can't think who else would send me a package."

"Well, open it, and let's see," Eilidh urged, her voice tight with excitement now.

With a huff of resignation, Neave did as bid, her nimble fingers untying the twine and peeling the leather back. The wrapping fell away to reveal a small velvet pouch of deep emerald green.

Both John and Eilidh looked on, fascinated, as Neave loosened the drawstring and tipped out the object within onto her open palm.

It was a necklace, and the finest one John had ever laid eyes upon. A large red ruby inlaid in gold glinted in the sun, hanging from a delicate golden chain.

"My word," Eilidh breathed. "I've never seen the like."

A small coil of parchment slipped from the pouch then, fluttering to the ground. John stooped down and retrieved it, handing it to her. "This should tell ye who it's from," he said with a wry smile.

Handing the precious necklace to Eilidh, who held it as if it were made of eggshell, Neave unfurled the parchment and cleared her throat before beginning to read. John knew that all the Munro sisters were good with their letters—something their late mother apparently had insisted upon. "To a woman who is lovelier than the first bloom of heather in summer. My heart beats for ye ... an ardent admirer." Neave sucked in a breath, lowering the parchment. Her gaze then swept over John and Eilidh as if seeking an explanation from them.

"Mother Mary," Eilidh murmured, awed. She then handed Neave back her necklace, her eyes huge. "It seems ye have captured someone's attention."

"Indeed," John said, his gaze flicking to the blood-red ruby. "Someone who has just spent a king's ransom upon ye." As he said the words, he felt his chest tighten a little. Ignoring the disquieting sensation, he flashed Neave a smile. "An ardent admirer indeed."

"But who could it be?" Eilidh was still staring at the necklace, clearly transfixed by its beauty.

"I've not the slightest idea," Neave murmured holding the pendant up by its chain. She then glanced at John, before frowning. "Ye don't think it's from Roy Morrison, do ye?"

John snorted before shaking his head. "I doubt he's the type to bestow gifts and declarations of love upon women." It was a blunt reply, yet it appeared to reassure Neave. Her furrowed brow smoothed.

"The smith?" Eilidh frowned, her gaze flicking from her sister to John. "Why would ye think it's from him?"

Neave heaved a sigh. "I shall tell ye later," she promised. Her attention settled upon the gleaming ruby. "What should I do about this then?"

"Ye don't have to do anything, dear sister." Eilidh flashed her a grin. "I'm sure yer admirer will make himself known to ye soon enough."

7

IMAGINED SLIGHTS

"YE MUST HAVE an idea of who sent ye the necklace?"

"None at all."

Jean's serious features tightened, and she gnawed at her bottom lip. "Think back, Neave, over the past months ... perhaps one of the Mackay chieftains currently in residence at Varrich took a shine to ye."

"Jeanie has a point," Eilidh agreed. "It may be no coincidence that yer gift arrived on the same day as the Mackay clan-chiefs."

Neave's lips pursed. She hadn't considered that.

The three sisters walked along the pebbly shore of the Kyle of Tongue. It was a still, bright afternoon, and the sun sparkled over the calm waters of the kyle.

Neave, Jean, and Eilidh walked at a deliberately slow pace, keeping well behind the couple they followed: John and Janneth.

The Mackay chieftains and their clan-chief had been locked away for the past two days in meetings, but this afternoon, Neave had invited John to join her, Jean, and Eilidh for a stroll. And, *coincidentally*, Janneth had also accompanied them.

It was the perfect occasion for John and Janneth to spend more time together.

Watching them walking side-by-side, Neave had to admit they made a striking couple: both tall, yet him with curly dark hair, and her with a gold mane so pale that it almost appeared silver in the sunlight.

Neave's breathing hitched then, her stomach hardening a little.

Janneth was fortunate indeed to have drawn the eye of a man like John. Much to Beth's chagrin, Neave spent little time thinking of her own future—but as her gaze lingered upon the couple, she wondered what lay ahead for her.

Beth was right, she thought then. *I spend my days worrying about everyone else's happiness. But what about my own?*

Sooner or later, she would have to focus on herself.

Reaching up, Neave's fingers traced the smooth surface of the ruby pendant. It was such a lovely gift, and recalling the message that had accompanied it made excitement curl in her belly. Her secret admirer had indeed appeared at the right moment. Perhaps it was time she started actively encouraging suitors.

"Let us list the Mackay chieftains who are yet unwed," Jean announced, as methodical as ever. "Robin Mackay of Melness, Breac Mackay of Balnakeil, Iver Mackay of Dun Ugadale ... and John Mackay of Aberach."

"Well, ye can discount that last name," Neave said with a shake of her head. She didn't know which of the Mackay chieftains—if it was actually one of them—was her mystery admirer, but it wasn't the laird of Achness.

"That leaves us with Robin, Breac, and Iver," Jean replied. Neave's younger sister then fixed her with a piercing look. "Think back on the past months ... on yer interactions with them."

Neave sighed. "I haven't had many conversations with any of the three," she admitted after a pause. "Robin Mackay of Melness is dour and unfriendly."

"That's only because his wife left him," Jean answered, her tone sharpening. "Few men would be smiling in his situation."

Neave nodded. Aye, she'd heard of that nasty business. Mackay's wife had betrayed him with his own brother. And then, if that wasn't bad enough, the pair had tried to murder him to take his lands for themselves. Fortunately for Robin Mackay, their plot had failed and they'd been forced to flee. It had happened nearly two years earlier, but when Neave had seen Robin Mackay's stern face at supper on the night of his arrival for these meetings, she'd realized he still nursed bitterness over it all.

No, she doubted Robin Mackay was her mystery suitor.

That left Breac and Iver.

"The young lairds of Balnakeil and Dun Ugadale are both handsome," Eilidh piped up. "And ye danced with both of them at Yule, Neave."

Neave's brow furrowed. Aye, she had, but she hadn't noted that either warrior was overly attentive toward her. However, she hadn't lavished much attention on them either. Neave knew she could be oblivious at times, and she wished now she'd paid more attention.

Neave stifled a yawn and pushed the remnants of her supper around her wooden trencher. She'd been enjoying the mutton stew and oaten dumplings when talk at the table had turned to the Sutherlands—again.

The conversation was becoming animated, and since such discussions tended to exclude any womenfolk present, Neave was getting fidgety. It had been a long day, and she was keen to retreat to the women's solar and put her feet up on a settle before the fire.

Across the table, Neave caught Janneth's eye. She then rolled her eyes dramatically, and Janneth grinned back. It was warm inside the great hall this eve, and Neave surmised that must have been why the lass's fair face was unusually flushed.

The clan-chief's table was packed, for all of his guests were present. The meetings had concluded, and the chieftains would all return home the following day.

"Sutherland should know better than to poke an adder with a stick," Hugh Mackay was telling Connor Mackay. The older chieftain's voice was an angry growl.

"He knows what he's doing," Breac Mackay spoke up. "He's just testing us."

Hugh scowled at this, but John replied before he could. "Aye ... or he's trying to get at me."

Breac's gaze narrowed. "Do ye really think this is personal?"

"It could be ... Robert Sutherland certainly hates John enough," Niel replied, his expression shuttered. "Nonetheless, I shall send men to help patrol our southern borders ... Achness shouldn't have to deal with this alone."

"And ye can count on support from Farr," Connor Mackay assured John with a tight smile.

"And from Balnakeil," Breac added. The young laird then leaned toward John. "Have ye thought about—"

Hugh Mackay slammed his pewter goblet down upon the table, cutting Breac off. "Enough!" he snarled. "I tire of listening to the opinions of a wet-behind-the-ears pup!"

Silence fell over the table.

Her boredom forgotten, Neave's attention swiveled to the laird of Loch Stach, marking his florid cheeks. She'd heard that after the death of his wife a few years earlier, Hugh had started drinking to excess. It was true, as she'd seen him slumped in his chair more than once during his regular trips to Castle Varrich, after a surfeit of ale.

But he wasn't in a drunken stupor this eve. Instead, his blue eyes glittered as he glared across at the chieftain of Balnakeil.

To his credit, Breac Mackay wore a surprised rather than angry expression at this outburst. Aye, he was young—no more than one and twenty—yet he was no 'pup'.

"Da," Janneth whispered, her blue eyes huge upon her delicately featured face. "Ye are being rude."

Hugh's mouth twisted. "No, lass ... I'm putting this lordling in his place."

"Hugh?" Niel spoke up, a warning edge to his voice.

Ignoring the clan-chief, Hugh leaned forward, pointing an aggressive finger in Breac's face. "I see ye, *lad*. The same blood runs through yer veins as that Robert Mackay ... treacherous whoreson that he was."

"Robert was my second cousin," Breac replied, his voice low and cold as shock faded from his face and ire ignited in his eyes. "I'll not take responsibility for his actions ... I was but a bairn when he betrayed his clan-chief."

"Old enough to listen to his whispers," Hugh growled. "Old enough to learn at his knee."

Next to Breac, Iver Mackay's face had turned hard. "Listen to yerself, Hugh," he muttered. "Do ye know how unreasonable ye sound?" The laird of Dun Ugadale was of a similar age as Breac, and the two were firm friends.

"Iver has a point," Niel said. The clan-chief sat in his carven chair next to Beth, a frown marring his brow. His gaze speared Hugh, even if the older man still glared at the laird of Balnakeil. "Robert betrayed us all ... and I understand yer resentment." Niel paused then, his dark-blue eyes shadowing. "But I also know that hate can eat a man alive if he's not careful. Let it go, Hugh."

"I can't," Hugh wheezed. "Every time I look across the table, I see Robert Mackay sitting there, breaking bread and drinking with us, while he plotted to usurp yer father and rule this clan in his stead." Hugh's florid face turned mean as he continued to glare at Breac. "Ye speak just like him too ... silver-tongued serpent."

"Enough," the younger chieftain growled back. "I'm my own man. And I've as much right to sit here as ye do."

"Whelp!" Hugh shouted, spraying spittle. "I was killing men when ye were still sucking yer mother's tit. How dare ye speak to me like an equal?"

"Da!" Janneth leaned toward her father this time and placed a cautionary hand upon his arm. "Please, don't—"

Hugh shook his daughter off.

He pushed himself up to his feet, swaying over the table as he stabbed a finger in Breac Mackay's face once more. "I've seen ye and Iver in a huddle ... just this afternoon, ye were discussing something outside Niel's solar ... but ye shut yer gobs the moment ye saw me. What was it?"

Breac's swarthy face tightened. "It was a private conversation ... of a personal nature. There was nothing underhand in it."

"If that's the case, why don't ye tell us of it?" Hugh swung his thick arm in an arc over the now silent table. The rest of the great hall had quieted now too, all gazes riveted upon the two arguing chieftains upon the dais. "Come, lad ... we'd all like to hear."

"As I said ... it was personal," Breac replied through gritted teeth. "Now why don't ye sit back down, ye great drunken oaf ... before ye make an even bigger fool of yerself."

With a roar, Hugh Mackay flung himself across the table.

Neave gasped, reeling backward as his booted foot nearly hit her in the face. The chieftain of Loch Stach was getting on in years, and heavyset, yet rage propelled him across the table like a missile from a trebuchet, scattering trenchers and goblets in his wake.

A meaty fist slammed into Breac Mackay's face, and the pair of them toppled backward off the dais.

Shouting erupted, the din echoing high into the rafters. Men jumped to their feet, gathering around the two struggling figures upon the rush-strewn floor of the hall, but no one made a move to halt them while they went at each other with their fists.

Neave stood up, watching in horrified fascination as Hugh head-butted Breac. The younger man grabbed hold of one of Hugh's ears and twisted. He then slammed a fist into his belly. The laird of Loch Stach's grunt of pain made Janneth cry out. Hugh's daughter's eyes were wild as she looked to the clan-chief. "Please! Stop this!"

Jaw bunched, Niel Mackay stood up. He then stalked around the edge of the table, gesturing to John as he did so. "Break them up."

John nodded, motioning to Connor Mackay for assistance. The two men closed in on the brawling chieftains, the gathered crowd drawing back to allow them access.

Together, John and Connor gripped hold of Hugh's broad shoulders and hauled him off Breac. However, the chieftain of Loch Stach was now incensed. His bearded face had gone the hue of liver, and he turned on them too, driving his elbow into Connor's belly before stamping on John's foot. His aggression took them both by surprise, and they released their hold on him.

It was long enough for Hugh to grab an eating knife from the table behind him. He then lunged at Breac once more.

This time, the younger warrior was ready for him. He rolled to his feet, ducking the swiping blade.

"Da, stop it! He's yer clansman, not yer enemy!" Janneth was hysterical now, tears pouring down her ashen cheeks. She rushed forward, heading toward her father, but Neave caught hold of her arm, drawing her back. She then placed an arm around the woman's waist, holding her fast. Hugh either didn't hear his daughter's plea, or he was past listening to reason.

"I'll gut ye, whoreson!" he roared at Breac, who continued to evade the blade. However, the laird of Balnakeil's face was taut and pale. Unarmed, he was at a distinct disadvantage. Aggression now crackled through the great hall of Castle Varrich, and Neave's skin prickled. Blood was certainly going to spill if someone didn't put a halt to this madness.

Connor and John closed in once more, although it was difficult for either of them to get close to Hugh. He circled Breac, like a wolf closing in on its prey, growling threats under his breath.

And when he lunged once more, events unfolded with lightning quickness.

Breac caught hold of Hugh's thick wrist, halting the knife as it flew toward his throat, while John leaped on Hugh from behind, grasping him in a headlock.

Hugh staggered back, bringing John with him, while Breac was forced to let go of his flailing arm. Roaring an oath, Hugh twisted in John's grip, his blade flashing.

Murmurs rippled through the hall at the sight of blood trickling down John's upper arm.

Hugh halted then, stopping his struggles so suddenly that John staggered, and would have fallen if Connor hadn't caught him.

Meanwhile, Niel had elbowed his way to the front. He now put himself before Hugh, yanking the man's knife away from him and hurling it onto the rushes. "Enough!" he snarled. "I'll not have my chieftains brawling like bairns over imagined slights. This is how the rot always sets in, man. The Gunns and the Sutherlands won't need to bring us down if we do the work for them ourselves!"

Hugh's blue eyes guttered. For the first time since the argument had begun, he appeared to be sobering up.

"It was over *nothing*," Breac muttered, reaching up to feel the large purple swelling that was coming up on his forehead. "I'm as loyal to ye as he is, Niel. I swear it."

Niel favored Breac with a curt nod before fixing Hugh with a glare.

A nerve flickered in the older man's bearded cheek. He was clearly still waging a war inside, yet now that his clan-chief stood before him, lucidity had returned. And when he glanced over at where John had placed a hand over his bleeding right arm, his mouth thinned. "Sorry, John," he rasped. "I forgot myself."

"Aye," Niel replied, a warning edge to his voice now. "Something ye won't do twice, Hugh."

8

TENDING TO A WOUND

NEAVE APPROACHED JOHN, her gaze riveted upon where blood oozed through his fingers. "God's bones," she said, noting his pinched expression. The man was in pain. "What has he done to ye?"

John managed a half-smile. "Don't fuss, lass … it's just a scratch."

Neave pursed her lips. *A scratch?* "All the same, let's get ye upstairs so I can take a look at it."

Around them, the excited murmurs from the crowd of warriors and retainers who'd witnessed the brawl rose and fell. Niel was still having words with Hugh, while Breac looked on, his brow furrowed. Neave could sense that John wished to linger, to ensure violence wouldn't erupt once more. Nonetheless, Niel had the situation well in hand now—and that arm needed seeing to.

She led him upstairs, to the women's solar, where she instructed Greta to bring hot water, vinegar, fresh linen, and catgut. And while they waited for the maid, John seated himself on the table that dominated the space, his hand still covering his injured upper arm.

"What the devil was all that about?" Neave asked. In truth, she felt shaky in the aftermath.

John shook his head as if trying to make sense of it himself. "Hugh took Robert Mackay's betrayal harder than most. These days, he's taken to seeing treachery everywhere."

"But in Breac Mackay?"

"The chieftain is young, cocky ... and does bear a startling resemblance to Robert. When Hugh's in his cups, he seems to forget they're not the same person."

Neave frowned. "Well, maybe it's time he cut back on his drinking."

John's mouth curved. "Aye, Niel will no doubt point that out."

The door to the women's solar opened then, and Greta bustled in with the items Neave had bid her collect.

"Do ye need any assistance?" the lass asked, brow furrowed as her gaze alighted on John's injured arm. She'd gone the color of milk, a reminder that Greta hated the sight of blood.

Neave favored her with a smile. "No, I should be able to manage from here ... thank ye, Greta."

The maid departed, trying and failing to hide the relief upon her face, leaving the pair of them alone inside the solar.

It felt odd to be sitting in this chamber with John, as this was a feminine space. Rather than the hunting and battle scenes favored by the clan-chief, the tapestry that hung from the damp walls depicted a bucolic scene of cottars working in the fields, flanked by cottages, with mountains in the background. Colorful embroidered cushions decorated the chairs and window seat, and the scent of drying herbs lingered in the air.

Turning to John, she reached for his fingers, gently lifting them from the knife wound. "Let's see what we're dealing with here."

"Are ye sure ye don't mind the sight of blood?" he asked, his brow furrowing. "Yer maid looked as if she was about to faint."

Neave snorted. "Hardly ... Greta is a sensitive lass, but few Highland women are stranger to such sights ... since our menfolk are always scrapping."

John raised an eyebrow at that, his lips twitching. "Ye never cease to surprise me, Neave Munro."

"Aye, and why's that?" she asked, washing away the blood so she could get a closer look at the wound. He was fortunate; the knife hadn't gone as deep as she'd thought, although the cut would definitely need tending to.

"I would have thought Jean was the sister with the healer's touch."

Neave shook her head. "Our mother taught all of us how to treat wounds … a skill that has come in handy over the years. I can't tell ye how many times Da has needed our help." She straightened up then, reaching for the small flask of vinegar she would use to clean the cut. "I will need to put a few stitches in … take off yer lèine."

When John didn't move, her attention flicked to his face. He was frowning, his gaze shadowed.

He didn't need to say anything: she could tell he didn't want to take off his lèine in front of her. Although he'd never said as much to her over the past months, she sensed he was embarrassed by his battle scars.

Deciding it was best to pretend she hadn't noticed, she made an impatient noise in the back of her throat. "Go on … I can't stitch yer wound while ye still have that lèine on."

She then turned and busied herself with readying the items she would need to tend him. He'd get over his embarrassment soon enough if she acted like a physician rather than a friend.

A moment later, she heard the whisper of fabric as he removed his loose black lèine.

She took the long-sleeved linen tunic from him and hung it over the back of a nearby chair. It was a beautiful garment, although it would need mending after Hugh's treatment. "I will see if I can fix that sleeve for ye, before ye head home," Neave assured him.

An instant later, her attention alighted upon his naked torso. She hadn't intended to gawk—as she didn't want to make him even more uncomfortable than he was already—yet she couldn't help admiring him.

John was lean, yet well-muscled. A number of scars— some silvered with age, others still puckered and pink— crisscrossed his torso. The deepest of them swept under his left nipple. Yet they didn't detract from the virility and strength of his torso. His shoulders were broad, his arms sculpted strength. He wore his artificial hand, strapped to his right wrist, this evening—as he always did for social occasions. The only time Neave had seen him remove it was when he practiced at sword play or wrestling. However, then he tended to let his sleeve hang over the stump that remained.

Clearing her throat, Neave glanced back to her healer's basket. Strangely, her breathing had quickened.

Keep yer eyes on the task, Neave, she chastised herself.

She picked up a clean cloth, moved close, and wiped away the blood that continued to leak from the cut. Then she unstoppered the flask of vinegar and trickled some directly onto the open wound.

John's hiss between clenched teeth warned her that it hurt—but this was necessary. Vinegar prevented wounds from festering. While the wound dried, Neave busied herself with threading one of her sewing needles with a length of catgut. Out of the four sisters, she was the most skilled at this task, for her embroidery and sewing were the neatest. Even so, she was wary of hurting him.

"I apologize in advance if this pains ye," she warned.

"I will weather it," he replied, with a grimace. "Go on."

His body tensed as she dug the needle into his flesh, pulling the lips of the cut together for the first suture. However, John didn't make a sound.

Mouth compressed, gaze narrowed, she deftly cut the catgut and knotted it before beginning her second stitch.

"Ye are stoic indeed," she observed as she worked. "The last warrior I sewed up, at Foulis after a skirmish, wailed like a woman giving birth."

John snorted, even if she noted a sheen now covered his skin. "I've had a lot of practice over the years," he replied between clenched teeth. "And this cut is merely a scratch compared to other wounds I've suffered."

Neave's brow furrowed. Indeed, after seeing the scars upon his torso, she wasn't about to contradict him.

The cut required six sutures, and Neave was also sweating by the time she finished. "There ... all done," she announced, before noting how pale John's face was. "Ye look like ye could do with a drop of wine ... I know I could."

"Aye," he said roughly. "Thank ye."

Neave crossed to the sideboard and poured them both two small cups. John took the one she offered with a wan smile. He then peered at the neatly sutured wound upon his upper right arm. "Ye weren't boasting of yer skill, I see."

Neave huffed. "I *never* boast, Mackay." She nodded to his sutured wound. "Of course, ye will need to have those stitches removed a few days after ye arrive home."

John nodded. Holding his cup up for a toast, he then took a gulp. Neave did the same, enjoying the fortifying heat. Standing near to John, she was all too aware of him, in the way she had been the day before in the garden. He'd stepped close to wipe away some dirt from her face, and she'd been acutely conscious of his proximity and the gentleness of his touch. It had unsettled her a little.

"Ye are wearing that pendant," John noted then, his gaze sweeping to the necklace that lay against her breast. "I've only just noticed."

Neave's mouth curved as she glanced down at the ruby that gleamed in the light of the cressets burning on the surrounding walls. "I thought if I wore it to supper ... my admirer might reveal himself ... if he was present." She pulled a face then. "But other matters overshadowed the occasion."

"So, ye have no idea of who it could be?" he asked, his gaze never leaving hers.

Neave shrugged. "My sisters keep insisting that I must know ... but I don't. We thought it might be Breac or Iver, yet I'm not so certain."

John's expression turned thoughtful. "Perhaps one of yer father's warriors pines for ye at Foulis Castle."

Neave inclined her head, arching an eyebrow. She hadn't considered that.

Seeing her reaction, John shrugged. "It's just a theory."

Taking another sip of wine, Neave cast her mind back to when she'd lived at her father's stronghold. One or two of George Munro's men had flirted with her over the past years, but she couldn't remember catching any of them favoring her with longing looks, or any who'd made a point of seeking her out.

"It's not a foolish one," she admitted. "I just can't think who."

"Well, a woman as lovely as ye is bound to have admirers," he replied, a wry note in his voice. "It's likely it's a man ye haven't yet noticed."

Taken aback by his compliment, Neave drank once more from her cup. Despite the soothing warmth of the wine, tension rippled through her. She was used to speaking frankly with John, yet there was something about this conversation that was different from others they'd shared.

She was suddenly mindful of the fact that she was a woman, and he was a man—and the reminder made her slightly on edge in his presence. The firelight kissed the lean contours of his naked torso, a sight that distracted her.

"Whoever yer admirer is … I just hope he's worthy of ye," John continued, his voice lowering. "Yer beauty isn't just in yer face, Neave. Ye are a woman a man can trust. I have appreciated yer friendship these last months."

Neave smiled back, even as embarrassment prickled her skin. "That's a kind thing to say," she murmured, wishing her cheeks weren't warming.

His gaze held hers. "It's the truth. Ye are loyal and would do anything for yer kin." He inclined his head then. "However, I've seen how ye are with men … how ye avoid capture, like a butterfly. When this mystery suitor reveals himself … will ye actually encourage him?"

Neave huffed a laugh and glanced away. "It depends … on whether I actually like the man."

He snorted. "Ye are skittish all right."

"Aye, well ... perhaps I'm not ready yet ... for things to change."

"What do ye mean?"

Neave forced herself to meet his eye once more. Talking about herself was indeed making her nervous. She wished they could steer the conversation onto other subjects. "I know I'll have to take a husband one day ... but I'm loath to leave Castle Varrich ... and my sisters." Her belly tightened then. "How can I keep an eye on them all, if I'm living elsewhere?"

His mouth lifted at the corners. "Maybe ye aren't meant to."

Neave harrumphed and pursed her lips. The notion was ridiculous.

Her attention settled then upon his wooden hand.

Setting aside her cup, she reached out, running her fingertips over the polished oak. "Someone made a fine job of this," she noted. It was a sincere observation, despite that she was eager to turn the conversation away from herself.

"Aye ... a carpenter at Achness made it for me," he murmured. "Although I'd rather have my real hand."

"Does it feel strange sometimes?" she asked. "I've heard the folk who lose limbs can sometimes feel like they're still there."

"Occasionally, when I'm lying abed, I will think I can feel the fingers of my missing right-hand twitch," he admitted. "I like to think it is the ghost of the hand that was severed ... coming back to haunt me."

9

YER HISTORY

NEAVE GLANCED UP to see John wore a smile, even if his gaze was shuttered.

Her attention shifted then, to the deep scar that slashed across his chest. "Did ye get that at Drumnacoub too?"

As soon as the question left her lips, she wished she could call it back. She knew John was uncomfortable about his injuries; she shouldn't be drawing his attention to them.

Their gazes met then and held for a heartbeat. Then John shrugged. "No, that one was courtesy of the Gunns … a skirmish with border raiders around five years ago," he replied. "The wound that nearly finished me off at Drumnacoub is on my back, under my right shoulder."

Neave shifted around, letting him twist so that she could see it. Her breath sucked in when she spied the deep, puckered crater there. She wished to reach out, soothe it with her fingers, yet she restrained herself. Instead, she murmured an oath under her breath. "How did this not kill ye?"

"Tess, the healer, knows what she's about," he replied with a wry smile. "A Sutherland warrior stuck me in the back with a pike, while his friend removed my sword hand with one blow of his axe."

Neave swallowed to ease the sudden tightness in her throat. She'd heard enough. No wonder John didn't usually speak of that terrible battle.

Yet now that John had begun talking about Drumnacoub, he seemed to want to finish the grisly tale,

"The bastard who took my hand plucked out my eye with his dirk as a second trophy, thinking I was done for."

Queasiness swept over Neave, and bile stung the back of her throat. "Savages," she muttered.

"That's war, lass," he said softly. "It makes barbarians of us all."

Drawing in a deep, steadying breath, Neave moved back to his front—and she tried to push aside visions of John lying there on the battlefield, helpless, and left for dead. The thought tied her belly in knots.

As she reached for the vinegar flask once more, she spied another long scar on the inner side of his right arm. "That one looks an old wound," she murmured.

"Aye, it is … I took that during a skirmish nearly ten years ago now … when Robert and William Mackay tried to bring down the Mackay clan-chief at a clan gathering."

Neave nodded, drizzling a little more vinegar on the sutures before cleaning up around the sewn wound with a fresh strip of linen. She then glanced up and met his eye once more. "Yer scars are like the pages of a book … they tell yer history."

He grimaced. "Aye, well … let's hope Janneth isn't reviled by them," he paused then, his gaze shadowing. "It's taken me a long while to get up the courage to woo a woman … and I'm still not sure Janneth will want a maimed husband."

Neave's breathing caught. "Yer scars aren't something to be ashamed of," she said, her voice roughening. "They are a reminder to all that yer enemies tried to kill ye and failed … ye are stronger than them, John Mackay." She paused then, her pulse quickening. "Only a woman with nothing between her ears would scorn ye."

Surprise rippled across John's face, his gaze widening at her bold words.

At that moment, the door to the women's solar flew open. Gasps followed.

Neave turned to see Jean and Eilidh standing inside the doorway, their gazes riveted upon her.

Neave went rigid. Although there was nothing illicit about what she and John were doing, she knew how the scene must look: John, naked to the waist, perched upon the table with Neave standing between his thighs.

Jean's cheeks flushed, her gaze darting around then as if she was aware she'd been staring and now wasn't sure where to look. Next to her, Eilidh's brown eyes were as wide as moons.

Jean then cleared her throat. "We thought ye might need some assistance … with John's arm."

"Aye," Eilidh murmured. "But I don't think ye do."

Neave stepped back from John. "It's all done," she said, injecting briskness into her voice. "John was a stoic patient indeed."

"And ye have a healer's touch," he replied.

Neave's cheeks started to burn. The intimacy of their conversation made her feel all strange and fluttery inside. Shifting back farther still, she picked up the lèine she'd discarded over the back of a nearby chair. "I will see to this now," she assured him.

"Thank ye, Neave," John slid off the table and rose to his full height before her. Neave felt tiny next to him; she sometimes forgot how tall he was. As he brushed past her, she caught the spicy, musky scent of his skin.

"Have things calmed down, below?" John asked Neave's sisters.

"Aye," Jean replied. "Hugh's very sorry for himself … now he's sobered up a bit." Neave noted then that although Jean seemed determined to keep her gaze upon John's face, Eilidh was openly staring at his naked chest. And there was no mistaking the genuine female appraisal in her youngest sister's eyes.

"Good to hear," John replied, making for the door. "I'd better go down and see Niel."

"How's that arm?" the clan-chief greeted John as he approached the dais. After leaving the women's solar, he'd returned to his bed-chamber and changed into a fresh lèine, before returning to the great hall.

"Sewn up, thanks to Neave," John replied.

In truth, he was a little off balance after the conversation he'd just had with Neave. He'd felt awkward when he'd first taken off his lèine so she could tend his arm, yet the discomfort hadn't lasted long. Neave always put him at ease, and he'd found that he'd wanted to tell her about Drumnacoub. And when she'd told him his scars were nothing to be ashamed of, he'd felt something loosen deep within his chest.

No one had ever spoken to him thus. Her words, and the gentleness in her voice, had been a much-needed balm—yet at the same time, he'd felt oddly exposed.

Spying Janneth at the table, John smiled. It pleased him she hadn't yet retired. Understandably, she'd been upset over her father's behavior, yet she was now composed. Janneth sat, pale and tense, nursing a pewter goblet of wine.

After the fracas, the great hall had emptied out and only a small group now sat at the clan-chief's table upon the dais. Hugh had retired, as had Breac. Niel reclined in his chair, Beth at his side, with Connor, Robin, and Iver across from him.

John slid into the empty seat next to Janneth and took the cup of ale Robin passed him, nodding his thanks to the laird of Melness.

"I'm so sorry for Da's behavior," Janneth murmured.

John met her gaze, smiling once more. "There's no need for ye to apologize, lass."

"No," Iver cut in with a snort. The chieftain of Dun Ugadale, a broad-shouldered young man with ice-blond hair, was scowling. "That's for yer *father* to do."

Janneth's throat bobbed. "He's not been the same since Ma died," she admitted, "although I know that's no excuse."

Iver's mouth pursed. "Breac has never done Hugh any wrong."

"I know," Janneth replied, her gaze shadowing. She leaned toward John then, a tremulous smile curving her lips. "I hope ye won't hold a grudge against the Mackays of Loch Stach for this, John? Despite his behavior tonight, ye know my father has a good heart. He will be truly sorry tomorrow."

John shook his head. "It's already forgotten, lass." He meant it too—he wasn't a man to hold onto slights. Hugh had injured him by accident. He would leave the matter there.

His gaze roamed over Janneth's face then. In the two months since Yule, he'd wanted to brave the snow and ice, and make the visit to Loch Stach to begin wooing the lovely Janneth in earnest.

But he hadn't.

If it hadn't been for Neave's insistence at Yule, he would never have even danced with her.

Neave's right, he told himself as he lifted his cup to his lips and took a sip of ale. *I'll lose my chance with Janneth if I continue to be so diffident.*

John had prepared himself for Neave's questions upon his return to Castle Varrich, and had largely succeeded in getting his friend to cease her interfering. Yet the fact remained that he still wanted Janneth Mackay of Loch Stach.

However, the lass didn't favor him with the soft, limpid gaze he wished for. She was kind and polite—but there was a reserve in her manner. She likely thought he didn't want her.

I need to change that.

It seemed Neave's counsel had come at just the right time. Despite that his gut still tightened at the thought of rejection, he had to put his fears aside and offer for the woman he wanted. He also needed to stop worrying about Janneth scorning him for his scars. The lass was gentle-hearted and kind. She would never treat him cruelly.

Around them, the conversation picked up. Niel was asking Robin about matters at Melness, and John and Janneth had a moment of relative privacy.

John caught her gaze once more, holding eye contact for longer than he usually would. He needed to be bold, to make his interest clear. "I must return to Achness shortly," he said, his voice low as their stare drew out. "But I shall be taking a ride along the shores of the kyle before I leave tomorrow morning ... will ye join me?"

10

BONNIER THAN A BLOOD-RED ROSE

Two months later …

"I DON'T BELIEVE it," Neave's voice caught as she held up the ruby brooch to the light. "Another gift?"

"There's another scrap of parchment with it," Eilidh noted breathlessly. "Read it."

Drawing in a calming breath, even if her pulse fluttered in her throat, Neave did as bid. It had been over two months since she'd received the pendant, but there had been nothing since then. In truth, she'd started to think her secret suitor had lost interest. "To a woman who is bonnier than a blood-red rose," she began. "My heart continues to beat only for ye … an ardent admirer."

Lowering the parchment, Neave's gaze slid over the faces of her three sisters. It was a rainy late-spring afternoon, just a couple of days before Beltaine. As was their habit, the four of them had retired to the women's solar for a few hours to sew, weave—and catch up on the day's events.

Beth was smiling at her, a hand lightly resting upon her swollen belly. The bairn was just over a month away now. "It's quite a gift," she murmured with a shake of her head. "Although, I do wonder at how shy this admirer seems to be."

"Aye, he's certainly taking his time to approach ye," Eilidh agreed. The youngest of the sisters sat at a loom by the window, working on a tapestry. "At this rate, ye will be a crone by the time he reveals himself. He needs to hurry up ... ye won't be young and pretty forever."

Neave snorted. "Thank ye for that reminder, Eilidh," she said crisply. "None of us will be."

In response, Eilidh pulled a face and stuck out her tongue.

"Eilidh's right though." Beth fixed Neave with a penetrating look. "Ye need to start encouraging men. Beltaine will be yer chance ... for there will be many men of marriageable age at the festival."

Swallowing her irritation, Neave pursed her lips. "Such things can't be forced," she replied. "I will find the right man for me at the *right* time."

Ignoring Beth's answering snort, she shifted her attention back to the blood-red brooch. Her ardent admirer had exquisite taste in jewelry. The brooch was expertly crafted.

A blend of frustration and excitement fluttered in her belly. *Who is he?*

"Some men can be timid with women," Jean pointed out then. "Have ye not caught any of Niel's men watching ye?"

Neave sighed before she pinned the brooch to the bodice of her kirtle. "Not one."

It was true. And nor had she received any visitors. Since Niel's last meeting, which had taken place on the cusp of spring, none of his chieftains had returned to Castle Varrich. The two chieftains her sisters had suspected of being potential suitors—Breac and Iver— had left Varrich the day following the incident with Hugh. Neither of them had sought her out beforehand, and neither man had contacted her since.

"Well, perhaps he will reveal his identity at Beltaine," Beth suggested with a wink, clearly not prepared to let the subject drop.

"Aye," Eilidh piped up, her eyes shining. "It is a time for lovers and new beginnings, after all. And the arrival of this gift, right before the festival, could be significant."

Jean muttered something about Eilidh's foolishly romantic heart, while Beth merely grinned.

And despite herself, Neave found a smile curving her lips. The sisters looked forward to Beltaine, as they did all the fire festivals that punctuated the year, yet Eilidh's excitement was feverish.

Neave's smile softened as she took in her sisters' animated faces. The four of them took delight in teasing each other and had their differences at times, yet she loved the banter between them. She was glad they'd all moved to Castle Varrich when Beth had wed Niel. She'd have hated to be without them.

"Maybe he *will* reveal himself," she murmured. Nervousness tightened her belly at the thought. Aye, whether she wished it or not, the time was coming when she would be taken from her sisters.

Trying to distract herself from such thoughts, she examined her hands, frowning when she noted the dirt encrusting her fingernails. It wouldn't do to turn up for the Beltaine celebrations with filthy nails.

Neave had been spending even more hours in the terrace garden than usual of late. With the spring flush, she'd been busy planting, weeding, and preparing beds for the wooden trays of seedlings she'd been cultivating. An overactive mind had also driven her outdoors, and she sought to quieten its chatter. An odd restlessness seethed within her these days.

John Mackay occupied her mind far too frequently of late.

Their conversation, that evening in the women's solar, haunted her. She found herself reliving what had passed between them, remembering the scars upon his body, and the story they told. She often lay awake at night wondering if John had continued his courtship of Janneth. The pair of them had gone riding together, the morning before they both departed for their respective holdings.

Neave should have been delighted he'd taken such an initiative, yet she'd been out of sorts afterward, had ended up quarreling with Jean over something inconsequential.

Of course, Neave hoped John would wed Janneth, and yet at the same time, she found herself feeling uneasy when she considered the possibility.

Her oscillating emotions wearied her.

"I think I'd better ask Greta to organize a bath for me later," she said, shifting her attention back to the here and now. "If my admirer is planning to make himself known, I must look presentable."

"Ye always look presentable, Neave," Jean sniffed, pushing aside a lock of frizzy hair that had escaped from the tight bun she wore. "Ye'd look lovely, even wearing a sack."

Beth sighed. "Aye, and at least ye don't look like a fattened goose … if I get any bigger, I shall start waddling."

All the sisters laughed, the merry sound ringing through the solar.

Eilidh fixed Neave with a coy look then, her mouth curving. "And when does John arrive?"

Neave stiffened, aware that all of her sisters were now watching her once more. It was impossible to miss the curiosity in their eyes. Of course, either Jean or Eilidh had told Beth about the scene they'd come across when they'd entered the women's solar that day. Ever since, whenever John was mentioned, they shared meaningful glances.

It was starting to vex Neave.

"I have as good an idea as ye, Eilidh," she said lightly, resisting the urge to scowl.

"Really?" Beth cocked an eyebrow. "Ye and he send missives to each other regularly."

"Aye," Eilidh agreed with a mischievous glint in her eye. "Have ye considered that yer ardent admirer could, in fact, be *John*?"

Neave burst out laughing. "Goose! He was there when the pendant and first love note arrived, don't ye remember?"

"I do," Eilidh replied, undaunted, "but he could have feigned surprise."

"And why would he do that?"

Eilidh's brow furrowed while she tried to come up with a plausible reply.

"It's all nonsense, anyway," Neave informed her sister when no answer was forthcoming. "John and I are nothing more than friends." She felt a slight twinge, deep in her chest, as she said these words. Hades, what was the matter with her at the moment?

"I've already told ye that I'm not sure unwed men and women can be friends," Beth said then, her expression thoughtful. "*Especially* if they find each other attractive."

Neave cast Beth a quelling look. "It's not like that between us."

Beth's expression turned incredulous. "So, ye mean to tell me that ye don't find John Mackay handsome?"

"He's pleasing indeed to look upon," Eilidh chimed in, earning a stern glance from Jean. She pulled a face at her sister's censure. "Don't be so prim, Jeanie … ye had a good look at his naked torso that day."

"Eilidh!" Neave snapped rigid in her seat. Of late, Eilidh had taken to surprising her with some of her comments. Before coming to Varrich, she'd been a dreamy lass, more interested in collecting flowers and playing with puppies and kittens than noting the virility of men. Yet in the past months, she'd made a few observations that made all three of her elder sisters blush.

"What?" Eilidh's oaken gaze widened upon her gamine face. "I'm stating a fact."

Neave's cheeks warmed. By blood and bone, she'd never been one to blush at the slightest thing. Usually, she'd been the sister to tease the others, the one to laugh easily. But of late, her mood was often introspective, and she was easily annoyed. Indeed, she'd lost a little of her sparkle, and she had no idea how to get it back.

"Enough of this babble," she informed her sisters crisply. "Janneth is arriving this afternoon, and I intend to find out if John has made any progress."

"He seems to be taking his time," Beth pointed out. "Perhaps he's not truly interested in her."

Neave shook her head, denying Beth's words. "Of course, he is."

"Welcome back to Varrich, Janneth." Neave approached the tall blonde woman who'd just dismounted her palfrey.

"Neave!" Janneth turned to her, a smile stretching her lips. "Ye are looking well ... green suits ye."

Neave grinned back. Indeed, this jade-green kirtle was one of her favorites. It was one of her lighter garments, and perfect for the balmy weather they were experiencing.

Moving closer to Janneth, Neave took in her friend's appearance. She'd wanted to pay her a compliment in kind, for Hugh Mackay's daughter was a rare beauty— but she noted that Janneth was much paler and thinner than she'd been the last time they'd seen each other.

"Janneth," she murmured, placing a hand upon her arm. "Is all well? Ye look strained."

Janneth nodded. She was still smiling, although Neave caught how forced the expression was. "I'm well enough ... just tired from the journey here."

It was a flimsy excuse, for Neave had heard the road to Loch Stach wasn't an arduous one. However, she didn't press the issue. "Come then." She put an arm around the taller woman's waist, steering her toward the keep as one of the stablehands led Janneth's palfrey away. "Let's pour ye a cool ale indoors."

A few yards away, Hugh was greeting Niel, his booming voice echoing across the bailey. The chieftain looked in high spirits this afternoon, and Neave noted that his face wasn't as high-colored as it had been on his previous trip to Varrich. Perhaps Hugh had eased up on the drinking. She hoped he had, for the last thing anyone wanted was for the laird of Loch Stach to ruin the Beltaine celebrations.

Neave didn't lead Janneth into the great hall, where they'd shortly be joined by the men, but instead, she took her upstairs to the women's solar. Her sisters weren't present at this hour. Beth was down in the kitchens, going over the planned meals for the coming days with the cooks, while Jean and Eilidh had gone into Tongue to help the locals prepare for the festival that heralded the first day of summer.

Neave and Janneth could have some time alone.

Greta brought them a jug of ale and two cups, leaving Neave to pour the drinks while Janneth seated herself by the window. Gazing out at the view, directly across the Kyle of Tongue, Janneth sighed. "This is such a lovely spot."

"Aye," Neave agreed with a smile. "I do love living here."

Janneth glanced her way. "It must have felt strange at first though, after growing up at Foulis Castle ... to suddenly find yerself surrounded by Mackays?"

Neave huffed a laugh. "It was," she admitted. "Although I've always had a thirst for adventure. When Beth suggested that I, Jean, and Eilidh joined her, I was delighted."

Janneth favored her with the ghost of a smile. "I've only ever known Loch Stach."

"Aye, but that will change soon enough," Neave replied, handing her a cup of frothy ale. Perching upon a stool a few feet away, she took a gulp of the cool, bitter drink. She then inclined her head. "Ye will find yerself a husband ... and make a new life elsewhere."

Did she imagine it, or did Janneth's fingers tighten around the cup at this comment?

"I suppose I will," she murmured. She then cast Neave a look under her eyelashes. "As will ye."

Neave took another sip from her cup. "Aye, it's a woman's lot ... few of us are rich or powerful enough to survive without a man's protection."

Janneth's mouth quirked. "Ye sound reluctant to wed. I would have thought ye a romantic … seeing as Niel and Beth are so happy together. And I hear yer father wed both his wives for love?"

Neave's eyes widened. Janneth's softly spoken demeanor hid a sharp, highly observant mind. "He did," she admitted, with a half-smile. "And, aye, all four of his daughters hope to wed under the same circumstances." She paused then, marshaling her thoughts. "But, how well do most women really know their husbands before they wed? What if we choose poorly?"

Janneth nodded as if she too had considered this. "It's indeed a leap of faith," she said, her mouth curving once more. Even so, her gaze had veiled.

Neave cleared her throat. Discussing what her own future held made her uneasy. She was happier focusing on other people's lives. "Have ye had any visitors to Loch Stach of late?" she asked lightly. It was a leading question, for although she and John corresponded frequently, he'd been frustratingly silent about how his courtship of Janneth was going.

Janneth nodded. "Aye … John Mackay of Aberach paid us a visit a fortnight ago."

Neave's pulse quickened. "He did?"

Janneth's gaze never left Neave's face when she replied, "Aye … he is good company. Charming, respectful … and he speaks very highly of ye, Neave."

Neave, who was in the process of swallowing another mouthful of ale, coughed. Eyes smarting, she blinked at Janneth. "He does?"

"Aye."

"Well, we became friends during his time living here at Castle Varrich," Neave replied. She tensed then, suddenly on edge. Surely, Janneth didn't believe her to be a rival for John's affections? That was the last thing she wanted—especially since it had been her goal since Yuletide to bring these two together.

She wondered then if she should mention that John only had eyes for Janneth. Her lips parted as she readied herself to tell her so. However, something in the woman's expression checked her.

Janneth's gaze held a look of caution. Neave realized then that she didn't wish to linger on this topic.

11

A DOG WITH A BONE

JOHN MACKAY DREW up his gelding, his gaze taking in the vista before him. Behind him, the small group of warriors he'd brought from Achness did the same.

Castle Varrich rose high against a pale-blue sky, the Mackay pennant fluttering in the breeze.

Smiling, John breathed in the sweet scent of grass and urged his heavyset horse onward. He'd lived at Varrich for four years after Angus Mackay's death, and had to admit that he missed the castle's grandeur.

Aye, he loved Achness, for it was where he'd grown up, and it held memories of his parents, but there was something about Varrich that made his skin prickle and his breathing catch.

It reminded him of what he'd fought for over the years, and it pleased him that the clan's head, Niel Mackay, had taken his rightful place.

Following the road around the base of the promontory, John continued to take in his surroundings as he listened to the rumble of his men's conversation behind him. The patchwork of fields around Tongue brimmed with produce this time of year, and on one of the hills, just outside the village, he spied locals building a great bonfire in readiness for the coming fire festival. Beltaine would take place the following eve. John's smile widened, anticipation curling within him.

It would be the perfect occasion to propose to Janneth.

Leaving the road, John and his men guided their horses onto a narrow path. John's gelding then picked its way up the promontory, mane and forelock ruffling in the light wind that rippled in from the kyle.

Upon leaving Castle Varrich two moons earlier, John had made himself a promise that he was done with hesitation. Janneth was a jewel indeed, and if he didn't make his intentions clear, another man would win her affections.

As such, John had written to her before making a trip to Loch Stach. The visit had gone well. Janneth had greeted him warmly, and Hugh had been delighted to host him. And then, when he'd mentioned to the chieftain that he wished to propose to Janneth at Beltaine, Hugh had slapped him on the back. "Ye have my blessing, John. I'd be honored to name ye kin."

Initially, John had planned to propose to Janneth while he was at Loch Stach. However, the lass had been a little skittish with him. They'd taken a few escorted walks together, but he hadn't had the chance to speak to her alone or to kiss her. He didn't want to be hasty, to push her before she was ready.

But Beltaine seemed the right time, and Janneth would likely know his intentions by now.

John's belly tightened, and he realized he was indeed nervous.

Neave's words that eve, when she'd stitched his arm for him, had galvanized him over the past weeks. Whenever he faltered, whenever he wondered if Janneth secretly scorned him for his missing hand and eye, he recalled her advice.

Yer scars aren't something to be ashamed of. They are a reminder to all that yer enemies tried to kill ye and failed ... ye are stronger than them, John Mackay.

Aye, he had much to thank Neave for.

John approached the summit of the promontory, his gaze straying to the path that led to the southern curtain wall, where Neave's beloved garden lay. A smile stretched across his face.

He was looking forward to seeing his friend again.

He didn't have to wait long—for as soon as he rode under the wide stone arch and into Castle Varrich's bailey, John's gaze alighted upon a woman dressed in green, her chestnut-brown hair fluttering in the breeze, crossing the cobbles, gardening basket tucked under one arm.

John's heart kicked against his ribs. Somehow, he'd forgotten how lovely Neave Munro was. He couldn't help it; his gaze roamed over her, taking in the gentle pink of her cheeks and the brightness of her hazel-green eyes. The dark-green kirtle she wore hugged her lithe form. She'd pulled her thick hair off her face and pinned half of it back, while letting the rest tumble down her back.

Upon spying him, Neave's gait faltered, her eyes widening. A heartbeat later, a wide smile flowered upon her pixie face. "John!"

Drawing up his gelding, John swung down and turned to Neave.

His first instinct was to step toward her and draw her into his arms for a hug—one that he firmly quashed. Such behavior was far too familiar.

Aye, they were friends—but they were also man and woman. There were some lines they had to be careful not to cross. The fact that John did notice how comely Neave was—when he was actively courting another woman—made uneasiness tighten his belly.

Fighting off the sensation, he grinned at Neave. "Off to yer garden?"

She nodded. "The weeds never sleep, I'm afraid."

"It's good to see ye, Neave," he found himself saying before kicking himself. *So much for self-restraint.*

Neave's bow-shaped mouth curved, her right cheek dimpling prettily. "And ye." Her eyes twinkled then. "Janneth tells me ye have paid her a visit?"

John rolled his eyes. "God's teeth, woman ... ye are like a dog with a bone. I thought I told ye to let that subject lie?"

Neave feigned innocence. "I have no idea what ye are blathering about ... I was merely making conversation."

John eyed her. "Aye, of course ye were."

Silence fell between them as their gazes fused.

Eventually, John cleared his throat. "Is Janneth here then?"

"Aye, the Mackays of Loch Stach arrived yesterday," Neave replied. "We've been catching up. I'm glad to hear ye are actively wooing her … do ye plan to propose soon?"

John muttered an oath under his breath, yet Neave didn't back down. "Well … do ye?"

"Aye," he growled. "Tomorrow eve."

Neave's eyes widened. "On Beltaine … a good choice."

"I hope so."

Neave took a step back from him then, favoring John with another one of her impish smiles. "Well, I shall let ye stable yer horse. Ye shall be looking forward to catching up with Niel." And with that, she walked away.

Frowning, John watched her go.

"Yer prisoner has fallen ill, Laird."

The announcement, uttered by Ewan Reay, the captain of Varrich's guard, made John glance up from where he'd been pouring himself a second cup of ale. He and Niel sat in the clan-chief's solar, at the table at the heart of the large chamber, while John filled him in about the continuing problem they'd had with sheep rustling on the Mackay-Sutherland border.

Niel frowned at this news. "Gunn?" The clan-chief's gaze settled upon the tall, broad-shouldered figure who had just entered the solar. Captain Reay was a big man whose presence tended to dominate any space he stepped into. This afternoon, he wore a severe expression, his grey-blue gaze narrowed.

Reay nodded. "He developed a wheezing sickness over the winter … but it seems to have worsened."

Niel's mouth pursed. Sitting back on his chair, he raked a hand through his long peat-brown hair. "Have ye called the healer to him?"

"No … I thought I should speak to ye first."

"Aye, well, a Gunn hostage is no good to me dead … send word to Tess."

"Aye, Laird … I shall see it done." With that, the captain turned on his heel and strode from the solar.

Silence followed the whisper of the door closing.

John didn't speak for a moment. Instead, he observed his cousin's face. Niel wore an expression he knew well: a look that was both a blend of stubbornness and thinly veiled irritation.

"Have ye had any more missives from Tavish Gunn?" John asked after a pause.

Niel shook his head. "He's given up pleading for his brother's release … for the moment."

John's gaze remained on the clan-chief, as Niel reached out and picked up his own cup of ale. He then took a deep draft. His face still hadn't softened. Niel Mackay had yielded on a number of things over the past year, and especially after his victory at Sandside Bay—a win that had nearly cost him his life. Nonetheless, there were some things he was intractable on, and the fate of William Gunn was one.

"Do ye have any plans to release Gunn?" John asked after a lengthy pause.

Niel's gaze swung his way. "No." His brow furrowed. "Don't tell me *ye* think I should … after all the trouble those bastards have caused us?"

John shrugged. Niel didn't like being questioned about the Gunns, yet his ire didn't bother John. They'd grown close since Niel's escape from Bass Rock, and John liked that he could be frank with his cousin. Like Neave, Niel had always put him at ease.

The thought of Neave, and their meeting earlier in the bailey, made John tense. The woman could be frustrating at times. She had a way of getting things out of him—even though he'd promised himself he'd remain tight-lipped about his plans regarding Janneth. It wasn't that he thought she'd go straight to Janneth and tell her. Instead, his courtship of Hugh Mackay's daughter made him want to create some distance between him and Neave.

Seeing her again had been both a pleasure and a disturbance. And, as always, Neave had flitted away before he could question her about herself.

"Like ye, I have a long memory where the Gunns are concerned," John replied, shoving thoughts of Neave aside. "Ye did well to take one of Tavish's brothers hostage ... and to hold him here ... for the Gunns will think twice about border raids or stealing cattle or sheep while William Gunn remains yer captive." John paused then, scratching his chin. "However, ye and I both know that the dungeon beneath the castle is a foul, damp place. I'm not surprised Gunn has sickened down there. If he dies, it could *worsen* relations between us and the Gunns ... it could spark new conflict."

Niel's face screwed up. "And what would ye have me do?" he asked, his voice lowering to a growl. He clearly didn't like John pointing this out, yet he couldn't deny the truth of his words. He'd probably already considered the eventuality.

John sighed. He'd tread carefully now. Raising the cup of ale to his lips, he took a sip while considering how to respond. "Sending Tess to him is a good start," he replied, his voice shuttered. "But ye might consider putting the prisoner to work."

Niel cocked an eyebrow, inviting him to continue.

"It'll get him into the fresh air and help keep him healthy and strong," John went on, warming to the idea as he spoke. "And, ye might as well make use of him. The cottars are always in need of laborers."

"And what if he tries to escape?"

John leaned back in his chair, his mouth lifting at the corners. "He won't if ye put him in irons."

12

EVERY LASS LIKES A ROGUE

THE RHYTHMIC POUNDING of the drums beckoned as Neave followed her sisters up the hill toward the Beltaine fire.

Most of the villagers had already gathered there, and laughter and singing rang out into the night. Lifting her chin, Neave spied the outlines of figures dancing around the fire. She smiled then, recalling Beltaines past. This was the second one she'd attended at Varrich, although the sound of the drums reminded her of all the occasions she'd danced around the roaring fire on a hill outside Foulis Castle.

Her mother had died just a day after Beltaine six years earlier.

Reaching the crest of the hill, Neave noted that some of the lasses wore yellow primroses and ribbons in their hair. The color evoked fire and was supposed to beckon the sun forth to ensure good weather for livestock and crops. It was a reminder that Beltaine was an ancient festival. Indeed, in nearby Tongue village, folk had placed boughs of hawthorn over the entrances of their cottages. The tradition invited prosperity but also paid respect to the *Aos Sí*, the fairy-folk. These days, most Highlanders followed Christ, yet many were still superstitious of the old ways.

Neave's mouth curved as she recalled her father's habit of always carrying salt in his pocket on the eve of Beltaine, "Just to keep the *Sí* in their place, lass," he'd once told her. "Otherwise, who knows what mischief they'd make?"

A sweet, nutty aroma drifted across the hillside then, and Eilidh, who'd arrived at the fire just before Neave, let out a squeal of delight. "We're just in time for the oatcake and caudle."

Following her sisters, Neave went to where women were ladling out the thick, sweet drink made from eggs, butter, ground oats, and milk upon the fire. Other village women also moved about the crowd, distributing wedges of oatcake.

"Good eve, Neave." A familiar male voice made her turn. John Mackay smiled down at her, his clear-blue gaze gleaming in the firelight. This eve, the laird of Achness dressed in black leather trews and a loose charcoal-colored lèine open at the throat. He wore a black velvet eye-covering.

"Good evening," she replied with an answering smile. "Ye look roguish when ye wear black."

His smile slid into a lop-sided grin. "It's not the eye patch?"

"Perhaps."

"A cup of caudle for ye, Neave," a woman asked, interrupting them. "And ye too, John?"

"Aye, thank ye, Mairi." Neave took the wooden cup the miller's wife offered. John also accepted a cup before holding it up to Neave in a toast.

"Here's to good fortune for us all," she quipped with another smile.

"And to new beginnings, lass."

Neave inclined her head before taking a step closer to him. It was noisy so close to the fire, as the drums continued to pound, and lads and lasses danced to the screech of a highland pipe. Nonetheless, she hadn't yet spied Janneth, and didn't want to speak of her, only to discover the woman was standing behind them. "Ye really are going to propose to Janneth tonight?"

John inclined his head. "Aye, I've already told ye that … are ye worried I've lost my nerve?"

There was no mistaking the challenge in his voice.

Neave raised her chin. "No … but ye were hesitant for so long, I thought—"

"Well, the time for hesitation has passed," he replied, cutting her off. A crease had formed between John's brows now, and Neave realized with a jolt that he appeared vexed with her. "If I wait any longer, I shall miss my chance." He paused then, his frown deepening. "I thought ye encouraged this match ... have ye decided otherwise now?"

Studying his face, Neave noted the glint in his eye. Indeed, John was determined this eve. However, her chest constricted, misgiving stealing through her. She'd spoken with Janneth again that morning, and had marked the pallor of her skin and her puffy eyes. She looked as if she'd spent the night weeping, but when Neave questioned her, Janneth had brushed her concerns off. "I always get irritated eyes this time of year," she told Neave. "That bothersome gorse is the bane of my life every summer."

Neave hadn't believed her.

Aye, she'd encouraged John to pursue Janneth, and had thought they'd make an excellent match. But she was now doubting her own judgment.

That morning, Janneth hadn't looked like a woman in love.

The urge to warn John of her worries wreathed up within Neave, and yet she checked herself. There was a fine line between helping and interfering—a lesson it appeared she was slow to learn.

She didn't want to ruin her friendship with John.

It was wise to let things be.

Neave took a sip of caudle. It was rich and sweet, a drink she usually enjoyed, although this eve it made her feel a trifle queasy. She noted that John hadn't yet touched his. "Of course not," she murmured. "Ye are right to offer for Janneth ... and Beltaine is an auspicious time to make a proposal." Stepping back from him, she cast her gaze around her. An instant later, she spied Janneth's silver-blonde hair. Hugh Mackay was making his way up the hill, arm-in-arm with his bonny daughter.

Neave's breathing caught. Janneth had looked pale and wan earlier in the day, but not so now. Clad in a silver-green kirtle, her silken hair tumbling over her shoulders, she looked like the queen of the *Aos Sì,* who'd emerged to dance with mortals for the evening.

"And here she is," Neave murmured, trying to ignore the tightening in her throat and chest. "Yer moment has arrived."

Janneth Mackay had never looked lovelier, and yet John hesitated to go to her.

Instead, he glanced over at the woman standing next to him.

Neave was also a vision this evening, in a butter-yellow kirtle that glowed gold in the firelight. She wore the ruby pendant and brooch her secret admirer had gifted her, both of which gleamed as if aflame. And yet her hazel-green gaze was shadowed, troubled. Their conversation had been tense.

They'd never rubbed each other up the wrong way in the past, yet tonight her words had nettled him.

After all, it was Neave who'd encouraged him to pursue Janneth. He didn't appreciate the caution he'd spied in her gaze earlier.

In truth, he'd approached Neave intending to ask her how she was faring. Her letters were entertaining and contained plenty of gossip, yet with few details about the woman herself.

But now the moment had passed.

Neave took another step back and gestured to where Hugh Mackay and his daughter approached. "Off ye go," she urged with a playful grin that didn't quite match her solemn gaze. "Ask her to dance before someone else does."

With a nod, John moved away. Janneth saw him approach, and she favored him with a smile.

It wasn't a radiant one, as he'd hoped, and his step slowed a little. However, he reminded himself that Janneth Mackay wasn't like Neave Munro. She had a more demure manner.

"Good eve, Hugh ... Janneth," he greeted father and daughter.

"And a bonny evening it is too," Hugh rumbled. His expression was a little abashed this eve as John approached. "I'm pleased that Niel invited us this year." The chieftain of Loch Stach's gaze surveyed the crowd, his face suddenly tensing. Following the direction of his stare, John turned to see that Hugh had spied Breac Mackay of Balnakeil. The young laird was laughing over something with Iver Mackay of Dun Ugadale.

"Look at them … those two are as thick as thieves," Hugh growled. "As Robert and William once were."

John frowned. He'd thought Hugh had vowed to let his suspicion of the lairds of Balnakeil and Dun Ugadale go. They certainly didn't want him causing another fight this evening.

As if echoing John's thoughts, Janneth placed a cautionary hand upon her father's arm. "Please, Da … ye *promised*."

"Aye," John agreed, injecting a warning edge into his voice. "Remember, I now bear yet another scar upon my arm thanks to ye."

The words were blunt, yet they had the desired effect. Hugh Mackay's face sagged, and he shifted his attention back to John. "I never intended for ye to get hurt, John."

"No, but that's what happens when ye let doubt take ye down dark paths," John countered, holding his eye. "Aye, Breac and Iver are fast friends, but there's nothing sinister in it. They are close in age … it is only natural." He paused then, letting his words sink in. "Ye need to let the past go, for it won't help any of us if ye cling to yer baseless suspicions."

Hugh's bearded jaw tensed at this, and John wondered if he'd offended him. Nonetheless, he'd had enough of bitterness and feuding within his own clan. He'd lost a hand and an eye to it—and right now, he didn't care if he offended his future father-by-marriage in order to make his point.

Breac and Iver had fought with them at Sandside Bay, and had both lost a number of their own men in the battle, as had Hugh. It was time for the chieftain of Loch Stach to focus his attention elsewhere.

Long moments passed, and then Hugh muttered an oath under his breath. "Aye, very well." When their gazes met, John was relieved to see no rancor there, just embarrassment. "Enough griping from an old hound … tonight is for the young." He looked at his daughter then, his expression softening further. "Isn't Janneth a fair sight?"

"Aye," John agreed, smiling. "Lovely indeed."

Janneth flashed him an embarrassed smile before she lowered her gaze. "Thank ye, John … ye look handsome … black suits ye."

"I've been told it makes me look roguish … although that wasn't my intention."

Janneth glanced at him, her eyes sparkling now. "Every lass likes a rogue."

John laughed, and the tension between the three of them dissipated.

"Well, ye could go on exchanging compliments all eve," Hugh interjected with a wry smile. "Why don't ye two join the dancers? I'll get myself a cup of caudle."

"Here, ye can have mine … I've not yet taken a sip." John handed him his untouched cup. In truth, he wasn't overly fond of the cloyingly sweet caudle, but he hadn't wanted to offend Mairi.

He then shifted his attention back to Janneth, and held out his left arm for her to take. "What say ye, Janneth, do ye fancy a dance?"

13

TOO LATE

NEAVE FINISHED HER cup of caudle and then nibbled on a wedge of oatcake. Lingering on the sidelines, she observed the celebration, rather than taking part in it.

It wasn't like her at all. And, as if sensing her mood, the men present hardly seemed to notice her. Not one asked her to dance.

In contrast, Neave's younger sisters were not so reticent, or invisible. Eilidh had even managed to drag Jean into the fray. Linking arms with Mackay warriors, the lasses laughed as they spun around the fire. A few yards away, Beth looked on. She was too heavy with bairn these days to dance. Instead, she stood with Niel. Arms wrapped protectively about his wife's midriff, the clan-chief's mouth was curved into a contented smile. Watching them, Neave's breathing hitched.

How pleased she was that Beth and Niel were so happy together. But at the same time, she couldn't help but be a little envious.

Janneth was right—she did want a love match. She ached for one. And now that she fully admitted it to herself, the intensity of the desire made it difficult to breathe.

Beltaine was an eve for *couples*, both old and new. Folk said that many a bairn took seed on this night, and indeed, a number of weddings took place in the months following this fire festival. As the night wore on, lovers would go 'green-gowning', leaving the fireside to seek a quiet, secluded spot, where they would lie together.

Neave's belly fluttered at the thought of doing something so daring.

Of course, few high-born lasses had such freedom, but just for an instant, she wished she could slip out of her own life and be one of those carefree, apple-cheeked lasses dancing around the fire.

Are ye no longer carefree? The question arose, unbidden. Just the year before, she'd danced around the Beltaine fire with abandon, but twelve moons on, she felt as if she'd changed. She wasn't as happy as she'd once been—yet she couldn't discern the reason. These days, helping those she loved didn't satisfy her like it once had. Tonight, the gnawing ache of loneliness tugged at her.

Taking another delicate bite of oatcake, Neave continued to watch the dancers. She wasn't hungry, yet eating gave her something to do, and an excuse as to why she wasn't joining the revelers.

At her sisters' urging, she'd worn her ruby pendant and brooch, in the hope that her admirer would spy them and make himself known tonight. But, still, none of the many warriors around the Beltaine fire approached her.

Maybe he's not here after all.

Disappointment gripped Neave's ribcage at the thought, and she suddenly felt self-conscious standing there in her finery, awaiting her ardent admirer. Perhaps someone was playing an elaborate prank on her.

Ruminating on this possibility, her attention traveled, unbidden, to where John and Janneth danced.

She'd told herself she wouldn't stare at them—yet she couldn't help herself.

Every time she tried to look elsewhere, her gaze returned to the pair, like a wasp to a pot of honey.

What a striking couple they make.

And they did: him tall, lean and dark—her slender and pale as the dawn.

Neave's throat started to ache then, and she reached up, rubbing it. What was wrong with her? She should be delighted for them, and yet suddenly felt on the verge of tears.

Daft woman, she chided herself. *This is what ye wanted, what ye have spent months helping create. Ye should be pleased.*

And she was—there was a certain satisfaction in knowing that she'd given John a push in the right direction. He looked happy this eve, laughing at something Janneth had just said, as they broke off from the dancing and retrieved cups of ale from a man who'd rolled a barrel up the hill for the occasion. The evening was drawing out now, many of the older folk retiring, while the young still danced and made merry.

Forcing herself to look away from John and Janneth, Neave noted that Breac and Iver had joined the dancers. Iver seemed to have taken a liking to Eilidh. The young chieftain of the Mackays of Dun Ugadale indeed drew the eye, with his sharp features, penetrating ice-blue eyes, and long white-blond hair that he wore tied back at the nape of his neck.

Despite her bleak mood, Neave's mouth curved. She wasn't surprised Iver was drawn to Eilidh—the lass looked radiant in the firelight, her delicate features flushed from all the dancing.

Jean had withdrawn from the fire now. To Neave's surprise, she saw her standing on the sidelines, a cup of ale in hand while she tried to draw Robin Mackay into conversation. Neave observed them with interest. Frankly, she was surprised Robin had made the trip from Melness, even though it was but a short distance from Tongue. The man's expression was hardly welcoming, and he was replying to Jean in short, terse sentences.

Nonetheless, Neave's plucky sister persisted.

The screech of the Highland pipe cut through the roar of voices around the fire, as the two musicians, their faces red with exertion, began another rousing song. Cheers went up, and many folk rejoined the dancers.

Yet John and Janneth didn't. Instead, he'd drawn her away from the throng, to where smoke drifted over the hilltop in a haze.

The laird of Achness wasn't smiling now. Instead, he wore an intent, serious expression.

Neave's belly clenched. *He's going to propose.*

Heart pounding, she tore her gaze away and stared down at the ground.

She should have been excited for them—for this was the moment they'd been building up to—but instead, she felt sick.

The urge to rush to them, grab John by the arm, and haul him away from Janneth reared up within her.

Of course, she'd do no such thing, yet the instinct made the queasiness in her belly intensify. Her hand, which held the remnants of her oatcake, tightened, crushing it to crumbs.

It hit her then, with the force of a smith's hammer between the eyes, that she was jealous of Janneth—jealous that the woman would soon be the wife of John Mackay of Aberach. Her stomach hurt now, and her breathing came in short, pained gasps.

The truth was that she wanted him for herself.

The devil strike me down, what have I done?

She wasn't sure when and how it had happened, but somehow, over the past weeks, her feelings toward John had changed, from friendship to something far more complex.

Tears stung her eyes, and her vision blurred.

Fool. Ye have fallen for yer best friend.

A man who saw her as a sister.

A man who was about to propose to the woman he wanted.

Neave couldn't stay by the fireside to watch. She couldn't bear to glance their way once more and see joy suffuse Janneth's face, or watch a smile of pride grace John's. The lass might have appeared out-of-sorts earlier in the day, but she was radiant now.

It would be a dirk-blade to the chest. One she likely deserved, for if she hadn't so eagerly pushed John in Janneth's direction, it likely would never have come to this.

Ever since that day when she'd stitched up his injured arm, things had been different between them. Somehow, their conversation had subtly changed the nature of their relationship. From that day forward, Neave had stopped seeing John Mackay as a friend. Indeed, her feelings toward him had been far more complex.

She just hadn't realized it until now.

And it was too late.

Swallowing hard, as a sob clawed its way up her throat, Neave let the oatcake crumbs fall to the ground and turned from the bonfire.

She needed to return to the castle, to get as far away from John as possible—before she did something idiotic, something she'd regret for the rest of her life.

Pushing her way through the milling crowd, she left the revelry behind. The glow of the bonfire lit up the hillside and the clusters of trees that ringed the base of the mound. After that, a path cut through the fields before forking: one branch traveling to the village, the other up to the castle.

As soon as Neave was out of sight of the crowd, the sob she'd been fighting escaped. Clapping a hand over her mouth, she hurried on, tears streaming down her face.

What an utter goose she was. Neave Munro, so bright and free, had just fallen into a trap of her own making. She'd been so fixated on helping John and Janneth, she'd completely ignored her own feelings, the desires of her own heart.

The grass was damp with dew, and she nearly slipped a few times, such was her haste. She also had to be careful not to trip over the rocks that studded the hillside. Tears now blinded her, and she tried to wipe them away. If she wasn't careful, she'd fall arse over tit.

She'd nearly reached the base of the hill, and the copse of hazel trees, when her step faltered, and she slowed.

Moonlight illuminated the hillside and the fields and promontory beyond, where Castle Varrich rose against a star-strewn sky. The walk through the fields and up to the castle was one she'd done many times on her own in daylight. But never at night. There were too many shadowed places along the way.

Foolish lass, she chastised herself, halting. *Ye can't walk back alone.* Deciding that she would have to dry her tears, go back, and fetch Jean and Eilidh, Neave started to turn.

A man's voice intruded then. "Neave!"

Turning, she scrubbed at her eyes. Christ's teeth, she didn't want anyone to see her in such a state. She'd hoped to pull herself together before she reached the top of the hill once more.

"Ye liked my gifts, I see, lass."

Peering up the hill, Neave spied a hulking silhouette advancing toward her, outlined by the glow of the Beltaine fire at his back. And then, as the man drew closer, she made out his features.

Neave froze.

Roy Morrison grinned, his eyes glinting. "And bonny ye look, too, wearing them."

"Janneth, will ye be my wife?"

The words came out in a rush, tumbling one over the other. It wasn't the proposal John had practiced in his mind. When he'd imagined this moment, he'd envisaged himself delivering the question with more assurance. As it was, his voice caught and he spoke far too quickly.

Janneth's gaze snapped wide.

For an instant, they stared at each other.

And then her gaze shuttered, her mouth turned down at the corners.

Without saying a word, Janneth had given him her answer.

And at that moment, John knew two things: firstly, that she didn't welcome his gauche proposal; and secondly, that she was going to refuse him.

"Ye look sad, lass," he murmured when the awkward pause between them drew out. Around them, the revelry continued. Lads, seated back from the fire, still beat upon their calf-skin drums—the sound like a steadily pounding heart. However, John's own pulse was now racing. "Is the prospect so terrible?"

She favored him with a brave smile, even though her eyes now gleamed. "Da told me ye intended to propose tonight, John … and if things were different, I'd be happy to be yer wife."

John swallowed, in an attempt to loosen the tightness in his throat. "If things were different?"

"Aye." Her gaze never left his. "I cannot wed ye … for my heart is already spoken for."

John stiffened, a chill sweeping over his body. Recovering, he forced himself to respond. "Ye wish to wed someone else?" he asked stupidly.

She nodded.

John scanned the surrounding crowd. He expected to see Janneth's mystery suitor standing nearby glaring at him, yet no one appeared to be paying them any attention. Hugh had pulled up a stool on the other side of the fire next to Niel and Beth, and the Mackays of Farr. He was currently ignoring his daughter as he chatted to the clan-chief and Connor Mackay.

Perhaps the man Janneth loved wasn't present this evening.

When he swung his attention back to her, he saw that she was watching him, her expression troubled. "I'm sorry, John," she murmured. "I hope ye aren't too disappointed."

Disappointed? He wasn't sure how he felt about her refusal of his proposal, yet the word didn't even begin to describe the maelstrom within him.

He hadn't been naïve enough to believe Janneth was in love with him—for such things took time—but he'd thought she had been taken by him, as he had been with her. Yet, as he thought back over the past weeks, he now realized that her coyness hadn't been down to shyness as he'd previously thought, but reluctance.

The chill dousing John from head to toe intensified. It felt as if someone had just emptied an icy bucket of water over him.

"And the man ye want," he began, surprising himself at how calm he sounded. "Is he here?" Damn it, he had to know.

A nerve flickered in her cheek, and John thought she wouldn't answer. But after a heartbeat, she did, her voice barely above a whisper. "Aye."

John's pulse quickened further, heat following the chill as embarrassment barreled into him. He suddenly felt like a jester, stumbling around a stage to the mirth of onlookers.

Only the fact that Janneth's expression was solemn, her gaze contrite, prevented him from becoming angry. The lass hadn't misled him on purpose—but all the same, humiliation bit deep.

"And will ye tell me who he is?"

Her throat bobbed. "Only if ye promise not to say a word to Da."

John's mouth thinned. He wasn't feeling in the mood to give such an assurance, yet after a moment, he nodded.

Janneth glanced left to where the dancers had slowed as the current song came to an end. And then John saw whom her gaze alighted upon.

The laird of Balnakeil was grinning as he stepped back from the dancers and took the cup one of the clan-chief's men passed him. Feeling someone's stare, he glanced up—and across the crowd, Janneth and Breac's gazes fused.

Breac's expression changed then. His smile faded, his tanned face tensed, and his gaze turned intense.

Glancing back at Janneth, John saw how the lass's face had come alive. His stomach dove then as he realized all hope truly was lost.

Not once in the past months had Janneth Mackay given him such a look.

14

INTENDED

"YE LOOK SURPRISED, lass … surely, ye knew those gifts were from me?"

Neave gaped at Roy Morrison, aware that he'd drawn closer and now loomed over her.

"No," she rasped, her heart fluttering in the base of her throat. "I had absolutely no idea."

"I must admit, those items were costly," he went on, not seeming to notice her horrified expression. "Talented jewelsmiths are a rarity in the Highlands, but I managed to find an Italian in Inverness with the skill I required." He flashed her another smile then, his teeth glinting in the darkness. "I spent every last penny I had on them too … but ye were worth it."

Neave swallowed. She couldn't believe this was happening. It was as if she were lost in a bizarre dream—one that she desperately wanted to wake from.

She and John had both agreed that Roy Morrison couldn't be her ardent admirer—the one who'd sent her gifts with romantic words. Indeed, it seemed impossible, and yet the man was admitting it.

"I was worried ye wouldn't wear them tonight," Roy said then, stepping closer still. He was a big man, and he towered over her. "But imagine my delight when ye did."

Neave's skin prickled. They stood alone at the bottom of the hill. The revelry and friendly glow of the bonfire suddenly seemed distant, and the shadows of the hazel wood reached out to embrace them.

She wasn't safe here.

"They were generous gifts indeed," Neave said then, finally finding her voice. She shifted right, intending to retrace her steps to the fire. If the man wished to speak to her, he could do so surrounded by a crowd. "And I thank ye for them … however, I would never wish ye to beggar yerself on my account. I really must give the gifts back."

She reached up then, cursing her trembling fingers, and unclasped the pendant. She had just started to unfasten the brooch when his large, rough hand closed over hers. Morrison had followed her and now blocked her path.

"They are yers, lass … as am I."

Neave dragged in a deep breath. She was in serious trouble here and didn't know how to extract herself. Her instinct was to spell it out to him, as baldly as possible, that she had no interest in him and that he had to take back his gifts.

But at the same time, good sense checked her.

The blacksmith was gazing down at her, eyes gleaming. By day they were a striking purple-gray, yet at night they appeared almost black. He was dangerous; she'd sensed it the first time she'd spied him staring at her at Yule.

Instinctively, Neave had known she never wanted to find herself alone with Roy Morrison. And yet here she was.

No, she had to tread carefully. And yet, she couldn't encourage him either.

"Ye must excuse me," she said softly. "I'm not feeling well … I must return to my sisters."

"What ails ye then, lass?" he asked, drawing closer still. His hand lifted and cupped her cheek. He then leaned in. "Nothing a kiss from yer intended wouldn't heal?"

Neave's heart bucked against her ribs. *Intended?*

"We aren't betrothed," she gasped.

"Aye, we are … when ye accepted my gifts, ye accepted my courtship."

"But I've already told ye ... I *don't* accept them."
Neave finished unfastening the brooch and stepped away
once more, pushing the two items of jewelry at him.
Morrison wasn't going to let her bow out gracefully, it
seemed. Other men would realize they weren't wanted
and allow her to return to the bonfire, but this one would
need some convincing. "Ye are overstepping."

"Am I?" he asked, his voice developing a hard edge.
However, he refused to take the brooch and pendant. "Ye
are an ungrateful wee bitch, aren't ye?"

Heat ignited in Neave's belly. "It seems so," she
replied, her own tone hardening. "Please take back the
jewels ... and ye can give them to a woman who wants
ye."

"I don't want another woman, Neave Munro." His
voice lowered to a tone that sent a warning shivering
across her skin. "I want ye ... and I shall have ye." Taking
the pendant and brooch, he then stuffed them into his
vest. "And if ye won't take my gifts, then I shall sell them
and use the coin to build us a grand home."

Neave's breathing caught. What was the man on
about? It was as if he wasn't listening to her, as if he
didn't care she wasn't interested. He'd already made up
his mind that she was his and didn't intend to be
thwarted.

Aye, she was in grave danger—and there was only one
thing to do.

Neave ran.

She was fast, even in long skirts, and terror gave her
feet wings.

But despite that Roy Morrison was a big, heavily
muscled man, he moved with frightening swiftness.

In just three paces, he caught up with her, one thick
arm hooking around her waist, and jerking her
backward.

Neave opened her mouth to scream, yet he cut it off
with his other hand.

And an instant later, he was dragging her away, back
down the hill toward the trees.

Terror sprang to life, writhing in her chest as she fought him. Morrison didn't need to state his intentions now: she knew he intended to rape her. And as soon as he got her into the trees, he would.

She had to do something to stop him.

But his grip was so strong, as hard as the iron the man forged. She couldn't wriggle out of his hold—instead, she had to use her wits.

Her father had taught his daughters how to deal with unwelcome suitors, with any man with wandering hands. "Go for the vulnerable bits," he'd told her as they returned home from hunting one day. Beth and Neave were both keen archers, and had enjoyed a deer hunt with their father. Both she and Beth had giggled at the comment, yet their father's brow had furrowed. "Mark me, lasses," he'd rumbled. "The groin, the eyes, or the throat are the best places to strike if ye ever find yerself in trouble."

And so, recalling her father's words, Neave stopped fighting Roy Morrison and flung herself against him, her right hand clenching into a fist.

Putting every ounce of her force behind her, she slugged him hard in the cods.

John decided it was time to leave the celebrations.

He'd already distanced himself from Janneth, watching as the woman made her way across to where Breac stood. The chieftain's gaze tracked her path, transfixed.

John didn't need to see any more of this.

It had taken much for him to cast aside his fears of rejection and propose to Janneth. Ever since his visit to Loch Stach, he'd found himself imagining what life would be like at Achness with her as his wife. He'd hoped to wed her soon, and to bring her home with him, but now that dream had soured.

Instead, he would ride through the gates of Achness broch alone, as always.

Turning, he scanned the surrounding crowd for Neave, but she was nowhere to be seen.

It was getting late, and she'd likely returned to the castle. However, he was surprised to see Jean and Eilidh still among the revelers. Surely, Neave wouldn't have left on her own? One of the servants, perhaps her maid, Greta, whom Neave was close to, must have gone back with her.

And with Neave absent from the crowd, John truly had no reason to linger.

Feeling oddly detached from his surroundings, he wove through the throng and made his way down the hillside.

Above, the full moon sailed high, a polished silver penny against the coal-black night, and the grass beneath his boots was slippery with dew. The sound of the drums, laughter, and music faded behind him, and he heaved a sigh, tension unraveling within him.

It had certainly been an evening to remember—although John wasn't sure he wanted to.

All he wished for now was his bed.

He was halfway down the hill when a pained male grunt reached him, followed by a rasped curse.

John's gait slowed. They were getting to the stage of the night when some couples would break off from the crowd and seek privacy nearby to couple.

He might be about to unwittingly stumble upon two lovers 'green-gowning'—although that noise hadn't sounded like moans of pleasure.

An instant later, a woman screamed. It was short, cutting off immediately, yet the hair on the back of John's neck prickled.

Something was definitely amiss here.

Gaze scanning the moonlit hillside, he advanced toward the hazel wood at its base—and there, just a few yards from the trees, he spied a large figure dragging a smaller one behind it.

John scowled. Even from this distance, he could see the woman wasn't willing.

He broke into a run, his feet sliding on the damp grass. He also had to be careful to avoid tripping over the rocks and small boulders that studded the hillside. If he wasn't attentive, he'd sprawl on his face.

A moment later, he called out, "Ye there … halt!"

At his shout, the woman appeared to struggle harder, her arms and legs flailing, her long hair swinging around her shoulders. She fought her assailant with everything she had, wriggling in his grip like an eel.

And with a vicious curse, her would-be-rapist smacked her around the head.

The man either hadn't heard John's shout or was ignoring him. Either way, he intended to continue.

John flew down the hill, balling his left fist as he went. And then, ducking around the big man's left side, he delivered a heavy punch—a haymaker—to the attacker's temple.

It was a brutal hit, one that could kill if delivered hard enough—and the man let out a pained grunt before he crumpled.

An instant later, John recognized both individuals: Roy Morrison and Neave Munro.

Twisting free of the blacksmith, as he sagged to the ground and released his grip upon her, Neave backed up. Her breathing came in short, ragged bursts, and her gaze glinted in the moonlight, wild with panic.

John moved toward her, his chest tightening. "Neave?"

She blinked, emerging from the terror that had turned her into a wild animal. "John!"

"Mackay of Aberach." Roy Morrison growled his name like a curse. He staggered to his feet, shaking his head. "Ye shall regret that."

John swiveled to face him. It surprised him Morrison had recovered so swiftly from that punch. Most men would be out cold.

His gaze narrowed as it swept over the blacksmith. "I recall telling ye to stay away from Neave Munro," he replied, his tone chilling.

In response, Morrison spat on the ground and turned to face him, his huge hands clenching and unclenching at his sides.

"Ye aren't her guardian," he snarled. "The lass wants a good plowing … why don't ye go back to the dancing and leave us to get on with it?"

John glanced Neave's way and saw she was staring at him, her heart-shaped face pale and taut in the moonlight. "Move behind me, Neave," he commanded.

Wordlessly, she did as bid.

John then shifted his attention back to Morrison, taking his measure. They were both tall men, yet the blacksmith was far heavier and stronger. That didn't bother John; he'd brought down plenty of big men in battle. But, even so, he considered the best way to fight him.

"I'll give ye one chance, Morrison," he said, rolling his shoulders to loosen the muscles, and letting his arms fall at the ready at his sides. He wore his fake wooden hand this eve and would have preferred to remove it before fighting. However, there wasn't time. The hand was secured tightly to his wrist and could be used as a weapon if need be. "Walk away right now … and we won't take this any further."

Roy Morrison sneered at him. "Don't waste yer words, *cripple*."

The blacksmith then bent his head and charged toward John.

15

A FIGHT IN THE DARK

NEAVE HAD WATCHED John fight before—sparring in the practice yard with a wooden sword or his fists—but she'd never seen him do so in a situation where his life was in actual peril.

It shouldn't have surprised her how quick and deadly he was, yet it did.

The John Mackay she knew had a ready smile and a warm, compassionate character. But the man who fought Roy Morrison bore no resemblance to the one she'd befriended.

John was a veteran of many battles. He knew how to stay alive—and despite that the blacksmith was a huge man, with brawny arms and a thick neck, John met his attack with confidence.

Sidestepping the first lunge, he tripped Morrison up.

The move enraged his opponent. Blistering curses rang out across the hillside as the blacksmith hauled himself to his feet and faced John once more. However, this time, he didn't charge him like a maddened bull. Instead, the two opponents circled each other, their guards up. Both men hunched a little, bringing their elbows against their ribs to protect themselves from blows.

Morrison began swinging punches with his right arm, strikes that John easily evaded, before counter-attacking with swift jabs of his left fist.

Looking on, it was clear to Neave that Morrison was expending the most energy, while John used his lighter build to his advantage, dancing out of reach or slipping punches by ducking his head. He stayed light and poised on the balls of his feet, which enabled him to change direction and keep his opponent guessing.

And all the while, the blacksmith got angrier. His face was now flushed, and sweat glistened upon his heavy brow.

Lunging at John, he hit him on the nose.

Neave slapped a hand over her mouth, to stop herself from crying out. The sight of blood trickling from John's nostrils made dread claw at her chest. He then shook his head to clear it and raised his fists once more, circling the blacksmith.

Heart pounding, twice as fast as the beating drums on the hilltop behind her, Neave backed up slightly.

What if John loses this fight?

Granted, he recovered swiftly from the blow and barely seemed to notice the blood, but Roy Morrison was a huge brute. If the blacksmith got his meaty hands around John's throat, he'd kill him.

Morrison landed a punch to John's shoulder, and another to his forehead. Neave couldn't help but think John had taken those blows on purpose, for they allowed him to get in close to the blacksmith, where he punched him hard just under the ribs.

The shocked wheeze of Morrison's breathing followed, and he staggered back.

John followed him.

The look on her friend's face made ice trail down Neave's spine, as did the fell gleam of his eye.

Pressing his advantage, John struck him hard in the jaw, driving the big man back farther. He then drove his wooden fist into Morrison's belly—hitting him with such force that the blacksmith sagged to his knees.

And then, to Neave's shock, he grabbed Morrison's head and drove it into his knee. It was a vicious move, and unsurprisingly, the big man slumped to the ground, groaning as he reached up and cradled his skull.

John stood over him, breathing hard. "Ye are no longer welcome here, Morrison," he growled, his voice rough with violence. "Tomorrow morning, I'm going to pay the forge a visit with the clan-chief ... and if we find ye still in residence, ye'll go on trial." He paused then, letting his words sink in. "Ye'll find that Niel Mackay doesn't look favorably on men who force themselves on lasses. He'll see ye castrated."

Morrison tried to crawl away, yet a swift kick to the ribs halted him.

"Did ye hear me?" John demanded.

"Aye," the blacksmith wheezed.

"Good ... I hope never to set eyes on ye again then."

Neave was scarcely breathing as she watched Roy Morrison haul himself to his feet. The big man's eyes were glittering, his face was twisted in pain, and his breathing came in agonized gasps, yet he still managed one last baleful glance in John's direction.

An instant later, he limped away.

Neave and John watched him go until the darkness swallowed him.

Dizziness swept over Neave, and she sucked in a deep breath before wiping her damp palms against her skirts. "John," she whispered. "Ye are bleeding."

Turning to her for the first time since he'd come to her assistance, he met her eye. The violence was still there, glittering in his gaze, although it was drawing back, and the man she knew was returning.

"It's nothing," he said roughly.

"Aye, it is." She approached him, before reaching up to inspect his nose. It was starting to swell.

John winced at her gentle touch, and a wry smile tugged her mouth. The man had just received a number of brutal blows without flinching. Anger had clearly prevented him from feeling any pain, although when the madness drew back, he realized his nose did, indeed, hurt.

"Is it broken?" he asked.

She ran her fingers down the bridge of his nose before carefully pressing the sides. "No ... just bruised." She drew in a steadying breath then. "But, if it's any consolation, Morrison will be feeling far worse than ye by tomorrow morn."

"He deserved more than a few bruises," John growled back, his blue eye glinting in the moonlight. "I wanted to kill the whoreson."

A chill shivered through Neave. "I tried to defend myself," she said huskily. "I even managed to hit him in the cods ... but he was too strong."

"I saw ye fighting him like a wildcat." John took her hand as she lowered it from his face, his expression turning solemn.

"Those gifts I received ... the pendant and the brooch from my 'ardent admirer'," Neave murmured. "It was *him* after all."

John's grip on her hand tightened, and his eye widened. "Christ's teeth," he muttered.

"I didn't realize he followed me when I left the fire," Neave admitted then.

John's gaze shadowed. "Ye shouldn't have been out here on yer own, lass."

Neave looked away, her pulse quickening. She couldn't admit to him that she'd left the bonfire in tears—that she hadn't been able to stomach watching him about to propose to Janneth.

"I was distracted," she admitted huskily. "But I realized my mistake halfway down the hill ... and was about to turn back when Morrison caught up with me." Forcing herself to raise her chin, she noted the crease between John's dark brows. "I was fortunate indeed that ye were nearby."

Their gazes held, the moment drawing out. Neave was aware then of how close they were standing, and that John still gripped her hand in his. She wondered then what *he* was doing down here.

"Why aren't ye up with the revelers?" she asked, trying to inject lightness into her voice. "I thought ye were proposing to Janneth tonight?"

John's face tensed, as did his fingers against hers. A moment later, he released her hand and stepped back. He then cleared his throat. "Aye, well ... things didn't quite go as planned on that front."

Neave watched him, her pulse accelerating further. "Excuse me?"

John sighed before reaching up and pinching the skin between his eyebrows. She'd only ever seen him do that a couple of times over the past months, yet Neave knew it was a sign that he was under stress.

"I'm feeling a little shaky on my feet," she admitted then, with a tremulous smile. "Shall we find somewhere to sit for a short while?"

He nodded.

Neave moved away, traveling a short distance up the hill to where a smooth boulder, big enough to seat the two of them, thrust out of the grass. Lowering herself onto the cool stone, she adjusted her skirts and drew in a series of deep breaths. Shock had left her weak-limbed.

She really did need to sit down.

Moments later, John settled himself down next to her. She glanced his way, studying his profile. He was looking sterner than she'd ever seen him.

"John," she said after a pause, resisting the urge to reach out and place a hand on his arm—better that she didn't touch him. "What happened?"

16

DENTED PRIDE

IT TOOK JOHN a while to respond. The silence after her question drew out for so long that Neave began to wonder if he would answer at all.

But eventually, he did.

"I did propose to Janneth," he said softly, not looking her way. "But she refused me."

Neave's skin prickled, as surprise and relief rippled through her. Yet she shoved the reaction aside and frowned. "Why?"

John's gaze swung to hers then. "She wants someone else."

Neave's breathing stilled. Her mind scrambled then, searching back to all the times she'd seen Janneth over the past year. She didn't recall spying Hugh Mackay's daughter favor any man with special attention. However, the lass's pale face and haunted gaze when she'd arrived at Varrich a couple of days ago, as well as her evasive answers when Neave had questioned her about John, suddenly made sense.

Neave's worries—ones she'd pushed aside when she'd seen Janneth happily talking and dancing to John earlier that evening—had been founded after all.

All the same, she was shocked to learn Janneth had another suitor.

"Oh, John," she murmured, her chest constricting.

"It doesn't matter," he said gruffly, looking away. His shoulders had tensed—clearly, the man didn't want her pity.

Yet it wasn't pity that moved Neave. "Aye, it does," she replied, swallowing to ease the tightness in her throat. "This is all my doing. I pushed ye to woo Janneth ... but I had no idea she had her heart set on another man."

He huffed a humorless laugh. "That makes two of us." His gaze snared hers then, his jaw firming. "Don't take the blame for this, Neave." His voice carried a sharp edge. "Aye, ye encouraged me ... but I'm no puppet to be moved this way and that. I wanted Janneth, and I pursued her. The decision to offer for her was mine." He paused then before reaching up and tentatively prodding his swollen nose. "In truth, it's my pride that's dented more than anything else. I've made a fool out of myself."

"No, ye haven't," she said softly. "It was just ill fortune. Ye weren't to know that Janneth's affections lay elsewhere. Don't let this put ye off approaching another woman in the future."

John snorted, and Neave stifled a wince. Courting Janneth hadn't been easy for him—especially in the beginning. Would this rejection embitter him? Would it make him distrust women from now on?

Goose-wit, what have ye done?

Silence fell between them, stretching out until Neave eventually cleared her throat. "Do ye know *whom* Janneth is in love with?" she asked, wisely changing the subject away from John.

He nodded, shifting his attention from hers. He then stared into the darkness. "Breac Mackay."

Neave's hands clenched upon her lap. That was a poor choice: Hugh Mackay couldn't stand the man. "It all makes sense now," she mused aloud. "Why Janneth has seemed on edge the past two days. She's been pining."

"Aye, she'll know her choice will enrage her father." John's voice was flat now, and he still stared into the distance.

Observing his profile, Neave twisted her fingers together. Her joints started to hurt, yet the discomfort made her focus. "What a mess this all is," she muttered under her breath.

John glanced her way then. Their gazes fused, and his expression softened. "Ye just narrowly escaped being raped, lass," he murmured. "Why are ye focusing on me?"

Neave heaved in a deep breath. In truth, she preferred not to think about how close she'd come to being brutalized by Morrison. The reminder now made sweat bead across her skin.

"I guess it's how I've always managed ... difficult situations," she replied, cursing the sudden huskiness in her voice. John was looking at her with such concern that the urge to crumple in his arms and weep against his chest assailed her. "If I look to helping others ... I don't have to dwell on myself."

His face tensed, and his lips parted as he readied himself to reply.

However, raised, angry, voices intruded, drawing his attention.

John glanced up to where the glow of the bonfire still illuminated the crown of the hill like a torch. Yet the drums had halted, and so had the music and laughter.

Neave frowned, even as relief barreled into her; she wasn't sure what John had been about to say to her, but she was glad he'd been prevented from continuing. She didn't want to talk about herself. "What's happening up there?"

John rose to his feet in one fluid, swift movement. "I don't know," he murmured. "Let us go and see."

Silently, Neave stood up and followed John back up to the revelers—and when they reached the bonfire once more, her attention swept the crowd, looking for the source of the argument. An instant later, she found it.

"How dare ye lay yer hands on my daughter?" Hugh Mackay stood before the chieftain of Balnakeil, one thick finger poking aggressively into the younger man's chest.

"Da!" Janneth had gripped one of her father's arms and was tugging at it, in an attempt to draw him away. "Ye don't understand."

Hugh ignored his daughter. Instead, his gaze gleamed, his bearded face twisted into a fierce scowl.

The laird of Balnakeil held his eye boldly. "Janneth has a will of her own, Hugh," Breac replied, his voice surprisingly calm considering the other chieftain's aggressive stance. "I took nothing that wasn't freely given."

"Ye were sticking yer filthy tongue down her throat!" Hugh jabbed once more at Breac's chest, yet the young laird still didn't react. "My daughter isn't yers to kiss. She's promised to another."

"Da ... that's not—"

"Silence!" Hugh roared, turning his ire upon Janneth then.

Eyes snapping wide at the violence of his response, she let go of his arm and stumbled back. The shock upon Janneth's face was so acute, it was as if her father had just struck her.

And then, to Neave's surprise, John shouldered his way through the gawking crowd toward the two chieftains.

"Hugh," he called out. "Enough of this ... Janneth and I aren't promised to each other. I already know she wishes to wed another ... and she has my blessing."

Hugh's attention snapped to John, and his jaw bunched. "So, ye know about this?" His tone was harsh, accusing.

John nodded.

"I love Breac," Janneth said then. John's appearance had bolstered her confidence once more, and she moved around, stepping up to Breac's side. "And I do wish to be his wife."

Hugh's mouth twisted. "Love? What do ye know of love, lass?" His bushy brows crashed together, and he sucked in a deep breath. He was now holding himself on a short leash. "Sheltered, pampered, and innocent in the ways of the world as ye are."

Looking on, Neave cringed at the harshness of his words. She couldn't blame drink for his rudeness either. She hadn't seen Hugh drinking tonight, yet it appeared that the rancor he held toward Breac Mackay hadn't eased over the past weeks, despite Niel's warning.

"This is my fault," Hugh went on, his voice roughening further. "I've always indulged ye … and after Shona died, I took ye everywhere with me … instead of leaving ye safely behind the walls of my broch, out of harm's way."

"I don't wish Janneth any harm," Breac cut in. The laird was frowning now, his tanned face strained. "I love her … and with yer blessing, I would wed her."

"Never," Hugh growled.

"Why not?" John had moved closer. He now faced Hugh, their gazes fusing. "I thought ye agreed to let the past lie? Ye gave Niel yer word."

A nerve flickered under one of Hugh's eyes, and he cast a glance at where the clan-chief had risen from his seat and moved to the edge of the crowd. Arms folded across his chest, Niel was watching the dispute with a veiled expression.

After living at Varrich for over a year, Neave knew that look. It signaled that Niel was vexed. He'd worn a similar expression when she'd burst into his solar that day and demanded he make things right with Beth.

"Letting the past go is one thing," Hugh growled, his gaze swinging back to Breac. "But joining my house with one that previously tried to destroy our clan is another."

"That's what letting the past go is, Hugh," Niel spoke up then. His tone was quiet, yet there was no mistaking the warning edge to it. "Perhaps a union between yer two families is exactly what is needed to heal things."

Hugh shook his head, his attention never wavering from where Breac and Janneth stood side-by-side. "There will be no wedding. And ye, lass, have shamed yerself, and yer mother's memory, by yer behavior this night."

Janneth flinched, and her eyes glittered with unshed tears. However, she raised her chin and continued to hold her father's gaze.

Neave's breathing quickened. She admired Janneth's defiance, yet it was clear her father wouldn't yield.

With a curse, Hugh stepped forward, grabbed his daughter by the upper arm, and dragged her from

Breac's side. Janneth cried out and struggled in her father's grip. "No, Da … let me go!"

"Hugh!" Breac moved forward, one hand fastening upon the chieftain of Loch Stach's muscled forearms. "Ye go too far."

"Stand down, whelp!" Hugh swiveled and shoved Breac hard in the center of the chest with his free hand. "Or I'll finish what I started last time."

"Hugh." Niel was suddenly there, in the thick of things, standing between the two men. "I think ye have said enough for tonight, don't ye?" The clan-chief's gaze bored into that of his chieftain. "Time to get a leash on yer tongue before it runs away with ye." Still staring Hugh down, Niel continued, "Breac, let go of his arm and step back. It's time all of ye retired for the night … I've no wish to have my Beltaine ruined."

The laird of Balnakeil scowled. "But—"

"Heed me," Niel cut him off, slashing through the smoky air. "Tomorrow we shall discuss this in my solar … with civil tongues."

"There will be no discussion," Hugh ground out, his cheeks reddening. "Janneth will not wed Breac Mackay … and I will not be convinced otherwise."

Niel's lean face grew hard. "So be it." His gaze fused with Hugh's then. "As her father, ye have the final word, Hugh … but mark mine. I will not have yer bitterness sour relations amongst the Mackays. I've already warned ye about stirring up trouble with yer clansmen. As such, ye leave me with no choice … I must fine ye for this transgression." Niel paused then, letting his words sink in, and when he continued, his voice was flinty. "Ye are to deliver one hundred head of cattle to Balnakeil broch by the end of the summer."

17

YE CAN'T MEND THIS

NEAVE ENTERED THE bailey, a basket full of onions under one arm. Their pungent smell filled her nostrils as she made her way across the wide cobbled space toward the large arched doorway that led into the bottom level of the keep—to the kitchens, stores, and bakehouse.

Gaze sweeping the bailey, she noted how quiet it was today. Aye, a few of Niel's men were nursing sore heads this morning, after a night of excess, but the hush was due to more than that.

The mood inside the castle was subdued.

Breac Mackay and his men had left with the dawn, returning to Balnakeil broch in the northwest of Mackay territory. He'd left without bidding anyone, even the clan-chief, farewell.

And Breac's departure had created an atmosphere of brooding tension when Niel, his kin, retainers, and guests had gathered in the great hall for the noon meal. Hugh Mackay wouldn't leave until the following morning, and although Hugh hadn't uttered a word as he'd enjoyed rich venison pie and braised kale, Neave had caught the gleam of victory in the chieftain's eye. Aye, he'd have to hand over a hundred head of his prized long-haired *coos* to the laird of Balnakeil, yet Breac Mackay wouldn't have his daughter.

Seated at his side, Janneth had been silent and wan. Her eyes were red-rimmed from weeping, and she'd barely touched the delicious meal.

Neave's chest constricted as she recalled her friend's unhappy face. She had to do something to aid her, yet she was completely at a loss as to a solution for this problem.

Entering the kitchens, she forced a cheery greeting to the cooks and handed one of the lasses the basket of onions. "Thank ye, Lady Neave." The lass beamed at her. "These will go a treat with tomorrow's mutton stew."

"Aye, well, there's plenty more if ye want any … just ask," Neave replied, keeping a smile plastered upon her face. In truth, she was tempted to hide away in her garden for the rest of the day. However, she couldn't bear the thought of Janneth weeping alone in her bed-chamber. Neave could lose herself in industry once the lass left Varrich, but at present, Janneth needed her.

Leaving the kitchens, she climbed the narrow stone steps to the entrance hall. Peeking through the doorway into the great hall, she saw that it was empty save two figures seated upon the dais: Niel and John were playing a game of Ard-ri, cups of ale at their elbow. Niel's two favorite wolfhounds sprawled under the table, both beasts soundly asleep.

Neave's gaze lingered upon John. The swelling in his nose was starting to go down, as was the one to his forehead—injuries he'd sustained coming to her aid.

Her belly clenched then. By blood and bone, she couldn't look at the man now without cringing.

He'd been hurt defending her—but that wasn't the worst of it.

Aye, he'd pursued Janneth at her urging, but there was a part of her that rejoiced to hear there would be no wedding.

I'm a terrible person.

She'd spent the last few months match-making, only to be relieved when things didn't go John's way.

Neave quickly withdrew. She didn't want John to see her watching him. Things had been strained between them since the night before. She'd seen him mid-morning and then again at the noon meal. Usually, he chatted amicably to her, teased her, and enjoyed her observations.

But today, he'd barely looked her way.

He'd insisted she wasn't to blame, yet his behavior indicated the opposite. He seemed almost uncomfortable around her.

Head bowed, Neave made her way upstairs. Her sisters would be gathering in the women's solar at this hour to sew, weave, and chat about the day's events. As a guest at Varrich, Janneth would have been invited to join them. But Neave knew Hugh's daughter wouldn't go.

Moving past the door to the solar, Neave made her way down the narrow corridor to the guest chambers. Halting before the last of them, she knocked softly on the door.

When no answer came, she leaned in and called, "Janneth ... it's Neave. Can I come in?"

Another pause followed before a husky voice responded. "Aye."

Letting herself inside, Neave's gaze swept around the small bed-chamber. A canopied bed dominated it, and the tiny single window was open, letting warm sunlight pool inside.

Nonetheless, Janneth sat next to the glowing hearth, a woolen shawl wrapped around her shoulders.

Seeing the paleness of her face, Neave's step faltered, and she halted. "Janneth ... ye are unwell?"

Janneth's mouth curved, her gaze bleak, before she shook her head. "Just heart-sick." She motioned then to the stool opposite. "Please ... sit down, Neave. It's good to see ye."

Neave did as bid, even if her belly clenched. Janneth was such a kind soul—even suffering as she was, she never forgot her manners. Pulling up the stool so that she sat close to Janneth, Neave reached forward and took her hands in hers.

Despite that it was a warm day outdoors, Janneth's slender hands were ice-cold.

"I hate to see ye suffer so," Neave whispered, her voice roughening as the urge to weep swept over her. "Is there anything I can do ... to help?"

Janneth sighed, the sad smile lingering on her lips. "There is nothing ye can do … Breac has departed, and Da has dug his heels in."

"But surely, he can be made to see sense?"

Janneth swallowed. "I'm not so certain," she whispered, the quaver in her voice betraying the grief that bubbled just under the surface. "He's as intractable as a mule when he wants to be."

"Maybe I should speak to him."

Janneth's gaze widened, chagrin flaring there. "No, Neave," she whispered. "That would only make things worse. I thank ye for yer concern … but ye can't resolve this." Her lovely features tightened then. "I must be the one to take the next step … whatever that may be."

Niel Mackay reached forward and knocked John's king off his throne. He then flashed him a grin. "Twice in a row, John … ye aren't on form today."

Pulling a face, his cousin sat back in his chair and dragged his left hand through his hair. "Aye, I'm a bit tired."

"Tired?" Niel arched an eyebrow, running a speculative gaze over the man opposite. "Not a little sore to lose Janneth to Breac?"

John snorted. "If I were, comments like that wouldn't help."

Niel raised an eyebrow. John was on edge today; he'd noted it the moment his cousin had joined him and Beth in his solar to break their fast. His gaze held a distant, brooding look that was quite unlike him.

"I wish I hadn't let the blacksmith go," John admitted then, his face hardening. "I should have hauled Morrison up to ye by the scruff of his neck, so ye could deal out justice … instead, he's now free."

Niel frowned. The pair of them had gone down to the forge before breaking their fast—to find it empty. The blacksmith had taken his tools and other belongings, saddled his garron, and disappeared.

The clan-chief's mouth thinned. If John hadn't interrupted him, the smith would likely have raped Neave.

Beth had been understandably enraged to hear what Roy Morrison had done, and upon returning from the forge, Niel had sent men out to track the blacksmith down. However, it was clear that John now blamed himself for being too lenient with him.

"Worry not, Morrison will have to run fast to escape Captain Reay and the others," Niel pointed out. "And if they drag him back here alive, I'll mete out justice … ye can be assured."

John nodded, his jaw still tight.

"Don't be too hard on yerself," Niel replied, pushing himself to his feet and stretching out his back. "Ye did what ye thought was right at the time. And thanks to ye, Neave is unharmed."

John's gaze shadowed. "Aye. I suppose ye are right." He then cast Niel a questioning look. "We usually play three games … where are ye off to?"

"I thought it time I paid my Gunn prisoner a visit," Niel replied. "Tess has been tending him … I want to see if he's going to rally."

Surprise rippled across his cousin's face, and he rose to his feet. "Do ye want me to join ye?"

Niel shook his head.

John inclined his head, settling back down upon his chair. He was clearly intrigued by Niel's enigmatic response. However, the clan-chief didn't enlighten him. He merely flashed his cousin a smile and nodded to the Ard-ri board between them. "We'll play that third game after supper in my solar … let's see if I can thrash ye again."

18

FORGED OF IRON

MAKING HIS WAY down the path below the castle, Niel wondered why he hadn't agreed to let John accompany him. He enjoyed his cousin's company and didn't get to see John so often these days.

But he wished to go down to the dungeon alone.

William Gunn had been on his mind increasingly of late. Niel wasn't sure whether it was his conscience plaguing him, or if it was unfinished business, but his gut told him it was time to finally pay his hostage a visit.

At the bottom of the promontory, he turned left, rather than taking the road that would lead him to Tongue village, walking the narrow dirt path to the dungeon.

Castle Varrich's dungeon was the oldest part of the fortress—a network of caves that local legend said had once housed the ancient people who'd settled this area. Sculpted out of the sandstone rock and facing north, the dungeon lay in shadow all year. It was a cold, damp place in summer, and unbearably so in winter.

Niel wasn't surprised that William Gunn had sickened—most of the prisoners kept in here over the years had.

Approaching the entrance to the large cave leading into the dungeon, Niel nodded to the two men keeping guard. Both individuals lurched to their feet, clearly surprised to see their clan-chief here.

"Laird," one of them greeted him, wide-eyed. "We didn't realize ye were paying us a visit."

"Neither did I," Niel replied with a smile. "No need to worry yerself, Eòin ... just tell me where to find Gunn."

"Take the left tunnel ... and it's the fourth cell to yer right." The young guard paused there. "The healer's with him."

Niel nodded before helping himself to one of the unlit torches hanging at the cave's entrance. "Good ... I wish to speak to her as well."

Ducking inside, he lit his torch from the cresset that burned there, letting it flare before he made his way into the belly of the dungeon.

God's bones, it was fouler in here than he remembered. The air had a musty, dank taste, and although most of the cells he passed were empty, the faint stench of excrement lingered.

He'd just entered the left tunnel, as advised, when Niel spied a tall, dark-haired woman walking toward him.

"Tess," he greeted her, halting. "How fares Gunn then?"

The healer stopped before him, her wide mouth pursing, even if her moss-green eyes were as warm as ever. "Better than he was," she replied. "I have been ensuring he drinks a draft of lungwort and horehound thrice daily, and have applied a warming poultice to his chest that has made his breathing easier." She paused then, her brow furrowing as her gaze grew serious. "Nonetheless, he will likely sicken once more in this place." The healer gestured to the dank darkness surrounding them. "There's no sunlight ... no air."

Niel stilled. Tess was a good-natured woman, yet he'd heard the chagrin in her voice. "Thank ye, Tess ... I shall keep that in mind," he replied coolly. "Good day."

With a respectful nod, the healer moved past him, her soft footfalls fading as she left the dungeon.

Niel listened to her go before he continued on his way.

A short while later, he stopped in front of William Gunn's cell. Holding his torch aloft, his gaze traveled to the figure lying upon a wooden pallet. A sack of grain had been propped up under the prisoner's shoulders, to ease his breathing. Even so, Niel could hear the wheeze and rattle of each breath Gunn took.

Indeed, he was poorly.

Moments passed while the two men eyeballed each other. The prisoner's face was cast in shadow, yet Niel could see the glint of his eyes.

Eventually, it was Gunn who broke the silence. His voice was reedy, weak. "Come to gloat, have ye?"

"No," Niel replied, favoring the prisoner with a cool smile. "Ye have been here for nearly a year now … I thought a visit was long overdue."

Gunn made a wheezing sound that may have been a cough or a laugh. And then he heaved himself up off his pallet and shuffled over to the bars. He wore a threadbare blanket around his shoulders, and as he approached, Niel raked his gaze over him.

The prisoner was lean to the point of emaciation, even thinner than Niel had been during his time at Bass Rock. His recent sickness had melted the flesh off his bones. A thick black beard covered the lower half of his face, and a mane of wild, knotted black hair made him look half-mad.

However, his purple-grey eyes were sharp and sane.

Niel's breathing hitched. That eye color was distinctive. At Inverness, over a decade earlier, he'd noted that both the Gunn clan-chief and his eldest son, Alexander, had eyes the color of summer storm clouds.

And yet, he'd seen someone else with eyes that same hue … recently.

An instant later, it hit him. Niel's pulse quickened as something that had niggled at him for months now finally fell into place.

"Do all yer brothers have the same eye color as ye, Gunn?" he asked.

William Gunn halted, his gaze narrowing at the abrupt question. His mouth then twisted. He drew in a labored breath and shuffled forward, closing the gap between them. Reaching out, his bony fingers fastened around the bars separating them. "And what's it to ye, Mackay?"

"A curiosity," Niel replied. Gunn's reaction told him that the answer was 'aye'. The light of the torch he held aloft flickered over the contours of William Gunn's face, highlighting every hollow and the grey pallor of his skin. "One is named Roy, is he not?" Niel's father had once told him the names of George Gunn's six sons, and he was sure 'Roy' had been amongst them. All the same, he wished for William to confirm it.

Gunn's features tensed, and once again Niel had his answer.

Silence fell between them, and when the prisoner replied, his voice held a harsh edge. "Aye, Roy is the third-born of us."

"And where does he reside these days?"

William Gunn scowled. "Around eight years ago, he tried to kill Tavish ... and was cast out in punishment. None of us have seen him since." The prisoner paused then, his gaze glinting. "But ye have met him, haven't ye?"

Niel nodded. "He goes by the name 'Roy Morrison' these days ... and until yesterday, he worked as the blacksmith here in Tongue."

Gunn's fingers tightened around the bars. "Why all these questions about Roy?"

"He tried to rape a woman and has now fled."

Clan-chief and prisoner stared at each other. After a pause, Gunn pulled a face. "Roy was always fond of forcing himself on lasses ... it sounds like he hasn't changed."

"He approached me last summer," Niel admitted then. He wasn't sure why he was telling his prisoner this, yet the words spilled from him. "He told me that if I wished to strike hard against the Gunns ... Dounreay was the place to do it."

William Gunn's face turned to stone. "Did he?"

"Aye, and when I asked why it mattered to him, he replied that he bore the Gunn clan-chief a grudge ... he was cagey though. I got nothing else out of him."

The prisoner's gaze glinted. "But ye took his advice."

"I did."

William Gunn's fingers tightened further around the bars, his skin turning white from the force of his grip, and his grey eyes now burned.

Not for the first time, Niel marveled at the Gunn fortitude. It was no wonder George Gunn had built such a reputation before his death, one that his sons ensured lived on. They were all forged of iron. Even sick and emaciated, the man before him was a fighter.

Niel stepped back from the cell, his gaze never leaving the prisoner's face. "The healer will continue to tend ye until ye are fully recovered," he informed Gunn. "After that, ye shall begin work in the fields each day."

Surprise flickered over Gunn's face at this news, although he recovered swiftly, his brow furrowing. "And why's that?"

Niel flashed him a hard smile. "Let's just say, it's in my interests that my Gunn hostage stays alive."

With those parting words, the Mackay clan-chief turned on his heel and made his way back up the dank tunnel.

It was a relief to step out into the sunlight and fresh air once more, and Niel sucked in a deep breath of it. He then turned to one of the young guards who flanked the entrance. "What are ye feeding him?"

"Porridge in the morning and vegetable pottage and bread for supper," the guard replied.

Niel frowned. "Well, ensure he gets meat every other day, and boiled eggs and bannock with his porridge from now on." The guard's gaze widened at this, yet Niel continued. "And starting tomorrow, the prisoner will join the cottars in the fields ... in shackles mind."

A moment passed, and the guard nodded. "Aye, Laird ... I shall see it done."

Niel nodded and moved off down the slope back to the path. However, after a few strides, he paused, turning to meet the guard's gaze once more. "And fetch him some decent bedding, Eòin ... the blankets he has are in tatters and likely crawling with vermin. Gunn is a valuable prisoner … I don't want him dying in our care."

"Aye, Laird." The man was staring at him as if he'd just lost his senses, but Niel didn't care. Eòin didn't know what it was to live inside a fetid cell with only the rats for company. But Niel did, and now he'd seen William Gunn, he couldn't leave him in such a state. It was indeed in his interests to keep the man alive, yet entering the dungeon had brought back chilling memories—ones he couldn't ignore.

Without another word, Niel turned and left the guards to their watch.

19

IN SEARCH OF JANNETH

"JANNETH IS MISSING!"

Hugh Mackay stood in the doorway to the clan-chief's solar, wild-eyed. He'd just flung the door open with such force it crashed against the wall. John lowered the wedge of bannock slathered with butter and honey he'd been about to take a bite of, while Beth's surprised gasp echoed through the solar.

A heartbeat passed, and then Niel responded. "Are ye certain?"

The chieftain of Loch Stach nodded, his large hands clenching and unclenching at his sides. "Aye! I've searched for her in the keep ... and in the bailey, stables, and beyond. She's vanished!"

John's pulse accelerated at this news. Lord, he hoped the lass hadn't done anything foolish.

He was already on edge this morning. The eve before, he'd hoped to talk to Niel again about providing more men to help defend his livestock and villages from the Sutherlands—for rustling and raids had become more frequent since early spring—but before he'd had the chance, Niel had informed him that Roy Morrison was actually Roy 'Gunn'.

Apparently, Roy had been exiled a few years earlier, after he'd tried to kill Tavish Gunn. It seemed he had been waiting for an opportunity to avenge himself against his elder brother, hence why he'd approached Niel the year before with his 'advice' to strike at Dounreay. After his cousin's revelation, John had lain awake late into the night, cursing himself doubly for letting the bastard go.

Nonetheless, they had to have a conversation about the Sutherlands. Despite that the Mackays had increased their presence along the southern border, their neighbors grew increasingly aggressive.

"Have ye checked the chapel?" Beth asked. "Janneth prays regularly there ... she might—"

"She's not there." Hugh's voice cracked then. John noted that the chieftain was dressed for travel, a light woolen cloak hanging from his broad shoulders. The Mackays of Loch Stach were indeed supposed to depart this morning and should have done so already.

Rising to his feet, Niel pushed back his chair.

Likewise, John stood up, his bannock forgotten. "We'll find her."

"I tell ye, she's not here," Hugh replied, shaking his head. His gaze glittered as it fused with Niel's across the room. "It's that whoreson Breac Mackay. He's taken her!"

"Breac left yesterday morning at dawn," John pointed out. "He'll still be on his way home."

"The swine will have doubled back." Hugh's face flushed red then. "He must have sneaked in here last night. He has—"

"He would have done no such thing," Niel cut in, scowling. "Get ahold of yerself, man. The castle gates are warded all night. My men would have alerted me if Breac returned."

"Were any others departing Varrich this morning?" John asked then, his gaze meeting Niel's. His mind was already racing ahead, going through various possibilities.

"Aye," Beth spoke up. "A grain merchant stayed here last night. He would have left early ... for he was heading into Sutherland territory next."

John's mouth thinned. "Then I'd say Janneth went with him."

Hugh spluttered a salty curse at this, his already high-colored face deepening to a dark red. His fisted hands now shook with rage. "She's going to meet him ... that bastard has put her up to this ... put her at risk ... I'll throttle him. When I set eyes on him, I'll—"

"This isn't helping, Hugh," John cut in. The chieftain of Loch Stach was raving now, barely coherent in his wrath. "Turning the air blue with yer oaths, and telling us all the ways ye plan to kill Breac Mackay, won't ensure yer daughter's safety." John met Hugh's eye, holding it steadily. "Now is the time for action, not anger. Let us go and ready our horses. We shall ride for Balnakeil this morning ... for that is surely where she's headed. If we hurry, we should catch up with her on the road."

Neave rushed down the steps into the bailey, picking up her skirts to avoid tripping in her haste. It was a warm morning, and the cloak she'd donned was making her sweat. However, she needed it for the journey ahead.

In the center of the bailey, John Mackay and his men were readying their horses to depart. Nearby, the laird of Loch Stach's expression was thunderous as he tightened the girth of his heavyset bay gelding.

Neave's pulse quickened. They were about to leave. She had to hurry if she was to join them.

"Neave," John hailed her as she crossed the bailey toward the stables. "What are ye doing?"

"Saddling my garron," she replied breathlessly. "Wait for me, John."

Glancing over her shoulder, she saw him straighten up from checking his courser's hooves. His features then tightened. "Ye aren't coming with us, lass," he informed her firmly.

"I am." Neave swung around to face him. Hugh had shifted his attention to her as well, and was looking at her as if she had just sprouted horns. "Janneth is my friend," she pointed out, "and if ye are going to hunt her down like a hind, she will need a woman to console her."

"We are not 'hunting her down'," John pointed out, frowning. "We're hoping to catch up with her ... to ensure her safety."

"Ye aren't welcome on this journey, woman," Hugh muttered. "Ye'll only slow us down."

John cut Hugh a sharp look before his gaze met Neave's once more. "Aye, ye won't keep up riding that fat garron of yers," he added, the furrow upon his brow deepening.

Staring back at the men, stubbornness rose within Neave. She squared her shoulders, lifted her chin, and eyeballed them. She'd slept badly over the last two nights, for her mind couldn't rest. In vain, she'd tried to think of ways to help her friend.

And now Janneth had fled.

Her friend was traveling without an escort. Anything could happen to her.

"She can have one of my coursers." Niel's voice carried across the bailey, and Neave turned to see the clan-chief standing at the foot of the steps to the keep, his arm around Beth's shoulders. Her sister held her chin high in a gesture that Neave knew well.

Beth wanted her to go with Hugh and John—and so did Niel, it seemed.

Neave nodded to the clan-chief, warmth spreading across her chest. But when she glanced back at John, she saw that he was now scowling. "Niel," he muttered, shaking his head. "This isn't—"

"Take Neave with ye, John," Niel replied, raising a hand to cut his cousin off. "She's right ... Janneth will need her ... and I know ye shall ensure she comes to no harm."

John stared back at him, his mouth thinning. However, after a beat, he gave a brusque nod. He then shifted his attention back to Neave. "We're leaving shortly," he said, his tone uncharacteristically clipped. "Ye'd better get that courser saddled."

Neave urged her mount into a brisk canter along the road that hugged the edge of the Kyle of Tongue. The road would take them south to where the kyle narrowed to the Kinloch River. From there, they'd cross the river before striking out west.

Balnakeil lay two full days' journey away, although Hugh was eager to catch up with his daughter before then. The grain merchant wouldn't likely be going any farther than the Kinloch River, and from there she'd be on foot.

Yet John had pointed out that, if she had coin with her, she could pay the merchant to take her to Balnakeil, or even buy a horse at the first village she passed. Kinloch hamlet lay on the other side of the bridge of the same name.

Hugh's face had hardened at John's words, and he'd kicked his feather-footed beast into a fast canter, forcing all those following to do the same.

A warm wind gusting in from the south caressed Neave's cheeks as she rode. Unlike her Highland pony, which had a short gait and a broad back, this mare had a long, smooth stride. The stable lad had told her the horse's name was Vixen—a fine name for a beast with a gleaming russet-colored coat. It was exhilarating to ride her, and despite that circumstances weren't the best, Neave felt the cares of the last few days draw back.

It was hard to feel worried or sorry for herself when she was riding fast, the sun bathing her face, the scent of grass and heather in the air. The rhythmic thud of Vixen's hooves steadied her.

However, when she glanced ahead, at John's back, her fragile sense of well-being shattered.

She hated knowing that he was vexed with her. John hadn't bothered to hide his irritation that Niel had allowed her to join them—and he hadn't spoken to her since they'd left Varrich.

What had happened to the easy rapport that had once existed between them?

In the past, he'd have welcomed her company and championed her cause, but, since Beltaine, the cooling of his attitude toward her hurt.

Neave's throat started to ache.

Aye, he *was* vexed with her over Janneth. It didn't matter that he'd denied it—his behavior revealed the truth. He held her responsible and resented her interfering ways.

And here she was, interfering again.

Neave reined in her mare, watching as John swung down from the saddle and went to speak to a man selling cabbages and onions on the roadside leading into the village. The sun hung directly overhead now, indicating they'd made good time so far. They'd just clattered over Kinloch Bridge outside the village, and allowed their horses a breather while John asked some questions.

"I wonder if he's seen her," Neave said, glancing over at the laird of Loch Stach. Leaning forward, she stroked her mount's sweaty neck.

Hugh frowned, his gaze never leaving John. "It's likely," he muttered. "This man's probably been out here since dawn."

Silence fell between them then. Neave supposed she was fortunate Hugh had even responded to her at all, for he'd not bothered to hide his ire when Niel provided her with a mount for the journey.

Instead of attempting to draw Hugh into conversation again, she shifted her attention back to John. His brow was furrowed as he continued to talk to the vendor.

Around her, an escort of ten men—warriors from both Achness and Loch Stach—had also drawn up their horses. The men watched John intently as he finished talking to the vendor and stalked back to them.

"He saw a grain merchant come by a few hours ago," John announced. "He had a lass traveling with him, perched on his wagon. She had her hood drawn up, but he saw she was blue-eyed with fair skin."

"Sounds like Janneth to me, Laird," one of John's men murmured.

"Aye," John replied, frowning, "but we need to know if they continued traveling together."

"My daughter wouldn't travel alone," Hugh ground out, his face paling. "She knows it isn't safe."

John's attention swung to him, his gaze shadowing. "Aye ... but desperation sometimes makes folk do foolish things."

They rode on into the village, where Hugh insisted on visiting the inn located just off market square himself. And while his companions waited—their horses' tails swishing at flies, listening to local merchants hawking their wares behind them—John became aware of Neave's gaze upon him.

Finally, the weight of her stare became too much, and John swiveled in the saddle, meeting her eye. "Aye, Neave?"

She was watching him steadily, her hazel eyes flecked with shards of green wide upon her elfin face. And as their gazes held, John tried to ignore the pull in his chest. He wished she wouldn't look at him like that. The wounded look on her face made him feel like a heel. Ever since leaving Varrich, he'd ridden ahead of her, and had resisted the urge to glance over his shoulder to make sure she was keeping up.

Of course, on that fine chestnut mare Niel had loaned her—curse the man for interfering—she was.

"Are ye annoyed with me?" she asked, her voice soft. They waited a few yards distant from their escort, and so it was unlikely anyone could overhear them.

Even so, John's mouth thinned. He didn't want to go into this now. "And if I am?"

Her throat bobbed. "Ye don't want me here."

John frowned. "This journey could be dangerous ... and who knows how things will go if Hugh and Breac face each other again. I'd feel happier if ye were back at Varrich."

Neave drew herself up, her fingers tightening around the reins. "If ye think this could end in violence, then it's just as well I'm here," she answered, her tone sharpening. "Janneth is my friend … I will not abandon her."

John's gaze narrowed further. "And did Janneth give ye any hint that she was planning to run away?"

A heartbeat followed, and then Neave shook her head, the defiance in her gaze dimming.

John pursed his lips. "Aye, well, perhaps ye don't know her as well as ye thought."

The inn-keeper at Kinloch hadn't seen Janneth. However, he sent them to the village's horse-trader, who admitted he'd sold a garron to a softly-spoken lass just a couple of hours earlier.

Janneth had parted ways from the grain merchant—and was now heading to Balnakeil unescorted, on horseback.

Hugh's bearded face was thunderous as they left Kinloch, although Neave marked the fear that now glinted in his eyes. She guessed his only child had never been allowed to ride out without being accompanied by at least one of his men. That wasn't surprising, for Neave's own father wouldn't have allowed any of his daughters to travel unescorted either.

Neave's belly clenched at the thought of Janneth meeting anyone on the road. There were plenty of two-legged predators throughout the Highlands who'd happily prey upon a woman alone—Neave's encounter with Morrison had been a harsh reminder of her own vulnerability.

A shiver rippled down her spine then. *He's out there … somewhere.*

With all that had happened since Beltaine, she'd almost forgotten the smith.

Almost.

Beth had told her that Niel's men were now hunting Morrison—but what if they never found him?

20

STILL FRIENDS

THE PARTY RODE on, over velvet-green hills, northward once more—but never caught up with their quarry. And as dusk settled over the Highlands, they found themselves at the hamlet of Hope. Nestled at the northern edge of a loch with the same name, the village—a sprawling collection of white-washed cottages—was big enough to boast a tavern. It also rented out a handful of rooms upstairs, although there weren't sufficient rooms for the entire party. John and Hugh's men would have to sleep in the stables with the horses.

Seated in the smoky common room, surrounded by the locals who fished the waters of Loch Hope and tended the black-faced sheep that grazed upon the surrounding hills, the travelers ate a simple supper of roasted mutton and oaten bread.

After a day in the saddle, Neave should have been ravenous. Nonetheless, her belly was in knots as she ate. She kept imagining what would happen if Janneth encountered the likes of Roy Morrison en route to Balnakeil. The possibilities her imaginings created stole Neave's appetite, and she ended up pushing her mutton around her trencher.

And as she did, Neave glanced often to where John sat speaking quietly with Hugh. They were discussing the quickest route to Balnakeil for the following day's journey—and which road Janneth would likely have taken.

It was difficult to know if she'd have opted for the longer, more heavily used road that circled south for a spell, or the lonely route across a ridge of rocky hills.

Neave's attention lingered upon John then, the knots in her belly tightening further. They hadn't spoken since their exchange at Kinloch, and his words still needled her. Reaching for her cup of ale, she took a large gulp. He was right though. Janneth hadn't trusted her enough to confide in her.

Neave dropped her gaze to her largely untouched supper. She was only trying to do some good, yet it seemed that the harder she tried, the bigger the disaster she made of things.

"Which road would ye have taken, Neave?" John asked, making her glance up. "If ye were traveling to yer lover?"

Both men were looking at her, acknowledging her for the first time since they'd sat down to eat.

Neave's cheeks warmed at the directness of John's question. She didn't have a lover, and even if she did, she had no idea what choice she'd have made in Janneth's place. However, the hopeful look upon Hugh's careworn face made her tense. She didn't want to disappoint him.

Mouth pursing, she attempted to concentrate. What if she were traveling to John, with her angry father in pursuit. Her cheeks started to burn at the thought, and her breathing quickened.

Aye, she'd have ridden the length of England to reach John Mackay. And she'd have taken risks she usually wouldn't have.

Neave was careful not to look in John's direction as she answered, "The road across the hills."

After supper, the proprietor cleared their empty dishes and brought another round of ales. Seated on the edge of the men, listening to the rumble of their conversation, Neave stifled a yawn.

Hugh and John were now discussing the journey ahead, having decided they would take the lonely road across the hills. Neave didn't know whether to be flattered or worried that they'd taken her advice. Even so, her gut told her that Janneth would travel that way.

Where is she now?

According to the tavern owner, there weren't any villages nearby, and the thought of her friend camping alone on the road made Neave feel queasy. No wonder a frown had marred Hugh's brow all evening.

"It's a mild night out," John noted finally, for he too had likely noted the worry upon Hugh's face. "If Janneth has found a spot under a tree or the lee of a hill, she will be comfortable enough."

"It's not the weather that concerns me," Hugh replied, viewing the younger man over the rim of his tankard. "But the fact that my daughter ... a lass who is innocent and sheltered ... is out there, unprotected." A nerve jumped in his cheek. "What if wolves approach her?"

Ice washed over Neave at these words, and her heart started to race. Lord, she hadn't thought about that.

"Wolves aren't on the prowl this time of year," John replied after a pause, and Neave's pulse settled. "They aren't hungry enough. Ye needn't fear such an attack."

Hugh's mouth flattened. Clearly, John's assurance hadn't eased his worries as it had Neave's.

"Janneth is stronger and cannier than ye give her credit for," Neave spoke up then, meeting Hugh's eye. It was a bold statement, yet over the months she'd known Janneth, Neave had noted her friend was astoundingly sharp beneath her gentle manners and sweet demeanor. "Aye, she has put herself in danger ... but she will be wary and on the lookout for trouble."

Hugh scowled. "She wouldn't need to be if she'd obeyed me."

Neave nodded, deciding that it was best they drop this conversation. She and John had endeavored to reassure Hugh, yet he wasn't in the mood to be comforted. Anger and betrayal bubbled too close to the surface this evening.

Rising to her feet, Neave winced. The muscles in her backside and thighs were already starting to stiffen up after a day in the saddle. Fatigue made her eyes gritty and her limbs heavy.

"We have an early start tomorrow," she murmured, favoring both men with a tired smile. "So I shall bid ye goodnight."

"Goodnight, Neave," Hugh rumbled.

Neave met his eye once more. "Don't worry ... we'll find Janneth in the morning."

Hugh nodded, his jaw tightening. "Aye, lass ... we *shall*."

Next to him, John inclined his head. "Sleep well."

Neave and John's gazes met a moment—it was the first time they'd looked squarely at each other all evening—and Neave's already knotted belly cramped. She didn't like the guarded expression on his face. The warmth that had once flowed so easily between them had dissipated. There was a distance between them now.

With a heavy heart, Neave left the common room and climbed the rickety stairs to the second floor of the tavern. Her chamber was at the end of the corridor, opposite John's. The tavern owner had shown them up earlier and allowed them to stow their bags.

Her room was small and simply furnished, with just a narrow bed, wash table, and chair, yet she was relieved to see the white-washed walls and wooden floor were all scrubbed clean, and the bedding appeared to be fresh. Despite that it was summer, a small brick of peat burned in the hearth. Candlelight illuminated the chamber.

With a sigh, Neave went to the tiny window and unlatched the wooden shutters, pushing them open. It was dark outside now, and the waxing crescent moon had just risen. Her window looked out over Loch Hope— an apt name considering the nature of their mission.

The still waters of the loch sparkled in the moonlight, reflecting its silvery glow.

Neave remained there awhile, gazing out at the view, and letting the day's tension unravel. But her belly continued to cramp.

It was bad enough that Janneth was somewhere out there in the darkness, but now John was guarded with her.

Letting out a heavy sigh, Neave reached up and rubbed the ache in her stomach.

Eventually, she shuttered the windows, stripped down to the lèine she wore under her kirtle, and crossed to the washbowl that had been left for her. She went through her ablutions swiftly before perching on the bed to brush out her hair. Ever since Beth's marriage, she hadn't shared a bed with any of her sisters, although Greta still slept upon a sheepskin by the hearth in her bed-chamber back at Castle Varrich. Usually, she and her maid would chat about the day's events as Greta brushed out her hair and put away her clothes.

It felt odd to get ready for bed on her own.

Putting aside her hog-bristle brush, Neave blew out the candles and climbed into bed. Tiredness dragged at her limbs. By rights, she should have fallen into a deep slumber.

Yet sleep eluded her.

Instead, she lay there, staring up at the shadowed rafters, ruminating over the events of the past days. Then John intruded on her thoughts.

Usually, she confided in her sisters about her worries. But not so this time. Aye, they'd all teased her about her friendship with John. Yet she hadn't said anything of the turmoil that now churned like a storm-tossed sea within her. It had taken her a long while to fully admit the truth to herself—but now that she had, it wouldn't let her go.

The idea of John taking Janneth as his bride had felt as if her heart were being ripped from her chest. She couldn't bear the thought—not when she wanted him for herself.

No, she hadn't said a word to anyone about her changing feelings toward John Mackay, but nor would she tell *him*.

The man had just been turned down by Janneth. He certainly didn't need Neave complicating his life as he dealt with rejection. After all, he'd confided in her about his fears regarding women; she knew just how hard it had been for him to overcome them to woo Janneth in the first place.

Aye, she would keep her feelings to herself—even if the need to clear the air with him about other matters roiled within her.

The night drew out, and slowly the tavern grew quiet and still around her as the last of the patrons departed and the proprietor cleaned up before locking the doors downstairs.

And still, sleep eluded Neave. She tossed and turned, but no matter what she did, she couldn't get comfortable, and her racing mind wouldn't quieten.

Eventually, muttering a curse, she sat up and threw the covers back.

"It's no good," she told the darkness, "ye will have to speak to him."

Neave rose to her feet and took a blanket from the bed, wrapping it around her shoulders in a makeshift shawl. She then took one of the doused candles, lighting it from the still glowing coals in the fire, and padded over to her door, lifting the bar that locked it from the inside.

She carefully opened the door and stepped out into the hallway beyond. It was late, far past the witching hour now. John would be asleep and likely wouldn't appreciate being woken.

Halting in the hall, Neave's resolve faltered. His good opinion of her mattered; she didn't want to vex him again.

She drew in a deep breath.

Ye aren't a coward, Neave Munro, she told herself firmly. *Things need to be said.*

Straightening her spine, she stepped close to John's door. She then knocked softly.

Long moments passed, and nothing happened. Perhaps she should knock louder. However, she didn't want to disturb Hugh, who slept next door to John.

Neave's fist hovered, and she was about to risk another knock when the scrape of the bar being lifted within stilled her hand.

An instant later, the door opened.

John Mackay stood there, blinking owl-like. Barefoot, he wore braies and an untucked lèine—garments he'd donned to answer the door. He also wore his eye patch, although she wondered if he ever took it off, even at night.

"Neave?" he greeted her, his voice husky with sleep. "What is it?"

"I wish to speak to ye, John," she whispered. "Can I come in?"

Rubbing his face, John sighed. "It's late ... why aren't ye abed?"

"I couldn't sleep. There's too much on my mind." Their gazes met and held. "Please."

John's brow furrowed. However, after a moment, he stepped back and gestured for her to enter.

His bed-chamber was the mirror-image of her own. John crossed to the bed and sat down, before gesturing to the chair by the glowing hearth. "Out with it, lass."

Closing the door gently behind her, Neave put the candle down upon the nearby table. Meanwhile, John's gaze remained upon her face, waiting for her to continue.

Neave cleared her throat. "I don't like it being like this ... between us. We used to be friends."

John frowned. "And we're *still* friends."

"Are we? Ever since Beltaine, ye look at me with exasperation in yer eyes. And ye have made it clear ye wish I'd stayed behind at Varrich." She sucked in a deep breath before continuing. "Ye think I'm pushy ... ye wish I hadn't played match-maker." She paused then, her voice lowering. "And, if it's any consolation, so do I."

Silence fell between them, and as it drew out, John folded his arms across his chest. "It's too late for this conversation, Neave," he murmured. "Why don't ye go back to bed, and we'll talk in the morning."

Neave shook her head, stubbornness rising. She wouldn't be able to sleep in such an agitated state. "Not before I explain myself a little. Perhaps then, ye will not think so badly of me."

John's features tightened. "I don't think badly of ye, Neave ... I just—"

"Please ... just let me say this." She drew in a steadying breath. "I'm sorry I interfered. I should have let ye find yer own way ... let ye approach a woman when ye were ready."

John sighed. "Ye don't need to apologize to me. I'm—"

"I wasn't always this way," she rushed on, cutting him off once more. "But when my mother sickened a few years ago, it upended my world. I'd had such a happy life before then. When Ma became ill, and no physician could heal her, I realized that the angel of death is ruthless." She swallowed hard, forcing herself on. She didn't like to speak of her mother's illness—in fact, it was a subject she'd never brought up with him before now. "I watched her belly swell with that growth inside her, as her limbs grew thin and wasted ... but I could do nothing."

She broke off there, aware that John's attention had never wavered from her face. His expression had softened. "Life can be needlessly cruel," he said finally. "I too know what it is to lose loved ones."

Indeed, Neave knew he'd lost both his parents young, although he'd never spoken of what had happened, and she'd never pressed him.

"Ever since Ma's death, I've found it difficult to let things be," she admitted softly. "If I see someone I care for suffering, I must help them."

He nodded. "Aye, although it's a habit that will get ye into hot water one day. Ye aren't strong enough to bend fate to yer will, lass ... none of us are."

Neave favored him with a wan smile. "I understand that now ... and I *am* trying to let go." She cleared her throat then. "Are we friends again, John?"

His mouth curved. "Daft woman, I told ye we are."

"Aye, but I didn't believe ye."

John moved forward, standing so close that Neave had to crane her neck back to hold his gaze. His nearness did strange things to her heart, and her mouth went dry. She grasped her blanket to her like a shield.

The silence drew out between them, and then, to her surprise, John reached out with his left hand and took her right one, drawing it away from where she clutched at the blanket about her shoulders.

The warmth and strength of his fingers made her breathing hitch, as did the tender look in his eyes. "I apologize if I've been distant with ye," he said gently. "I've just needed some time to myself." He paused then, his expression softening further. "But never think it's because I don't care. I will always be here for ye, Neave … *always*."

21

THE ONLY THING I HAVE LEFT

JOHN SPIED BALNAKEIL first, the crenelated top of the broch rising above a stand of pines.

Turning in the saddle, he waved to Hugh. "We're here!"

The chieftain of Loch Stach shifted his gaze north to where John now pointed, his already severe expression hardening further. "Good," he growled. "I'm looking forward to having my reckoning with the shit-weasel who stole my daughter."

John frowned. "Breac hasn't stolen Janneth … she followed him of her own free will."

Hugh's mouth twisted. "She would never defy me like this … not without encouragement. No, he put her up to this … and I will gut him for exposing her to such danger."

John clenched his jaw, forcing down the urge to argue with Hugh. The man was as intractable as a bull, and the glint in his blue eyes warned he'd merely dig his heels in if John pushed the issue.

Instead, this discussion would have to wait for when they stood face-to-face with the laird of Balnakeil.

John hoped that Janneth had indeed reached here safely. As they'd discussed at length, it was risky for a woman to travel alone, even a Mackay in her own territory. There were rogues all over the Highlands who preyed upon those traveling on their own—and they would make sport of an unescorted lady.

Pushing the nagging worry aside, for he'd find out soon enough if Janneth had arrived without incident,

John shifted his attention from Hugh to where Neave rode her spirited chestnut mare a few yards behind him.

Her cheeks were flushed from the wind and exertion—the afternoon was waning, and they'd spent another tiring day in the saddle. Yet, despite that he glimpsed the worry upon her face, there was no mistaking the warmth in her hazel-green eyes when their gazes met.

A little of the tension in John's belly—in anticipation of the coming meeting between Breac and Hugh—eased.

Neave Munro never failed to surprise him.

He'd been taken aback when she'd woken him in the middle of the night. But the sight of her standing barefoot in the hallway—a blanket wrapped about her slender shoulders, her chestnut-brown hair cascading down her back, and her gaze imploring—had made it impossible for him to send her back to bed.

And the hurt in her eyes, the vulnerability on her face, while she'd told him about her mother, had made him feel like a heartless bastard. She was right, of course, he *had* been irritated by her meddling, especially when she'd insisted on accompanying them to Balnakeil. However, he should have realized that Neave's drive to help others was rooted in her past.

He'd surprised himself too, when he'd reached for her hand and told her he'd always be there for her. He'd meant it. His throat had thickened as he'd said the words, a wave of tenderness assailing him. A prickling sense of awareness had followed at the feel of her fingers against his—a sensation that had unbalanced him. He'd sent Neave back to bed shortly after and retired to his own.

Yet he'd lain awake for a long while afterward.

Ahead, the trees drew back and a sturdy sandstone tower hove into view. It sat back from the coast, where reed-covered dunes rolled down to a golden-sand beach. A village surrounded Balnakeil broch, the pitched roof of the kirk piercing the pale blue sky. This was John's first visit to Balnakeil, and he had to admit the broch's setting was a lovely one. The afternoon sun highlighted the yellow hues of the sand and the broch's walls, making it appear bathed in honey.

Slowing his courser to a walk, he allowed Hugh to draw alongside, while Neave fell in behind them. Hugh and John's warriors brought up the rear.

"Try to give the man a chance to explain himself," John warned as they approached the open gates, "*before* ye draw yer dirk."

Hugh snorted before casting him a scowl. "He'd better talk fast then."

The travelers passed through the gates, under a stone arch and an iron portcullis, riding into a wide outer ward.

And to John's surprise, Breac Mackay was there to meet them. Clad in a loose black lèine and dun-brown braies, his dark hair tied back at his nape and a dirk strapped to his hip—the man looked as if he was expecting trouble.

A tall, lissome woman with pale-blonde hair stood at the laird's side.

John let out a slow breath. He glanced across at his companions and spied his own relief reflected on Neave's face. Likewise, Hugh's shoulders sagged a little. At least the lass had arrived at Balnakeil without any harm befalling her.

Janneth's gaze never strayed from her father's face as he drew up his horse and swung down from its back.

And then, to John's dismay, the chieftain of Loch Stach drew his dirk and stalked toward Breac.

Leaping off his courser, John followed him, his long legs overtaking the older man easily. He then placed himself in front of Hugh, forcing him to halt.

"Easy there, Hugh," he warned, ignoring the chieftain's glare. "Let them both speak."

Hugh's bearded jaw bunched, and John thought the man might charge him, and attempt to shove him out of the way.

However, moments passed, and he didn't move.

Meanwhile, Neave had dismounted her mare, and now warily approached.

"So, ye have stooped to abducting women now, have ye?" Hugh snarled, moving left so that he could meet the laird of Balnakeil's eye.

Breac's swarthy features tensed, his dark brows crashing together. His lips parted, as he readied himself to respond, yet Janneth cut him off. "This was no abduction, as ye well know, Da." Her cheeks were flushed, ire glittering in her usually gentle blue eyes. "Breac left Varrich, thinking he would never see me again … but I decided to take fate into my own hands." She took a step forward, her gaze fusing with her father's. "I knew the grain merchant would be departing with the dawn, so I paid him to take me with him. Clad in a cloak, with my hood pulled up, none of the guards asked any questions. The merchant took me as far as Kinloch, where I bought myself a pony and continued on alone."

The steadiness of the woman's voice surprised John. He'd once thought Janneth too timid for such a bold act, yet she'd now proved him mistaken.

"Janneth speaks the truth, Hugh," Breac said then. "I would never have asked her to make a two-day journey on her own … nor would I have insisted she join me without yer blessing."

"Good," Hugh growled back. "That being the case, ye can hand her over. We'll be leaving now."

"No." The firmness in Janneth's voice cut through the warm afternoon air. "I won't be leaving with ye, Da. I'm staying here, with Breac … and this evening, we shall be wed."

"Ye will not!" Hugh roared back, taking a menacing step forward. John reached out, gripping the laird by the shoulder, but Hugh shook him off. "I forbid it!"

"Hugh!" Breac was scowling now as he moved close to Janneth and placed an arm around her shoulders. "I love yer daughter and will do everything in my power to give her a good life. This is what she wants … why would ye deny her happiness?"

Hugh's mouth twisted. "Happiness?" he spat out the word as if it were something foul. "This isn't about her …

it's about ye. This is yer revenge, isn't it? Ye didn't like me challenging ye at Varrich, so ye decided to rip my daughter … the only thing I have left … from me."

John's chest tightened at the rawness in Hugh's voice. Aye, he was enraged, yet something else had just emerged.

The only thing I have left.

Hugh Mackay had grieved deeply when he lost his wife. And since then, his daughter had provided companionship. He never went anywhere without her.

The mood in the outer ward shifted then, and Neave stepped up next to Hugh. She reached out, placing a gentling hand upon his arm. To John's surprise, he didn't shrug her off.

"Ye were always going to lose her, Hugh," Neave pointed out softly. "Whether to Breac, or another. Janneth wasn't going to remain with ye forever."

"Aye," he admitted roughly. "But to a Mackay of *Balnakeil*? These bastards betrayed the clan, tried to take power for themselves."

"They did," Neave agreed, her gaze never wavering from Hugh's. "But Breac fought by yer side at Sandside Chase. Admit it … the man has never given ye any *real* reason to doubt him."

John watched Neave, warmth spreading through him. He'd never known a woman like this one: a beguiling combination of vulnerability and pluck. Neave genuinely cared about others and ended up putting herself last.

He wondered then, how she was feeling in the aftermath of Beltaine. It must have come as a shock to discover Roy was her suitor.

Had she hoped another man would approach her that eve?

He'd been so taken up with his own disappointment, he hadn't asked her.

John studied Neave's elfin face, wondering at the sudden tightness in his chest. Neave was lovely—it wouldn't be long before another man sought her hand, one she might welcome.

Heedless to the direction John's thoughts had veered off in, Hugh's mouth pursed. He then shot Breac a dark look. "I saw ye and Iver that afternoon at Varrich ... whispering together like conspirators. What were ye discussing that could not be freely voiced with the rest of us?"

Breac inclined his head, his gaze glinting. "I was telling Iver that I was in love with yer daughter," he replied. "An admission that I thought it best not to shout across the room."

John couldn't help it; his mouth lifted at the corners. He remembered that day. They'd just finished a long meeting with Niel and were helping themselves to cups of wine. Hugh would have indeed choked on his tongue if Breac had made such an announcement.

"Da, please." Janneth shared a long look with Breac before she stepped away from him and crossed the cobblestones to her father. Neave dropped her hand from Hugh's arm and moved away. John also shifted back, giving father and daughter the space they needed.

Hugh's gaze glittered when Janneth stopped before him. She then reached out, taking his left hand—for his right still gripped a dirk. "I know ye miss Ma ... but so do I," she murmured. "Our grief is shared."

The chieftain of Loch Stach's face sagged. "Why couldn't ye have fallen in love with someone else, lass?" His voice was raspy now. "John's a good man. He'd have made ye happy."

John fought a cringe. Christ's bones, why did Hugh have to drag him into this? Janneth had already made her preferences clear. He didn't wish to be a woman's second choice.

As if sensing his awkwardness, Janneth flashed John an apologetic smile. She then fixed her attention on Hugh once more. "And he'd be a fine husband ... but it's Breac I love." Her mouth curved then. "I recall ye telling me that my grandfather wasn't pleased when Ma told him ye were her intended."

Hugh huffed. "Auld Callum MacVane was a mean-tempered curmudgeon," he muttered. "That's not the same thing."

Janneth arched a delicate eyebrow. "Isn't it?" She stepped closer to Hugh, her hand tightening around his. "Breac is as loyal to this clan as ye are … and if ye take off yer blinders, ye know it." Her throat bobbed. "I *will* wed him, Da … with or without yer blessing … but having ye with us this evening, when the priest binds us, would mean the world to me." Her gaze shone then, her voice growing husky as she continued, "Ye haven't lost me, Da. Ye will *never* lose me."

22

BITTERSWEET

THE MERRY STRAINS of a harp and a flute echoed high into the rafters of the hall of Balnakeil broch. Seated upon the dais, watching as Breac Mackay led his wife onto the floor, Neave smiled.

Things had ended well after all.

Hugh had agreed to the union grudgingly—but at least he'd agreed—and just an hour later, Neave had stood at John's side at the foot of the steps to Balnakeil's kirk, watching as the priest wed Janneth and Breac.

Taking a sip of wine from her pewter goblet, Neave glanced right at where Hugh sat, watching the newlyweds.

Her smile faded.

Hugh hadn't said much over the last few hours. She'd expected him to look sullen or to see him silently fume—but instead, he simply appeared sad.

His face seemed to have aged over the afternoon and evening. He was slumped in his chair, and had barely touched the fine meal of roast venison or the plum wine Breac's servants had poured him. Despite that he'd acquiesced in the end, he clearly wasn't overjoyed about this wedding.

Neave's mouth thinned. Perhaps it was just as well that Hugh wasn't drinking. She remembered what happened the last time she'd seen the man in his cups.

"Janneth looks happy," she said then, drawing Hugh's attention.

"Aye," the chieftain rumbled, his gaze narrowing. "Let's hope she stays so."

"Breac adores Janneth," Neave persisted. "Ye can tell by the way he looks at her."

Indeed, the laird of Balnakeil's face shone with joy as he spun Janneth around the floor.

Hugh grunted, although he didn't deny Neave's observation. It was hard to, with the evidence right before him.

"It's not easy, Hugh ... being left alone," John said then. The pair of them had deliberately flanked Hugh this evening, deciding that it was best not to let the man brood in a corner. "I remember well what that feels like."

Hugh glanced John's way, his eyes shadowing. "Aye, John," he replied, his voice softening. "But at least I'm a man grown. When Sìomon and Deirdre drowned, ye were but a bairn." His features tightened then. "I still miss yer father, ye know ... Sìomon was a good friend."

Listening to this, Neave's breathing stilled. "Yer parents drowned, John?" she murmured, leaning forward so that she could see past Hugh to meet his gaze. "Ye never said."

His mouth curved into a tight smile. "Aye, well ... it's not something I enjoy discussing." He glanced down then, toying with his goblet of wine. "They went swimming one day near the falls, not far from Achness broch. It wasn't a wise decision, for there had been recent rains and the river was swift ... Ma was swept away, and my father jumped in to save her." He paused there, his voice lowering. "They were both lost."

"Such a waste," Hugh muttered. "They were young ... with everything before them."

"Aye," John replied. "I was eight at the time, and their only surviving child ... for my brother and sister both died in infancy. I was too young to rule Achness, so the steward, Murtagh, looked after things until I came of age."

Neave listened to this tale, her chest tightening.

She and John had known each other nearly a year and a half now, yet they'd both avoided difficult subjects in their conversations. She hadn't confided in him about the scar her mother's illness had left, and he'd never told her about his parents.

Reaching up, she rubbed at her aching breastbone. She'd been blessed with a noisy, close-knit family, yet John Mackay of Aberach was truly alone. During the time she'd known him, she'd caught glimpses of his loneliness, but hadn't realized just how deep it went. Her discovery made Janneth's rejection all the more poignant.

Neave had thought she knew John Mackay of Aberach, yet did she really?

The music changed then, shifting into another lively jig. John set down his tankard and rose to his feet. He moved past Hugh before extending his left hand to Neave. "I do believe we have never yet danced together, lass," he said, flashing her a boyish smile. "Let us remedy that."

Neave's heart started to race, although she hid her nervousness with a smile of her own and stood up. "Are ye sure ye can keep up with me?" she teased.

His smile widened. "Let's see, shall we?"

Taking her hand, John led Neave out onto the floor. An instant later, they joined the circle of dancers.

Neave discovered that John *could* keep up with her. Of course, she'd seen him dance with Janneth and noted how well he carried himself. Just like when they'd sung together at Yuletide, they anticipated each other and moved seamlessly through the dance. John knew how to lead, and Neave laughed as he spun her around and then caught her against him.

However, her heart felt as if it had lodged in her throat. The blend of gentleness and strength in his hand, as he guided her, was playing havoc with her pulse. She hoped he couldn't feel it.

As much as she enjoyed it, this dance was a bittersweet reminder of what she couldn't have.

Breathing hard, John led Neave back to the table after the dance. He found himself reluctant to let go of her hand, although he ignored the impulse and released her. He was glad he'd cast aside his usual reticence to dance this eve. After a few glasses of wine, he'd started to feel restless. Dancing with Neave Munro was like racing at a gallop across wide hills on a summer's day: wild and free.

Perhaps he'd ask her for another dance before the celebrations ended.

Taking his seat upon the dais once more, John picked up his goblet of wine and took a sip.

"Watching couples dance always reminds me of when I met Shona MacVane," Hugh said as Neave resumed her place next to him. "It was at my cousin's wedding … and I knew the moment I set eyes on the lass that I'd make her mine." John glanced the chieftain's way, to see that his face had softened and his blue eyes had grown misty. "As bonny as a summer's dawn, she was … and we danced all evening." Hugh pulled a face then. "Until Shona's overbearing father dragged her away."

"But ye didn't let him put ye off," John said with a smile.

Hugh shook his head. "The die was already cast. I knew without doubt that I'd met the woman I'd one day wed. And, from that day on, I pursued her."

John listened to the older man's words, his smile fading. His gaze then shifted back to the dancers, where Breac and Janneth were now gliding around the floor in a courtly *basse danse*. The happiness in Janneth's eyes shone like the stars on a clear night.

She was with the man she truly wanted, and that man wasn't him.

John should have been seething with jealousy right now, should have been bitter about losing her. But instead, all he felt was a strange sense of relief.

Hugh would have fought for Shona, but John had stepped aside for Breac without complaint. The chieftain's story reminded him of what he'd known since Beltaine: that not only was he the wrong man for Janneth, but she wasn't the right woman for him either. Aye, he admired her, but his pulse didn't quicken at her touch, and he didn't turn into a grinning fool whenever she smiled at him.

John glanced over at where Neave was watching the dancers. A pretty blush graced her cheeks from dancing, and her eyes gleamed in the light of the cressets upon the wall behind her. His gaze lingered upon her, as his belly tightened.

The woman who did that was his best friend.

Neave and John left Balnakeil shortly after breaking their fast the following morning.

To Neave's relief, Hugh decided to stay on in Balnakeil for a few days—a decision that had pleased Janneth.

The two friends hugged in the outer ward as the sun peeked over the eastern walls surrounding the broch and warmed the cobblestones.

"It looks as if ye shall have fine weather for yer journey back to Varrich," Janneth said, glancing up at the cloudless sky.

"Aye, let's hope so," Neave replied with a smile.

The women's gazes fused then, and a flush rose to Janneth's cheeks.

Of course, Neave was curious as to how the wedding night had gone—as she had been with her sister Beth. But, whereas she'd questioned her elder sister boldly, she wouldn't take such liberties with Janneth.

Even so, the flush to the woman's cheeks, and the sparkle in her blue eyes, told Neave all she needed to know.

"Thank ye for coming all this way with my father," Janneth said softly. She glanced over at where John stood—holding their horses, saddled and ready to leave— and flashed him a smile. "My thanks to both of ye ... Da needed yer counsel yesterday."

John's lips quirked. "Perhaps ... but it was *ye* who brought him around in the end."

Janneth nodded before her own smile faded. "He looked so sad last night ... like a beaten man."

Neave reached out, taking her friend's hand. "He will come right ... just give him time ... and ensure ye pay him plenty of visits in the coming months. He'll pine far less if he knows ye aren't abandoning him." She thought then of her own father. She hadn't seen him since Samhuinn. She missed his good-humored face and warm hazel eyes, but took solace in the knowledge that he was happily wed to Laila, and now had a son to carry on his line.

"I would never abandon him," Janneth assured her huskily, squeezing Neave's hand. Her attention flicked between Neave and John, before her expression lightened and her mouth curved once more. "I'm glad Da listened to me in the end ... but I truly couldn't have persuaded him without assistance from ye both." Her smile widened then. "Ye make a formidable team."

They rode south under the wide arc of a blue sky and a blazing sun, John's men behind them. Along the way, they passed a few travelers, merchants mostly, journeying between the various holdings in Mackay territory. Neave also spied shepherds, tending flocks of black-faced sheep on the hills. The men raised their hands in greeting as the party cantered by, and the travelers waved back.

"Did Beth tell ye about the blacksmith ... before we left Varrich?" John asked unexpectedly.

Neave cast him a surprised look. "Roy Morrison? No." She suppressed a shiver at mention of the man.

"Niel has discovered that the name isn't Morrison, but Gunn," John replied, brow furrowing. "He was cast out of Castle Gunn a few years back after he tried to kill his elder brother … hence why he wished for reckoning against Tavish Gunn."

Neave sucked in a shocked breath. "And Niel's men are still hunting him?"

"Aye … although I suspect they won't catch him … the bastard is as slippery as an eel."

Seeing the severe look upon his face, Neave brought her mare in close, reached out, and placed a hand upon his forearm. "Don't blame yerself, John."

His jaw clenched. "I made a mistake letting him go."

"Yer mercy does ye credit," Neave replied. She then favored him with a soft smile. "Ye likely thought a man needs a second chance."

He snorted. "Not Roy Gunn."

Silence fell between them, although tension still rippled across John's face. Neave wished he wouldn't take responsibility for Gunn. Aye, he probably should have hauled the man up before Niel, yet she'd been relieved when John had sent Roy stumbling off into the darkness instead.

She'd just wanted to be rid of the man.

A strong wind gusted in off the kyle when John and Neave rode up the last stretch of the path toward Castle Varrich the following afternoon.

As they approached the gates, John twisted in the saddle, his gaze alighting upon Neave. He then flashed her a disarming grin that made her belly somersault. "Home at last … how are ye faring?"

"Saddle sore and hungry," she grumbled.

Both of those were true, although she wasn't as grumpy as she feigned.

In truth, she'd wanted the journey to last longer, for she'd enjoyed these past two days traveling alongside John. The evening before, they'd broken their journey at the same point they had on their way to Balnakeil—at the village of Hope.

The tavern owner had welcomed them as old friends, slapping John on the back, and asking him how things had gone in Balnakeil. It appeared the man had noticed Hugh Mackay's black mood, and had worried for the fate of the chieftain's daughter.

He was relieved to hear that she was safe and well.

It had been a sultry evening, and the tavern owner left the doors open, allowing the air, sweet with the scent of grass and heather, to drift indoors. Seated in a booth in one corner of the quiet common room, Neave and John had enjoyed a supper of coarse bread, blood sausage, and cheese washed down with tankards of ale. John's men gathered around a table a few feet away, teasing each other good-naturedly.

And like the previous time she'd eaten there, Neave had found it difficult to enjoy the meal. The food was delicious, yet John's presence across the table distracted her. It had occurred to her then, with a sickening sensation that made it hard to force down her stew, that she could no longer enjoy her friendship with John Mackay.

Not when she didn't see him as a friend anymore.

After supper, she'd retired to her bed-chamber and lain awake for hours pondering the situation. She had been relieved she and John managed to patch things up, but knew there was no going back to how things had been.

And now their journey was ending. Tomorrow John would likely set off for Achness once more. Who knew when she'd see him again?

Perhaps that's for the best, Neave counseled herself, even as her throat constricted. *Ye can't continue pining for him like this.*

She certainly couldn't approach him—not after everything the man had endured of late.

No, she had to let him go. Once he did, she might be able to pull herself together and get on with her life.

23

TAKING A RISK

"YE ARE QUIET this eve," Niel Mackay noted. He poured out two cups of wine and carried them over to the fireside. Despite that it was high summer, the evening was cool. The sky outside the glassed window was the color of old bone. "Did something happen at Balnakeil ye haven't yet told me?"

John glanced up from where he'd been staring at the dancing flames. Taking the cup his cousin offered him, he then shook his head and favored him with a weary smile. "Worry not, Niel ... things have been resolved there."

"Why the distracted look then?" Niel asked, settling himself down opposite John. "I didn't realize I was so boring."

John snorted. They both knew that wasn't the case.

However, Niel was a sharp man, one that missed little—and he'd marked John's odd mood ever since his return that afternoon.

Taking a sip of wine, John tried to pinpoint the reason for his distraction.

It had been a relaxing afternoon and evening. He and Neave had joined Niel, Beth, and the Munro sisters for supper—a lively meal during which Jean and Eilidh insisted Neave recount what had happened at Balnakeil. Neave had obliged, and John was happy to let her do so without any help from him.

Instead, he'd watched Neave as she spoke, his gaze tracking the delicate movements of her hands, the way her cheeks dimpled when she smiled. Aye, she was fatigued from the journey, yet she was a natural storyteller. She had everyone at the table spellbound.

No, John had no idea why he felt out of sorts.

"I've never had a Beltaine like this one," he admitted after a pause. "I'll be going back to Achness for a rest."

"Aye, between Janneth and Roy Gunn … ye have been kept busy," Niel replied.

John's mouth thinned at the mention of Tongue's former blacksmith. Niel had informed him during supper that Captain Reay and his men had returned that morning empty-handed. Gunn had either left Mackay lands or hidden himself expertly. The news left John uneasy—perhaps that was the reason for his quietness this eve. He had the nagging sense that he hadn't seen the last of Roy Gunn.

John had first thwarted and then humiliated him. Gunn wouldn't likely forget.

"I'm sorry things with Janneth didn't work out," Niel continued, his gaze never leaving John's face. He clearly thought disappointment was the cause of John's subdued mood.

John shrugged. "Don't be … we weren't meant for each other. She wed the man she wanted."

"So ye aren't sore over it?"

"No."

Niel's lips curved into a wry smile. He then leaned back in his chair and crossed his long legs at the ankle. "It looks like Beth was right," he murmured. "She said ye weren't smitten with Janneth."

John frowned. The smug look on his cousin's face was starting to irritate him. "Did she?"

"Aye … my wife misses little," Niel continued, still looking exceedingly pleased with himself. "She whispered to me after supper that ye didn't take yer gaze off Neave once while she told us about what happened at Balnakeil."

John stiffened, his fingers tightening around his cup. Heat rolled over him, his skin prickling in embarrassment. He hadn't realized he'd been gawking at Neave so openly. He also didn't like to think Niel and

Beth had been discussing him. He was a private man and preferred to keep his business to himself.

But the way Niel was grinning now, it was as if he was privy to some secret that John had yet to be let in on.

"Keep smirking like that, and I'll plant my fist into yer mouth," John growled.

Niel paid him no heed. Instead, he leaned forward, his gaze spearing John's. "So," he drawled. "When are ye going to talk to Neave?"

John stared back at him. And when he eventually found his tongue, he only managed to rasp, "What?"

Niel sighed, leaning back once more in his chair and setting his cup down on the table beside the fire. "I thought no man could be as thick-headed as me when it came to women ... but ye seem to be doing yer best." He paused then, his eyes narrowing. "If ye want Neave, ye'd better offer for her ... before someone else does."

John's grip on his cup was so tight now that the wood creaked. His heart was racing as if he'd just taken the three flights of stairs at a run, and his limbs had gone oddly weak.

Aye, he wanted Neave, yet it wasn't as simple as that.

After the disaster with Janneth, his gut clenched at the thought of humiliating himself again. He and Neave were close, but what if she saw him only in a 'brotherly' light? An unwelcome admission could ruin their friendship forever. He inwardly cringed as he imagined her eyes shadowing as Janneth's had when he'd proposed to her.

Could he take such a risk?

The door to the solar crashed open then, with such force that both men started.

Captain Reay burst in, out of breath from his race up the stairs.

"God's teeth, man." Niel rose to his feet, scowling. "Don't ye know how to knock?"

"Apologies, Laird," Ewan Reay panted. His gaze then shifted to where John had put aside his cup of wine and stood up. "But a man has just come from Achness ... the

Sutherlands have started raiding along the River Oykel ... and they've torched two of yer villages."

John sucked in a sharp breath. "Which ones?"

"Brae and Doune."

John whispered a curse, heat igniting under his ribs. His gaze then cut to Niel. "They've never raided this close to Achness before ... the bastards are virtually on my doorstep."

"And they won't stray so near again," Niel muttered. His sharp-featured face had gone hard, his eyes narrowed. "Gather as many men as ye can," he instructed Captain Reay. "We ride out within the hour."

Ewan Reay nodded, before turning on his heel and leaving as abruptly as he'd arrived.

Niel then turned to John, their gazes fusing. "It looks like Sutherland is spoiling for a fight."

"Aye," John growled back. "Then we shall give the bastard one."

Cutting across the bailey, which was now filled with horses, dogs, and men, John made for the gates.

They would be departing soon, but he had to see someone before he did.

Neave.

He'd looked for her in the great hall, and then the women's solar—and even her bed-chamber. Unlike her sisters, who were in the kitchens helping fill packs with food for the warriors, Neave was nowhere to be found.

There was only one place he hadn't looked.

The garden.

Passing under the stone arch, John cut right, taking the path to the terrace garden. It was growing late in the day, yet the sun still hadn't set; dusk drew out this time of year. They would be able to cover some ground before night settled over the Highlands.

The wind, which had been gusting earlier, had disappeared, and stillness settled over the promontory like an indrawn breath. The air felt charged, as it often did before conflict.

John's jaw clenched. The viciousness of the Sutherland attack made fury boil in his guts. Two villages razed, and lord knows how many of the villagers maimed or killed. The people of Achness looked to him as their protector—and he'd failed them.

Soon, he would do his best to mend this mess, yet before he departed from Varrich, words had to be said.

Embarrassment be damned. Battle had a way of making a man's priorities clear. He wouldn't leave this castle without speaking honestly to Neave, without telling her how he felt. He just hoped she saw him as more than a friend. There had been times over the past days when he'd marked a softness in her gaze as she'd looked at him. But there was only one way to know the truth.

Striding into the garden, John pulled up short, his gaze sweeping the terraces. He'd expected to see Neave at one of the beds, on her knees, her basket at her side as she pulled up weeds.

However, she wasn't there.

For a moment, he thought the garden was empty— and then he caught sight of a small figure, sitting at the top of the garden, her back against the wall of the keep.

Spying him, she hurriedly got up and dusted off her skirts. John climbed the steps and approached her. Neave's cheeks were flushed and her shoulders tense, as if she was embarrassed at being caught idling. Indeed, it was odd to find her not at work. Neave was the most industrious woman he'd ever known. Clearly, she hadn't come to the garden to work, but for solitude.

Perhaps the churning emotions within him showed on his face, for worry creased Neave's brow when he drew near. "What's wrong?"

John pulled up a few feet from her. "Have ye not heard?"

She shook her head. "Heard what? I've been here since supper."

"The Sutherlands have razed two of my villages ... not far from Achness. We're riding out now to confront them. Niel and his men are joining me."

Neave whispered an unladylike oath and stepped close, her hazel-green eyes widening. "Ye are going to fight them?"

"Aye ... it's likely."

Their gazes met and held, and suddenly, it felt difficult to breathe.

This was his chance—and he would seize it.

Clearing his throat, he stepped close. "I had to see ye before I left, Neave," he murmured. Reaching down, he brushed away a lock of hair that had fallen over her eyes. Neave was staring up at him, her rosebud lips parted. A friend didn't look at a man like that. Something deep within his chest unknotted. At that moment, he knew he didn't need to worry about Neave rejecting him. This scene wouldn't end in his humiliation. "I needed to do this."

And without another word, he leaned down and brushed his lips across hers.

He went gently at first, for this was new for them both, and then more firmly. A gasp escaped Neave, emboldening him further. A heartbeat later, his tongue swept her lips apart, and the kiss turned passionate. His left hand slid up to cup the back of her neck, before his fingers tunneled through her hair, spanning her scalp as he explored her mouth with slow, sensual determination.

Lord, she tasted sweet: like heather honey.

It was a kiss that made her heart race and her head swim.

Neave responded, her tongue tentatively sliding against his—and the groan that rumbled low in John's throat when she did so told her he welcomed her eagerness. She placed her hands flat against his chest. His heart pounded under her right palm, the heat of his body embracing her through the thin material of his lèine.

A tingling excitement curled in the cradle of Neave's hips, and she melted into the kiss, losing herself in the heat of his mouth, his questing lips, and tongue.

When they drew apart, both of them were breathless.

John stared down at her, his gaze gleaming.

"Mother Mary," she murmured before giving a shaky laugh. "What was that?"

"Something I should have done months ago."

"And why now?" Neave still couldn't believe John had just stridden into the garden, announced he was about to go off to fight the Sutherlands, and then kissed her. *And what a kiss.* Aye, in the past days, she'd dreamed of him looking at her as he was now, but everything was moving so swiftly. She couldn't keep up.

After supper, she'd slipped away to her garden. Her sisters had wanted to hear everything about Hugh's confrontation with his daughter and Breac Mackay, and the wedding that followed, but telling the tale had drained her. And when Niel and John retired upstairs to the clan-chief's solar afterward, she'd begged off joining her sisters in the women's solar.

Heaviness had dogged her steps as she made her way to her sanctuary, her throat tight with the need to weep. During supper, John had confirmed that he'd be departing for Achness with the dawn. She wouldn't see him again for a while—and when she did, both their circumstances might be different. There seemed to be no hope.

As if sensing her confusion, John's mouth curved. "Because when a man knows what he wants, he shouldn't hold back."

Neave stared back at him, her breathing coming in quick gasps.

"Ye caught my eye, ye know," he continued. "On the day ye and yer sisters arrived at Castle Varrich. Why do ye think I sat next to ye?"

Neave huffed a laugh. "I thought it was the only empty seat left."

His gaze seared hers. "There were plenty of empty spaces at the table that day ... as ye well know." His hand then cupped her cheek. "I'd never met a woman like ye. Ye are beautiful, yet ye didn't flirt, didn't look at me in any way that could be construed as amorous." He paused then, swallowing, as if nervous. "After Drumnacoub, I'd become shy around women ... embarrassed at being maimed ... but ye didn't look at me with pity in yer eyes, or deliberately avoid glancing at my eyepatch or my missing hand. I enjoyed yer company so much that I told myself ye were nothing more than a friend... and I believed it too."

"As did I," Neave whispered back, her throat thickening. It was time she spoke plainly as well. "Until Beltaine ... and then I realized I'd made a terrible mistake in match-making ye and Janneth. I'd pushed ye into her arms ... when I wanted ye for myself."

John's gaze widened at her revelation. "Och, lass ... what a pair we are," he murmured. His thumb traced a gentle path down her jawbone to her chin, before lightly skimming across her lower lip. His touch made Neave shiver with need. "I can't believe I didn't see what was right in front of me," he said, shaking his head.

"We've both been blind," Neave whispered.

His mouth curved into a sensual smile that made Neave's pulse flutter at the base of her throat. "Aye," he murmured. "But not any longer."

And with that, he leaned down and kissed her again.

24

DEATH AND DEVASTATION

"HE KISSED YE?" Eilidh's excited squeal arrowed through the women's solar. "When I saw the pair of ye in here that day … I *knew* there was something between ye!"

"As did I." Jean wore a smug look upon her face as she lowered the cup of warmed milk she'd been sipping, her grey-green gaze settling upon her elder sister.

"We all did," Beth added. Seated by the window, she had a knowing glint in her eye. "I was wondering when ye'd both come to yer senses."

Neave rolled her eyes. "Well, it seems, *everyone* knew before we did," she huffed.

Indeed, she was embarrassed that she hadn't noticed the gradual change between her and John. And even when she *had* admitted her feelings to herself, she'd been afraid to approach him. Janneth's rejection had been a blow, and she'd thought he was now wary of women.

The change in their relationship had happened so swiftly, she felt dizzy in the aftermath. Her lips tingled as she remembered the passionate kiss John had left her with.

"It's sometimes that way," Beth replied with the knowledgeable air of a wedded woman. "These things are easier to spot from afar … it's not so easy when yer heart is involved."

Neave nodded, wrapping her fingers around the cup of milk she hadn't yet taken a sip from. That was indeed the truth. She then stifled a yawn. It was getting late, and the sisters all needed to go to bed. However, once Niel, John, and a party of sixty warriors left the castle, they'd been too on edge to retire. "I'm relieved John and I were able to clear the air," she murmured finally, even as her belly tensed. "Especially since he's now gone off to fight the Sutherlands."

Beth and Neave's gazes fused, a silent message passing between them. Beth hid it well, yet Neave had spotted the tension in her sister's shoulders, and the faint groove between her eyebrows. She didn't want Niel going into battle again—especially after she'd nearly lost him during the last one. She also now carried his bairn. What if it grew up fatherless?

"Niel and John will both be fine," Eilidh assured them, her gaze flicking between Beth and Neave. She had picked up on the look they'd shared. "They're both warriors of renown."

"Aye, but that doesn't make them immortal," Jean pointed out with a frown. "As ye well know."

Eilidh scowled. "God's teeth, Jeanie, I was just trying to make them feel better. Why do ye have to be so grim?"

"I was just stating a fact. Battle is—"

"That's enough, Jean," Beth cut in, rising to her feet. "All of us know what battle entails ... and I'd rather not go to bed tonight dwelling upon it."

Jean's cheeks flushed at the reprimand, her gaze dropping to her cup. "I'm sorry, Beth ... I didn't mean to worry ye. It's just that Eilidh shouldn't make ye assurances like that."

"Perhaps not, but she meant well."

Jean's eyes filled with tears. "As did I."

A brittle silence fell over the solar then, a rare occurrence when all four of the Munro sisters were gathered together. Usually, it was difficult to get a word in edgewise.

Neave looked at each of their faces, all a little pale and pinched with worry. Her sisters' expressions likely mirrored her own. Despite that her eyes burned with fatigue and her muscles were sore from riding, she would sleep fitfully tonight.

Today had been strange indeed, for it had brought both joy and upheaval, both hope and fear. Her breathing quickened then, dizziness sweeping over her at the thought that John might never return to her. She didn't want to linger on the risks, yet Jean had unwittingly slapped her across the face with reality.

John Mackay wasn't invincible. One stolen moment in her garden might be all they would share.

"We've made good time," John announced, twisting in the saddle to meet Niel's eye. "We'll reach Achness by noon."

Niel responded with a nod, his gaze shifting then to scan the surrounding pinewood. "We'll need to be careful," he replied, his hand straying to the hilt of his dirk. "The Sutherlands might have traveled upriver."

John shook his head at this suggestion. "They won't get past Achness … my men will have made sure of that."

Niel cocked an eyebrow at his cousin's assurance, yet John didn't waver. Achness wasn't a large holding; nonetheless, it had a strong fighting force, and Murtagh would have sent out patrols following the attacks on Brae and Doune. "That's reassuring to hear," the clan-chief replied after a pause.

They rode along a rutted road that was only wide enough to allow horses to ride two abreast. The wind roared through the pines this morning, the sound mingling with the chatter of the River Cassley alongside. Behind them, the conversation of the warriors was a low rumble.

John's attention shifted once more to the road ahead, and he urged his horse into a brisk canter. Niel did the same, and the two of them surged ahead. They were both keen to reach Achness, and to gather John's men so that they could ride south to the River Oykel.

"Ye have the look of a man eager to spill some blood," Niel observed as he drew up alongside John.

Glancing across at his cousin, John snorted. "Do I?"

Niel flashed him a wolfish smile in reply. His dark hair flew behind him, and his cobalt-blue eyes were bright.

John looked away, frowning. "This might come as a surprise to ye, Niel … but I don't revel in war. I never have." A heaviness settled in his gut at the admission. "All I ever wanted was to live in peace at Achness, surrounded by pines, tilled fields, and a rushing river. But it seems that from the moment I was old enough to wield a blade, I've been fighting." He swallowed then, for resentment had grabbed a stranglehold around his throat. "There's never any respite from it … if our own clansmen aren't trying to stick a dirk in our backs, it's the Gunns or the Sutherlands. Is it any wonder so few warriors live to see old age?"

John fell silent then, suddenly embarrassed by his outburst.

He'd never been so candid with anyone on this topic before—and his clan-chief cousin wasn't the best choice. However, his emotions lay close to the surface this morning. Fury at the Sutherlands simmered within him, yet there was frustration too.

He and Neave had only just found each other. He didn't want Robert Sutherland's reckoning to shatter his future before it had a chance to begin.

Clearing his throat, John glanced back at Niel. He'd expected to see censure, or even scorn, upon his cousin's face, for Niel Mackay—like his father before him—had come out of the womb looking for a fight. But, instead, Niel wore an introspective expression.

"Don't mistake me," John continued. "I'll fight till they drag my last breath from me, to defend Mackay land … to protect my kin and clansmen … but that doesn't mean I have to like it."

Niel's mouth quirked, even if his gaze was now solemn. "I once lived for the thrill of battle madness in my blood," he admitted after a pause. "It brought me alive in a way few things ever could ... but ever since Sandside Chase, I can understand why old dogs lose the hunger for a hunt."

John snorted. "Ye are hardly an 'old dog', cousin. I'd say yer change of heart has more to do with Beth than yer age."

Their gazes fused, and Niel's mouth curved. "Aye ... and I shall return to her." There was no doubt in the clan-chief's voice. His gaze glinted then. "But not before we find the men who torched yer villages ... and send them all to hell."

The shadows were lengthening, the day drawing toward dusk, when a force of over one hundred Mackay warriors slipped through the forest like wraiths.

Dirk gripped in his fist, his longsword hanging at his waist, John slowed his gait as dry bracken crunched underfoot. Gaze narrowed, he scanned his surroundings. It was dark amongst the trees, despite that the sun hadn't yet slipped behind the western horizon. He didn't like fighting at this time of day—not since losing his left eye. After Drumnacoub, he'd adjusted well to being able to see only out of his right one, but when the light was dim, his peripheral vision wasn't the best.

He would need to rely on the men flanking him to spy anything amiss.

As he'd promised, they hadn't seen any skulking Sutherlands en route to Achness. Upon arrival at his broch, Murtagh had updated him and Niel on the situation. There hadn't been time to rest or eat more than a few mouthfuls of bread and cheese before they'd departed Achness once more—this time on foot. Although they couldn't travel as fast this way, they had stealth on their side.

Murtagh had reported that the Sutherland men weren't on horseback either. Instead, a number of them had been spotted that morning, stalking the banks of the River Oykel.

John's mood had blackened at this news.

It sounded to him as if Robert Sutherland was attempting to draw a new boundary between the Mackays and the Sutherlands, much farther north than the existing one, upon the River Oykel.

Emerging from the trees, John crouched down in the long grass. Ahead the river glittered in the last rays of evening sun. At this point, the Oykel was a wide, shallow river, studded with rocks, although it could be deep and fast flowing both up and downriver.

Doune was their destination now, for the village was the closer of the two that had been attacked. No one had returned to either hamlet since the survivors of the raid had fled and raised the alarm.

John's jaw clenched. It was time for him to see the devastation for himself. He also wanted to draw the Sutherlands out—for they'd be keeping an eye on the villages they'd razed.

Glancing right, he caught Niel's eye. He then pointed to the river and nodded.

His cousin nodded back, and together they moved toward the grassy banks of the Oykel. Their men followed, and moments later, they were all fording the river. Icy water surged up to John's thighs, making him suck in a breath. Teeth gritted, he pushed on, and, upon reaching the far bank, took refuge in the trees once more. It wouldn't be long before a Sutherland scout spied them, but he wanted to get to Doune before one did.

John had seen plenty of death over the years. Even so, bile stung his throat when he walked into the ruins of the village. Doune had once been a quiet, yet prosperous, hamlet, nestled on the south bank of the River Oykel. Its inhabitants fished the river and lived in peace.

But now nothing remained of it, except the charred skeletons of cottages and storehouses, some of which still smoked. Bodies lay everywhere, bloodied and twisted. Most of them were men, who'd picked up pitchforks and shovels to defend their home—but there were women and children amongst them too.

John stopped before the body of a lad, of no more than six or seven winters. He'd had his throat cut.

"Filthy whoresons," he muttered, his heart now pounding like a battle drum against his ribs. This was a violation of his lands, *his* people. "Ye shall pay for this."

Nostrils flaring at the burned odor that mingled with the stench of blood, John forced himself on, picking his way through the dead. Around him, Niel and the others fanned out. They'd ordered some warriors to keep watch on the riverbank in the meantime, while the others secured the southern perimeter.

They didn't want to be taken unawares.

A few feet away, Niel muttered a salty curse of his own. Turning to his cousin, John watched him straighten up from peering inside the shell of a cottage. Its turf roof had half collapsed. Niel's face had gone pale, yet his gaze smoldered. "They burned a family alive in there."

The pounding of John's heart increased in tempo. It was hammering so hard it echoed in his ears now. Heat rolled over him, fury chasing away all other thoughts or cares. Robert Sutherland had struck hard, in order to get his revenge on his enemy, but now the need for a reckoning of his own stirred in John's blood. This devastation and death wouldn't go unpunished. Time narrowed to that moment as he locked gazes with Niel.

An instant later, shouting erupted to the south, shattering the stillness of the gloaming. Both men reached for their dirks before Niel cast John a harsh smile. "Looks like we've flushed the pheasants out of the grass."

"Aye," John replied, his fingers flexing around the bone hilt of his dirk. "Let's show them a Mackay welcome."

25

UNFINISHED BUSINESS

NEAVE WAS IN the granary, helping take an inventory, when the men returned.

The clatter of hooves against cobbles, followed by shouts and barking, echoed across the bailey and through the granary's open door.

Neave's fingers clenched around the stub of charcoal she'd been using to mark a ledger, her heart bucking hard against her breastbone. The inventory forgotten, she thrust the ledger at the lass who was halfway through counting sacks of barley, turned, and raced outside.

It was chaos inside the bailey, and she drew up sharply, to avoid being trampled by horses. Her gaze darted from face to face, of each man in the milling crowd before her—searching for one in particular.

She spied Niel Mackay first. The clan-chief's face was drawn, and he had a cut across his forehead, one that had already started to scab. However, his gaze was triumphant, and Neave knew then that their campaign had been successful.

She held her breath, her hands clenching at her sides. *Where's John?*

She spied him then. He'd just drawn his courser up behind the clan-chief. His dark curly hair was mussed from the wind, his face tired, yet he appeared unhurt.

A relieved breath gusted out of Neave.

She drank him in, noting that he was looking toward the keep, to where Beth, Jean, and Eilidh were making their way down the stone steps.

Neave's heart leaped once more.

He was looking for her.

In the meantime, the crowd parted for Beth and her sisters, allowing the clan-chief's wife to welcome her husband back.

Niel swung down from his courser and closed the gap between him and Beth. He then gathered her tenderly against him, difficult for her belly now stuck out before her like the prow of a ship, before he kissed her.

Watching them, Neave's throat constricted, tears pricking the back of her eyes.

The past five days had been difficult, and the tension within the keep had grown with each new dawn. That morning, Beth had even broken down as worry for her husband became too much. Likewise, Neave had wept.

Five days and no word. What had happened to them?

But here were Niel, John, and their men, their voices echoing off the stone walls once more.

"John!" Neave stepped forward, her voice catching as he swiveled, his gaze spearing hers.

And the intensity she spied there made time stand still for an instant.

Her surroundings drew back: the clatter of horses' hooves, the excited yipping of dogs, and the roar of voices lowering to a dull murmur.

All Neave could focus on was John.

They stared at each other, and then a slow smile spread across John's face.

Joy barreled into Neave, causing her breathing to hitch. She wanted to look upon that smile daily for the rest of her life. She couldn't breathe without it.

John dismounted his horse then and headed toward her. However, Neave was already moving, pushing her way through the press toward him.

They collided in the midst of the bailey, ignoring the hoots and whistles from the surrounding men. John picked Neave up, spun her around—and then kissed her passionately, his mouth slanting across hers.

Neave didn't care that they had an audience. Instead, she linked her arms about John's neck and kissed him back wildly. The feel of his lean strength against her, the heat of his body, made her forget where they were.

Eventually, they drew apart to realize that the noise in the bailey had quietened. A sea of grinning faces surrounded them. Neave's sisters were amongst the onlookers, and all three of them were beaming.

Blushing now, as propriety caught up with her, Neave leaned against John's chest, burying her face in the crook of his neck.

"It's good to have ye back … safe," she murmured, sinking into his embrace once more.

"Aye … the Sutherlands were waiting for us," he replied, his voice a rumble in his chest. "They'd decided to push their border north … it was indeed a ploy to draw me into battle." He paused then. "But we bested them … and made sure that enough Sutherlands survived to limp home to tell their clan-chief the tale."

Neave drew back once more, her chin tilting as her gaze sought his. "So, it's over?"

His mouth curved, even though his gaze was solemn. "Aye … for the time being."

His left hand raised then, his fingers stroking her cheek tenderly. The moment drew out, before he finally spoke. "Lass, our time in this world is so short … I don't want to waste an instant more of it. We've known each other awhile now … and I can't imagine life without ye. I want to awake every morning with ye in my arms." He paused then, swallowing. "Neave Munro … will ye do me the honor of becoming my wife?"

Neave drew in a shaky breath, warmth rolling through her. "Aye," she gasped. "A thousand times over, 'aye'."

A wide smile stretched his face, and he lowered his head once more, his mouth capturing hers.

"So, when's the wedding?" Niel's voice intruded, and they broke apart, turning to the clan-chief. Niel stood next to Beth, one arm about her shoulders. His gaze twinkled as he met his cousin's eye.

"As soon as we can arrange it," John replied without hesitation.

"Wait." Neave's hand fastened around John's forearm. With all the excitement, they'd overlooked something important. "I'd like Da and Laila to be present when we wed."

John nodded, his gaze warm upon hers. "Then I will send a rider out to Foulis, at first light tomorrow."

Roy Gunn crouched low in the heather, watching the patchwork of fields below.

It was dangerous to travel this close to Tongue and the path that wound its way up to the fortress above, but he'd taken the risk anyway.

He had to if he was to spy his quarry.

Roy's jaw clenched, as did his fists. After Beltaine, he'd hidden away and let his bruises heal. Finally though, hunger had forced him out.

The day before, he'd gone into the tiny hamlet of Ribigill to pick up supplies, and had heard two women gossiping while they picked out cabbages at market.

Apparently, the Mackays had just returned, victorious, from a skirmish with Sutherland raiders. And soon there was to be a wedding at Varrich. John Mackay of Aberach would be taking Neave Munro as his wife— and the ceremony would take place as soon as the bride-to-be's kin arrived from Foulis Castle.

The news had been a punch to the face.

Roy had frozen to the spot, his senses reeling.

Of course, he should have realized. That whoreson had wanted Neave for himself. It all made sense now— how he'd warned Roy off before Beltaine, and then had suddenly appeared when Roy had gotten Neave alone.

He'd been looking for her.

Roy had bought his supplies in a daze, before stumbling away from Ribigill. He hadn't slept that night. Instead, he'd tried to think of a way to get even.

Drawing in a deep, steadying breath now, Roy surveyed the fields below, where cottars toiled under the midday sun.

One of the figures drew his eye. A tall, lean man with wild peat-dark hair and a beard. He was clad in a sweat-stained lèine and braies and wore iron shackles around his ankles. The chains hampered him a little, yet the man still managed to work. At present, he was tilling the soil with a hoe.

The wind caught at his unkempt hair, blowing it back from his proud face.

Roy's mouth thinned. Even at this distance, he recognized his youngest brother. He'd heard that Niel Mackay had taken Will prisoner, and had hoped the Mackay clan-chief would mount Will's head on a pike outside the castle gates.

Instead, he'd put him to work in the fields.

Will didn't look well. His face was pale and gaunt, his color ashen. His clothing hung off him, yet he stayed upright and continued to toil alongside the cottars.

Roy's gaze narrowed. Out of all his siblings, William was the one he'd clashed with the most. Aye, he'd been jealous of Alexander—although he'd minded his brutal elder brother—and then he'd resented Tavish for taking his father's place as clan-chief. These days, his hatred for Tavish pulsed like a hot coal in his gut. Yet Will had always rubbed him up the wrong way.

Right from when they were lads, Will had goaded him. He had a smart mouth, and although Roy had pummeled him with his fists numerous times when they were bairns, his younger brother always managed to get the last word.

The last time they'd physically fought, Roy felled Will, and was kicking him as he lay on the ground, when Tavish had intervened. If he hadn't, Roy would have killed him.

Roy glared at his brother as he worked. With any luck, Will would live out the rest of his days as a prisoner of the Mackays—if sickness didn't end him first.

At that moment, he spied figures making their way down the promontory above. Shifting his attention from his brother, Roy peered at the group.

Three women, followed by two men.

And when they reached the bottom of the hill and crossed the bridge that would take them into Tongue, Roy's breathing slowed.

One of the women was Neave. She was still some way off, but her chestnut-brown hair was distinctive, as was her jaunty stride and lithe frame, encased in a form-fitting dark-blue kirtle. He recognized her companions too, for he'd seen them many times in Tongue: her sisters.

Roy's gaze shifted to the two men trailing the women. They were big warriors with dirks at their hips. Roy's mouth thinned. An armed escort.

Of course, John Mackay knew Roy was still at large. It looked as if he was now protecting his bride-to-be.

Breathing a curse under his breath, Roy reached up to his belt and removed the leather pouch hanging there. Then, tearing his gaze from the women and their guards, he tipped the ruby brooch and the pendant he'd once gifted her onto his palm.

Roy gazed at the jewels. Sunlight glinted off the rubies. These two pieces had cost him every last penny he'd had. Fortunately, his skill as a blacksmith had earned him plenty of coin over the past years—but even so, these gifts were the costliest items he'd ever purchased.

And that ungrateful wee bitch had thrown them back in his face.

Life had been hard for Roy after his elder brother cast him from Castle Gunn. For the first time in his life, he'd made close acquaintances with hunger and cold. He no longer had a warm hearth and a soft bed to return to each night. Days would pass without a proper meal. He'd fought for scraps in alleyways with stray dogs and stolen eggs from fowl coops to keep from starving. For the first year or two, he'd scratched a living, before a smith in

Inverness had taken him on as an apprentice. The memory of those hard years remained with him still.

It made Neave's rejection all the more galling.

Roy swallowed, his fingers closing around the brooch and pendant. He needed to return to Inverness, to find a buyer for them. He should leave Mackay lands, put all of this behind him, and start afresh.

But still, he lingered.

He couldn't leave with unfinished business.

His gaze flicked up once more, traveling to where one of the sisters—a slender lass with delicate features—had just laughed. It was a merry, joy-filled sound, one that even caused a few of the cottars to glance her way.

Will also straightened up, his gaze shifting to the women. All three of them looked back at Will. They were closer now, and Roy spied the curiosity upon their faces.

His attention returned, once more, to Neave. Aye, she looked bonnier than ever—a woman in love. In the past, just the sight of her would cause his wits to scatter, his heart to pound, and his mouth to go dry. Even now, his pulse quickened at the sight of her.

He wanted to stalk the lass. If those two warriors hadn't been escorting them, he'd have followed the three Munro sisters into Tongue, watched from the shadows, and pounced when the moment was right. Three small women would be easy enough to handle. And then he could drag Neave away and finish what he'd started at Beltaine.

Roy's breathing caught at the thought before he scowled.

Neave Munro was beyond his reach for the moment. If he wanted her, he'd have to remove the man who'd thwarted him.

John Mackay of Aberach.

Roy's fingers tightened around the brooch and pendant, the sharp edges of the jewels digging into his palm, but he paid the pain no mind.

He had time to lie in wait for the chieftain of Achness, for the Munros would have to travel up from Foulis Castle, four days' journey to the south, to reach Varrich.

In the meantime, Roy would sharpen his blades and ready himself to strike.

26

ONE THING AT A TIME

"THAT'S WILLIAM GUNN, isn't it?" Eilidh whispered, her oak-colored eyes wide.

"Aye," Jean murmured. "No one else would be working in the fields with iron shackles fastened around his ankles."

"He has a wild look to him," Eilidh replied, her gaze never leaving the man.

Neave shifted her attention from her sisters, taking in the prisoner's appearance with interest. Indeed, he was ragged, thin, and wild-haired, although the intensity of his stare was hard to miss. When Eilidh had laughed, he'd straightened up from tilling the earth with a hoe, his gaze settling upon them. "He does," she agreed, her tone speculative. "However, so would ye, if ye'd been locked up in Varrich dungeon for nearly a year."

"I heard he got ill," Jean said then. "A breathing sickness that would have claimed his life if Tess hadn't tended to him."

"And if Niel hadn't told the guards to start feeding him properly," Neave added, with a wry smile. She'd heard the whispers within the keep. Niel had paid his hostage a visit, it seemed, and in the days since, folk had spied William Gunn out in the fields.

"Just as well," Jean murmured. "If he dies, it'll be likely to restart the feuding ... Niel will know that."

"Beth told me that when Niel saw Gunn in that dark cell, it brought back memories of what it was like for him at Bass Rock," Eilidh said. Neave glanced her way to see that the youngest of her sisters was still watching Gunn, her usually smooth brow furrowed. "Perhaps that's why he's become more lenient … he knows what it is to suffer so."

"Perhaps," Neave mused. Ever since Niel had returned from the north, and his bloody reckoning against the Gunns, the clan-chief's attitude had altered. Aye, he'd ridden out to deal with the Sutherlands without hesitation, yet he no longer spoiled for a fight.

Neave didn't imagine Niel would ever look upon the Gunns as friends, but his leniency toward William Gunn revealed that he wished to leave the feud behind him. While Gunn was his hostage, the man's kin would think twice about raiding Mackay villages or stealing their livestock.

But it appeared Niel wasn't interested in making his prisoner suffer needlessly.

Neave smiled, pleased at this change in their clan-chief's attitude. Now that the Sutherlands had withdrawn from John's lands, perhaps they could all live in peace.

"Come." She beckoned to where Eilidh and Jean still lingered on the path. "The seamstress will be wondering what's keeping us."

Jean nodded, moving after her. Yet Eilidh hesitated. Her youngest sister was still staring at William Gunn as if a wulver stood in the midst of the field. And likewise, the prisoner boldly looked back at her. Misgiving tightened Neave's belly then, causing the warmth of contentment that cocooned her to ebb just a little.

She worried a little about Eilidh sometimes. The lass was a sweet soul, and kind to a fault, yet she could be flighty and impulsive. She didn't want her to develop an unhealthy fascination with William Gunn.

"Don't stare at him so, Eilidh." Jean's voice echoed Neave's own misgiving. However, unlike her elder sister, Jean didn't hesitate in sharing her thoughts. The youngest two Munro sisters were very close in age and as such bickered the most. She was frowning at Eilidh now, chagrin upon her face. "Ye will only encourage him."

Eilidh snorted, although she did as bid and moved off down the path with her sisters. "Encourage him to do what exactly?" she asked, arching an eyebrow at Jean. "The man's in chains."

"Da!" Neave flew across the cobbles and collided with her father, laughing as his arms went around her and squeezed tight. "Ye arrived sooner than I'd expected!"

"We left the day after receiving yer missive, lass," George Munro replied. He drew back then, his gaze shining as he gazed down at her. "Ye didn't think we'd make ye delay yer wedding, did ye?"

"I'm so glad ye could come."

"We wouldn't have missed it for anything." Laila stepped up next to her husband, a wide smile upon her face.

Drawing back from her father, Neave's gaze went to the bairn in the sling across her stepmother's chest. The babe had a thick head of brown hair, a cherubic face, and bright eyes. "Oh, Laila ... he's a bonny wee lad," she murmured.

Laila flushed with pleasure. "Aye, I'd say Fionn will be the image of his father when he grows up."

The Munro clan-chief beamed at his wife's words.

"Welcome, Da ... Laila!" Neave turned to see Beth approaching. She was trying to move quickly, although that was difficult with her belly so large. Neave frowned. The healer, Tess, had told her she should start her 'lying in' now, with the birth just a couple of weeks away—but Beth had insisted on coming out to meet her father.

"Look at ye, Beth," Laila greeted her. "I know exactly how uncomfortable it feels."

"Aye." Beth halted before them and patted her protruding belly. "Especially in this heat."

Indeed, this summer had turned out to be the hottest in years, and even though Neave was wearing her lightest kirtle, she was still sweating. Beth's cheeks were flushed, and a light sheen covered her face. Likewise, her father and Laila, and the escort of warriors that followed them, all looked hot, bothered, and in need of a cool tankard of ale.

"Ye are radiant," George Munro said, moving to Beth, and taking her hand. "It warms my heart to see ye so happy, lass." He glanced then at Neave before winking. "And hopefully ye and John will start a family soon too."

Neave rolled her eyes. "Aye, Da … one thing at a time."

Her father nodded, his gaze shifting between his two eldest daughters. His gaze shadowed then, his smile faltering just a little. "I wish yer mother were alive to see ye both now," he murmured. "She'd be so proud."

"Oh, Da," Neave whispered back, her voice catching. "She's looking down on us … I'm sure of it."

"Munro!" A male voice echoed across the bailey, drawing their attention. A moment later, Neave spied her betrothed striding toward them. As always, the sight of John made Neave's belly flutter. Leather encased his tall frame today, as he'd just come back from a boar hunt with Niel and his men. Over the past days, since their return home, the pair hadn't had a moment alone. Preparations for the wedding had swept them both up. It was to be a grand affair, and all of the Mackay chieftains had been sent invitations.

Neave's sisters accompanied her everywhere, and she hadn't even had an opportunity to take a walk with him on her own. As such, she and John had to content themselves with lingering glances and the accidental brush of their hands.

John was smiling, his gaze warm as he clasped arms with the Munro clan-chief. "It's good to see ye again, George."

27

VISITING THE SEAMSTRESS

"YE CAN'T COME inside," Neave warned John. They were crossing the humpbacked bridge to the path that would lead them into Tongue. "It brings ill luck for a man to see his bride's gown before the wedding."

John snorted. "Ye don't believe in such superstitions, do ye?"

A stern look from Neave told him that she did.

His mouth quirked into a grin. "Very well, lass ... I shall keep guard outdoors."

"Worry not," Eilidh piped up. "I will stand near the door and make sure he doesn't peek."

Neave laughed. "And I'm glad to hear it."

John was accompanying Neave to the seamstress in Tongue. Beth was too heavy with bairn to come down to the village for the final fitting, and Jean was busy in the kitchens, overseeing the preparations for the following day's wedding banquet. However, Eilidh had been only too happy to join her elder sister today.

As she walked, Neave glanced up at the overcast sky. The air was heavy, and the day had a brooding, watchful quality to it. "I hope it doesn't start raining," she mused aloud. "Perhaps we should have *ridden* into Tongue."

"It won't rain until later," John assured her, "and making the trip on foot ensures we get to spend more time together."

Neave flashed him a smile. Indeed. She'd been pleased when he'd intercepted her and Eilidh, in the bailey on the way out of the castle, and offered to join them.

The trio continued into the village, past the kirk and the clusters of squat stone cottages with thatch roofs. They saw a number of locals on the way in, all of whom called out to them and waved.

Neave grinned back and greeted them in kind. The folk of Varrich and Tongue had welcomed the Munro sisters with open arms. After living here for a year and a half, she felt a strong sense of belonging.

Would she feel that way in her new home?

Glancing John's way, she caught his eye once more. "What are the folk like ... at Achness?"

"Much the same as here," he assured her. "It's a smaller community. My broch is half the size of Castle Varrich, although Achness village thrives." He paused then as if sensing her worries. "They will adore ye, Neave."

"Of course they will," Eilidh replied. Her younger sister was smiling, although her oak-colored eyes were veiled. Neave didn't need to question her to know she wasn't looking forward to the day Neave would leave them. For the first time ever, the sisters would soon be separated. "Neave brings sunshine wherever she goes." Eilidh flashed Neave a teasing look then. "When she's not sticking her beak into other folk's business."

"Eilidh!" Neave gave her sister a look of mock censure, even as John laughed.

"She knows ye well," he answered.

It was market morning, and as such, crowds thronged the dirt square at the village's heart. Tongue's market drew in vendors and folk from many miles around. Passing an enclosure where a farmer was haggling with a man over a flock of noisy, honking geese, Neave smiled.

She would miss this market too.

They crossed the square, weaving amongst the women carrying wicker shopping baskets, bairns who chased each other through the crowd, and the clusters of stalls selling everything from freshly cut cabbages and kale, to live fowl and goats. The seamstress's small workshop lay on the far side of the market square, in an alley.

However, it took a while to reach their destination, for every few paces, men and women hailed them, offering the couple their congratulations on their upcoming wedding.

John was loved here, for he'd ruled Varrich after Angus Mackay's death until Niel had returned from Bass Rock. Men slapped him on the back, while women grabbed Neave by the hands, their gazes gleaming with excitement.

Eventually though, the trio broke free of the press and entered a narrow lane. It was a shadowy alley, festooned with washing that they had to duck under to reach the seamstress's workshop, halfway down.

"Go on in then," John told the women. He then leaned up against the rough stone wall, folded his arms across his chest, and crossed his legs at the ankles. "I promise to behave myself."

"We shouldn't be too long," Neave assured him.

"Take as long as ye need," he replied.

Ducking inside, they entered a cramped space illuminated by lanterns. The seamstress, a tiny woman named Mòrag, perched on a stool before the hearth. Upon her lap sat a pale gold gown. She was stitching the hem, her gnarled fingers working with surprising dexterity. It wasn't a cold day, yet Mòrag was getting on in years. As such, she appeared to welcome the warmth that the small brick of peat threw out.

A wide smile bloomed across her lined face—removing at least a decade in an instant—at the sight of Neave and her sister.

"Lady Neave ... yer arrival is timely indeed." Nipping off the thread with her teeth, she then put aside her needle. "I've just finished yer gown."

Mòrag then rose stiffly to her feet and held up the garment for Neave to inspect.

Neave's breathing caught when her gaze alighted upon the lovely garment. The material shimmered as if it had caught the sunlight itself. The bodice was low and embroidered with tiny daisies, and flowers also adorned the long bell-sleeves and the hem of the gown.

"Oh, Mòrag," Neave murmured, her throat thickening. The last time she'd seen the gown, it had lacked all the embellishments. "Ye have such talent."

"Aye," Eilidh breathed. Moving forward, Neave's younger sister traced the embroidered flowers with her fingertips. "How did ye get this done so quickly?"

"My daughter and granddaughter both helped with the embroidery," Mòrag admitted. "We worked night and day to get it done in time."

Neave's vision misted. "I appreciate ye going to so much trouble."

"Och, well … only the best for ye, lass." The elderly woman's gaze glinted with pleasure, a smile creasing her face once more. "Let's see how it looks on ye."

John shifted position against the wall, listening to the rise and fall of excited female voices within the seamstress's workshop.

He couldn't make out their words, but from her tone, Neave appeared to be pleased with her wedding gown.

John smiled, a sense of well-being unlike any he'd ever known settling over him. He wanted her to be pleased—and he'd make it his mission in the weeks, months, and years to come to bring his wife as much joy as possible.

It wouldn't be a difficult task though, for Neave was a light-hearted woman who sought to find the good in all things. He knew in his gut that they'd be happy together. Their friendship had allowed the usual barriers between couples to be broken down early on. He'd been himself around Neave, and she'd been natural in his presence.

Nothing in his life before now had ever felt so right.

Glancing up at the strip of grey sky above, John hoped the weather wouldn't turn for tomorrow. Even so, the heaviness in the air warned him that a summer storm was approaching. The air was sticky, uncomfortable to breathe.

Nonetheless, nothing could dim John's mood today.

Now that George Munro had arrived, he and Neave could finally be wed.

This time tomorrow, ye shall be standing before Niel and swearing yer vows, he reminded himself. He should have been a little nervous about that—after all, he was eight and twenty and still unwed. Instead, he just felt as if, finally, his life made sense. John had known periods of loneliness over the years. Losing his parents young and then being thrust into lairdship at the age of seventeen had made him grow up faster than most. And then a succession of conflicts had taken up his time. His maiming had changed him, and there had been times since then when he'd wondered if he'd ever take a wife.

But now all those worries and the gnawing emptiness he'd sometimes felt had gone.

Life would be very different at Achness broch with Neave's vibrant presence. He wanted to ensure she was happy there.

Still smiling, John closed his eye and relaxed against the wall. *When we arrive at Achness, I will—*

John's thought cut off then as the scrape of a booted foot on dirt made his senses snap alert. With his eye closed, his hearing had sharpened, and although the scuffing sound was faint, it was unmissable.

His eye flew open, and he pushed himself off the wall, just as a huge man barreled through a screen of washing. The crisscrossing, low-hanging lines cut off John's view of the market square a few yards distant—he hadn't seen his attacker coming.

Roy Gunn raised his dirk high, the thin blade gleaming despite the dull day, and went for his throat.

There was no time for John to draw his own dagger, which he always carried at his hip, no time for him to do anything but duck out of the way.

Gunn smacked hard against the wall, his breath gusting out of him. Then, snarling a curse, he whipped around and lunged for John once more.

John circled him, ducking again as the swiping blade whistled past his face.

Roy Gunn's storm-grey eyes glinted, his heavy-featured face set in an expression of grim determination. It was a look John instantly recognized, for he'd seen it numerous times upon the battlefield.

A killing rage had Gunn in its grip.

There was no time to wonder how the bastard had managed to make his way back to Tongue unseen, or how he'd known John was in this alleyway.

Instead, John's entire focus was on avoiding that wickedly sharp blade.

And, unsurprisingly, Roy Gunn was good with it.

John jumped aside again. The dirk caught one of the sheets drying on the line nearest, the ripping sound of rending material filling the alley.

Gunn snarled another curse, and John took his chance, drawing his own blade.

His opponent's mouth twisted as the pair circled each other. "Ye think ye can beat me, *cripple*?" His voice was goading. "How good are ye with yer left hand?"

28

DEAD OR ALIVE

"IT'S PERFECT, MÒRAG." Neave wriggled from the gown, stepped out of it, and carefully bundled it up in her arms. She then handed it back to the seamstress. "I can't think of anything that would make it better."

The elderly woman beamed. She lay the gown out on a nearby table and rolled it up, ready to be carried back up to Castle Varrich. "That warms my heart, lass. A woman should look as bonny as a fairy queen on her wedding day."

"And she will do," Eilidh assured her. "I picked bluebells and snowdrops to weave through Beth's hair when she wed Niel ... and I will go in search of meadow flowers when we leave here, before the rain sets in."

"That's a fine idea," Mòrag replied with a nod. "The heather is in full bloom on Beltaine Hill at present ... and I saw some bonny primroses growing near the kirkyard."

Listening to the two women discussing flowers, Neave smiled. She then stepped back into her kirtle and began lacing up the front.

A loud thud intruded then, making her glance toward the door. Pale daylight filtered through into the interior of the workshop, yet she could see nothing. Dismissing it, she continued to lace up her bodice. Her simple blue kirtle was much easier to don than the gown. It had taken Eilidh a while to fasten her up at the back and then loosen the laces after the fitting.

A rough male curse cut through the humid air at that moment, causing Eilidh to break off mid-sentence. Face tensing, the lass turned toward the door. "What was that?" She then moved away from Mòrag, clearly intending to find out.

Alarm tightened Neave's chest, her instincts kicking in. "Eilidh, wait!"

However, it was too late. Her sister had already reached the door and peered through it.

And an instant later, Eilidh reeled back, her eyes wide when she whirled around. "John's fighting someone out there!"

"Who?"

Eilidh's face had gone as pale as milk. "The blacksmith … they've drawn their dirks."

Neave's heart leaped into her throat, and she rushed forward, squeezing past her sister to see for herself. Jaw clenched, she looked out into the alleyway to see John and Roy Gunn circling each other. John lunged forward then, attempting to slip under his opponent's guard. The thin blade of his dirk whistled through the air, narrowly missing the smith's chest.

Frozen in the doorway, Neave stared at the men, a chill sweeping over her.

What the devil was the blacksmith doing back here … and why had he attacked John?

The coldness in her limbs intensified. Gunn was deranged. If the man was capable of attempting to murder his own brother, he was capable of anything. He hadn't liked being bested by John at Beltaine, and had come back to deal with him.

Ducking another savage attack, John glanced Neave's way. His face was grim, his jaw set. "Get inside," he grunted before swinging his attention back to his opponent.

Gunn was relentless. Mouth twisted in a rictus, he came at John repeatedly, trying to back him into a corner. But John was faster, nimbler, and he wielded the dirk in his left hand as if he'd been born favoring his left rather than his right.

A pained grunt filled the alley as John's blade found its mark, slicing Gunn's lèine and cutting into his chest. Dark blood flowered across the soiled material, and

Gunn's hiss of pain filled the alleyway. "Now it's my turn to make ye bleed," he snarled.

Neave placed a hand to her throat, trying to calm her erratic breathing.

God's teeth, she couldn't let this go on. She couldn't just stand here and watch Gunn kill the man she loved.

Swiveling, she collided with Eilidh, who was peering over her shoulder. She pushed her sister aside and retreated into the workshop, surveying the interior for something she could use as a weapon.

Mòrag had settled back onto her stool by the fireside, her face sagging with concern as she waited the fight out.

Neave wouldn't do the same. Spying the iron poker leaning up next to the hearth, she grabbed it and made for the door.

"Careful, lass!" Mòrag called out, fear causing her voice to tremble. "Ye'd do well to stay out of this."

Neave ignored her.

Eyes as wide as moons, Eilidh stepped aside to let Neave move past her once more. "What are ye going to do?" she hissed.

"I don't know," Neave replied honestly. "But if I've got a weapon in my hands, I might be of some help to John."

Eilidh's lips parted once more as if to argue with her, but perhaps seeing the fierce look upon Neave's face, she held her tongue.

Neave peered outdoors again to see that the knife-fight had become more desperate, more violent. John was bleeding now, from a cut to his right forearm. Blood ran down his wrist, dripping off his wooden hand—yet he paid it no mind. Sweat glistened off his face as he ducked and swiped at his opponent, catching Gunn once more across the chest.

Snarling another curse, the blacksmith kicked out, attempting to knock his opponent off his feet. John stumbled and would have righted himself, if Gunn hadn't charged into him, slamming him hard against the wall of the alley.

A scream rose in Neave's throat, her heart now slamming hard against her breastbone.

It had to be now, while Gunn was going in for the kill.

Ignoring her sister's startled gasp behind her, she gripped the poker with both hands and darted forward. She then slammed her weapon hard against the back of Gunn's neck.

It was like hitting the solid trunk of a mighty oak—the impact was jarring and nearly made her drop the poker.

Roy Gunn grunted, his dirk slipping from his fingers. The weapon thudded onto the dirt at his feet. Reaching out to steady himself, he collapsed against the wall as John drove his dirk into his side.

Things moved quickly after that.

Despite that his opponent had just stabbed him, Gunn launched himself at John and head-butted him, sending him reeling. He then swiveled to face Neave.

His face was red, his dark-grey eyes wild and glazed with pain. His once grey lèine was now scarlet, soaked with his blood. Panting a curse, he lunged forward, ripped the poker from her hands, and flung it away. He then grabbed her around the throat, walking them both back so that she was pressed against the wall opposite.

Neave struggled, kicking at his legs and clawing at the hands that now tightened around her throat. However, the man's grip was Herculean. He didn't budge an inch. She was vaguely aware of Eilidh screaming, even as her lungs started to burn.

And then, the vise-like grip upon her windpipe loosened.

Choking, Neave slid down the wall, her hands reaching up to cover her aching throat.

Roy Gunn slumped sideways, a dirk buried to the hilt in his side.

Breathing hard, his own gaze shadowed with pain, and a purple swelling coming up on his forehead, John went to Neave, hunkering down next to her.

"Love," he rasped. "Are ye hurt?"

She shook her head. "I'm fine," she croaked. Her gaze then snapped left to where Roy Gunn had just crawled off, leaving a trickle of crimson blood behind him. "Don't let him get away, John!"

Mouth thinning, John gave a curt nod and turned, diving through the blood-splattered sheets in pursuit of Gunn.

His head throbbed in time with his thudding heart, yet John clenched his jaw and tried to ignore it—instead, he pushed his way through the lines of blood-smeared sheets, following the trail out of the alleyway and into the market square beyond.

Bursting out of the narrow lane, John halted, glancing left and right.

Curse it, he'd never seen this square so busy. It seemed that all the neighboring villages had emptied out and converged on Tongue this morning. News of his imminent wedding had clearly spread, and there was a festive air. A piper stood in the midst of the crowd, the wail of his Highland pipe cutting through the din of excited voices.

And Roy Gunn was nowhere to be seen.

Aware that he was attracting concerned looks, for he stood there blood-splattered and wild-eyed, John made for the stall nearest, where a man was selling turnips. "The man ye're after cut straight through here a few moments ago," the vendor told him, his gaze wide. He then gestured to the center of the square. "He was bleeding like a stuck pig ... he won't go far."

"Aye," another vendor—a man standing next to a carefully stacked pile of onions and garlic—added. "He looked half-crazed ... he almost knocked me down."

"Wasn't that Roy Morrison?" One of the shoppers asked.

"The name's Roy Gunn," John growled, shouldering his way through the press to follow in the direction the vendor had indicated. "And he's now got a price on his head."

John searched for Roy Gunn, yet he never found him.

Although he was badly injured, with John's dirk buried in his side, he was a slippery bastard. And even with half the men in Tongue hunting him—for news of a reward from John Mackay of Aberach for Gunn's capture spread like the pox through the market square—he eluded capture.

One of the villagers rode up to the castle to inform the clan-chief, and Niel and his men joined the hunt. They used dogs to track the fugitive, although his scent ended at the river that flowed into the Kyle of Tongue.

Gunn had taken to the water.

Standing on the bridge, rage hammering in his ears, John looked out over the kyle. The shallow sea loch wasn't easy to swim across, especially now as the tide was turning. Instead, he imagined that Gunn had waded upriver, hoping to lose himself in the hills.

Next to John, Niel muttered an oath. "I don't understand how he can disappear so easily," he growled. "The man must be half-fish to be able to escape by water."

John's mouth twisted, and he was about to answer when a voice interrupted them.

"Laird." Captain Reay approached upon a courser, his face creased into a deep scowl. "We found his camp in a valley north of here ... a garron and his smith's tools. He hasn't been back to retrieve them."

"No, there's no way he'd have made it, injured as he is," Niel replied. "Instead, he's using the river to elude us." The clan-chief then turned to the gathered crowd of men on foot and horseback surrounding them, and the panting wolfhounds. "Half of ye are to follow the river upstream. It breaks off into a number of burns farther up ... make sure ye follow each one and search the valleys surrounding them." Niel's gaze then narrowed. "The rest of ye are to scour the shore of the kyle ... just in case he was daft enough to try and swim across."

Muttering followed this comment. Few folk could swim well enough to attempt such a crossing.

"If he tried it, we'll likely find his body washed up somewhere," Ewan Reay pointed out.

Niel's mouth pursed. "Good." His gaze swept over the amassed crowd. "One hundred silver pennies to whoever catches Roy Gunn," he announced, doubling the sum

John had promised them earlier. "Bring him in dead or alive, it matters not."

29

TEMPTED

JOHN WINCED, HIS breath hissing between his teeth. Glancing up, Neave cast him an apologetic smile. "Sorry … I'm trying to be gentle."

With a sigh, John shook his head. "Ignore me, lass … I'm in an ill-mood this eve."

Putting aside the bottle of vinegar she'd just used to clean the cut to his forearm, Neave straightened up. They sat in John's chamber, perched on the edge of his bed. "I can't believe Gunn slipped our net … again."

John's usually good-natured face drew taut. "Neither can I," he muttered. "But they've been out hunting him for hours now … with horses and dogs … and he appears to have vanished."

"But that wound ye dealt him." Neave suppressed a shudder as she recalled his dirk, buried to the hilt in Gunn's side. "Surely, he couldn't have survived that?"

John's mouth thinned. The look on his face made a response unnecessary.

Roy Gunn was hard to catch and even harder to kill, it seemed.

Shifting her attention back to the cut on John's forearm, she was pleased to see it was a shallow one. "Ye'll be relieved to hear ye are only going to need a couple of stitches," she informed him. She then glanced up, her hand going to the swelling upon his forehead. "I have some salve that should make this go down by morning."

John snorted, his mouth curving in a humorless smile. "A fine pair ye and I shall look on our wedding day." He reached out then with his left hand, his fingertips tracing the livid marks upon Neave's neck. She watched his clear blue eye darken and his jaw clench. "I hope that bastard is lying in a ditch somewhere, gasping his last breath," he growled. "I hope he's suffering."

Neave swallowed. The ruthless edge to his voice reminded her—as it had when Roy had attacked her at Beltaine—that John wasn't lightly crossed.

Their gazes met and held, while his fingers traveled up her neck to her jaw. "Yer bravery is commendable, mo ghràdh," he murmured. "But please don't scare me like that ever again."

My love. The endearment made Neave's pulse kick up a notch. "I had to do something," she replied softly. "I couldn't stand by and watch. What if he'd killed ye?"

John's mouth quirked. "Do ye think he would have?"

Neave drew in a deep breath as irritation flared.

Men. Their arrogance was both appealing and aggravating. She knew John was a battle-hardened warrior and that he could hold his own in a fight—he'd recently proved that, once again, against the Sutherlands—but Roy Gunn had fought with a viciousness borne of desperation and hate.

"He *might* have," she pointed out, her voice then caught as she continued. "And I couldn't have borne it, John."

Their gazes fused, a weighty silence stretching between them.

"Aye, we'll stand before Niel bruised and battered tomorrow," she whispered huskily. "But at least we're alive."

He favored her with a soft smile. "And I'm grateful … I just don't like seeing an enemy get the better of me."

"He hasn't," she replied firmly. Her mouth pursed as she reached for the catgut in the healing basket she'd brought into the bed-chamber. "Fear not, Roy Gunn won't have a pretty end."

She then selected a needle and glanced up, meeting John's eye once more.

His eyebrows lifted. "This will be the second time ye've sewn me up, lass."

"And I'm hoping it will be the last."

His smile turned rueful. "I don't need any more scars … I'm already riddled with them."

Neave placed a hand upon the stump of his wrist, for he'd removed his wooden hand. "I don't see yer scars, John," she said softly. "I never have."

John fell silent while Neave sewed the wound with neat sutures. She then bound his arm with linen.

Watching her face, as she finished securing the bandage, he was aware of the rapid thud of his heart. Her last words had moved him more than she knew.

He waited until she'd gathered her things and placed them back in the basket, before reaching out and catching her hand in his.

"I've found a treasure in ye, lass."

Neave glanced up, her hazel-green eyes luminous. Her mouth then lifted at the corners. "Have ye?"

"Aye," he said huskily, drawing her to him. "Come here."

He pulled her onto his lap, his mouth finding hers.

It was a gentle kiss, yet a sensual one. His lips brushed against hers a few times before his tongue teased them apart.

And, as she had on the last occasion he'd kissed her, Neave melted against him.

A groan rumbled in John's chest. He kissed her with languid determination, his tongue slowly dueling with hers.

Heaven help him, she tasted too good to resist. Ever since his return from fighting the Sutherlands, and his proposal, he'd been unable to get a moment alone with her. He'd ached to kiss her again—and now they sat alone in his bed-chamber, he stole his chance.

The kiss deepened, turning wild now. However, having her perched on his lap wasn't enough. He wanted to feel her lithe body pressed up against his. Rising to his feet, John lowered Neave to the floor. He then drew her to him.

They fitted perfectly, and when Neave linked her arms about his neck—pressing herself harder still against him, welcoming the feel of his arousal—John forgot himself.

With a groan, he walked her back, pressing her up against the nearby wall. "God's teeth, woman," he ground out, as his mouth left hers and kissed its way down her jaw to her throat. "Ye drive me insane."

Neave gasped. She writhed against him, her fingers delving into his hair as he trailed kisses down her throat. He was gentle there, for the skin was bruised and he didn't want to hurt her.

Breathing hard, he drew back, his gaze spearing hers. "I'm burning up with need for ye," he growled. "I'm so close to dragging ye to my bed, tearing off yer clothes, and losing myself in ye."

"Do it then," she gasped, her eyes glazed with need. "I want this as much as ye."

"Neave." His voice was pained now. "I'm tempted ... so tempted."

Neave stared up at him, her lips, swollen from his kisses, parting. "Then give in to the temptation, my love."

Lord help him, he wasn't made of stone. "But, don't ye want to wait until tomorrow? We'll be wed then ... and I—"

Neave lifted her hand, placing a finger upon his lips to silence him. Her eyes gleamed, her chest rising and falling sharply. "Tomorrow is only a formality," she murmured. "Make me yers now ... in the only way that truly matters."

Her words freed him. Dragging in a deep breath, John moved away and bolted the door to the bed-chamber. He then returned to her, reached for the laces at the front of her kirtle, and began unlacing them. As he did so, he noted that his fingers trembled with eagerness.

It was as if he'd never lain with a woman before.

Once the laces were loosened, Neave wriggled out of her kirtle. It pooled at her feet, leaving her standing before him in nothing but an ankle-length lèine.

John stepped close once more. He then cupped her right breast and lowered his mouth to it, suckling her hard nipple through the thin linen of her lèine.

Neave writhed under him. She gave a soft cry of disappointment when his mouth left her breast, only to melt against him once more when he transferred his loving to her other one.

And when he rose to his full height once more, his lips capturing hers in a deep kiss, she trembled in his arms. His mouth mated hers, in a dance that mimicked the act he now craved.

He ached to be buried to the hilt inside her.

Pulling away, John reached down and yanked his lèine over his head, tossing it aside.

Neave watched him, her cheeks flushed, her lips parted.

John drank her loveliness in.

An instant later, she launched herself at him, linking her arms hard around his neck and pulling his head down to hers for a passionate kiss.

John forgot all else.

Her lips tasted so sweet, and her warm, pliant body felt so right in his arms. It was as if she'd been made for him.

Eventually, Neave tore her mouth from his, her breathing coming in pants as she trailed her mouth down his neck, her lips and tongue exploring the hollow of his throat, the planes of his chest.

John sucked in a gasp when she grazed his nipples with her teeth, before soothing each with her hot tongue. And then, when she dropped to her knees before him, her tongue tracing a wet path down from his navel to the waistband of his braies, his stomach muscles quivered.

He couldn't believe she was so being so bold—and it thrilled him. He shouldn't be surprised really, for Neave's saucy, teasing temperament should have told him that despite her inexperience, she'd be a lusty, willing lover.

All the same, his pulse quickened further when she unlaced his braies and pushed them down.

His rod sprang up to meet her, just as eager as he was to be touched.

Neave murmured an oath under her breath. She then cupped his bollocks with one hand, the other wrapping around his engorged length.

John couldn't help it; he let out a long groan.

"I don't know what to do," she murmured, her voice rough with need. He glanced down to see Neave was staring up at him, her lips—swollen from their kisses—slightly parted, her expression eager. "Will ye show me, John?"

Swallowing hard, John resisted the urge to haul Neave to her feet, throw her on the bed, and plow her.

The woman had no idea what she was doing to him.

"Aye," he rasped. "Here ... like this." Reaching down with his left hand, he adjusted hers around the base of his shaft. "Hold firmly, and then move up ... nearly to the tip ... that's it." His voice turned strangled. It was hard to speak when her fingers were wrapped around him like that. She eagerly followed his instructions, her other hand stroking his bollocks as she worked his rod.

"It's growing even bigger," she whispered, the awe in her voice making him choke back a laugh.

"Aye, lass." John closed his eye, his hand going to her hair, his fingers tangling in the soft, heavy waves. "It tends to when treated so well."

Neave gave a soft, throaty chuckle, the sound so sensual that John's belly muscles clenched hard, heat gathering at the base of his spine.

Lord, he didn't want to spill now, not when they were just getting started.

Neave slowed her hand then, her gaze fusing with his. The rasp of their breathing filled the chamber, while a flush spread across her cheeks. "Can I ..." She faltered then, before clearing her throat and trying again. "Can I ... suck on it?"

John went rigid, lust slamming into him with such force that an animal groan tore from his throat. The blend of innocence and seduction in this woman was turning him witless. "Aye," he rasped. "If ye wish."

A delighted smile curved Neave's lips at his response. And then she dipped her head, and put her mouth over the end of his rod, sucking him eagerly.

John threw his head back, another groan ripping from him. His fingers tightened against her scalp. The feel of her lips and tongue was too much. He couldn't endure this, not without exploding into that sweet, sinful mouth of hers.

Breathing hard, he stepped back and reached for Neave, drawing her to her feet. "That's enough of that," he growled.

"Why?" Her eyes were large on her heart-shaped face, and there was disappointment in her voice. "Weren't ye enjoying that?"

God's teeth.

"Aye," he replied, before reaching down and grabbing the hem of her lèine. "But this isn't just about me." He drew her thin tunic up, over her head. Neave helped him by raising her hands high above her.

A moment later, the lèine fluttered to the floor, and Neave Munro stood before him—gloriously naked.

30

PERFECT

JOHN STARED AT her.

"Ye are exquisite," he breathed, taking in her long, slender limbs, the gentle swell of her hips, and the dip of her waist. His gaze then settled upon her small, pointed breasts. In the glow of the guttering hearth in the corner of the chamber, her nipples looked like two ripe berries, ready to be devoured.

And sinking down before her, he did just that.

He'd enjoyed suckling her through the material of her lèine, yet now there was nothing separating them.

Neave started to make soft, mewing cries as he lavished attention on each breast, her fingers sliding through his hair, her fingertips digging into his scalp, urging him on. Eventually, John pulled back, rising to his feet once more.

His mouth slanted over hers, their tongues tangling, as he turned her, moving them both back toward the bed. And then, when the back of her knees hit the mattress, he placed his left hand between her breasts and gently pushed her down.

Neave went willingly, her arms reaching up for him.

The sight of her there—her richly-hued brown hair fanned out across the pillow, her pert breasts, their nipples glistening from his loving, straining toward him—made tension coil tighter still in the pit of John's belly. Sweat beaded his skin, and his shaft jerked, demanding to be inside her.

Clenching his jaw, John fought the primal urge.

His rod would have to wait a little longer yet to be satisfied.

Stretching out over Neave, his mouth claimed hers once again. He held himself up on his right elbow, while his hand traced a path between her breasts, and down her belly, to the soft chestnut curls between her thighs.

And when Neave parted her legs to give him access, and he felt her wetness and heat, need shuddered through John.

Her arousal, her wanting, was only too evident, and when he slid a finger deep inside her, she arched her hips, begging for more. John removed his finger before thrusting into her with two this time. He then curled his fingers upward and was rewarded by a rush of wet heat against his hand. Neave shuddered against him, while John continued to stroke his fingers deep into her.

Neave writhed, her fingernails racking his back.

Heat pulsed like molten ore through John's body. It was too much—he couldn't wait any longer.

Tearing his mouth from hers, he spread her thighs wide, took hold of his shaft, and guided it into her.

She was tight, yet so wet that he slid into her easily. However, since she was a maid, he did so slowly, watching her face all the while.

Neave's eyes went wide, her breathing quickening. "Oh, John," she whispered, her voice low and needy.

"I'm not hurting ye, am I, mo ghràdh?" he asked huskily.

Aye, she was his love. This woman was his everything.

"No," she sighed. "It's ... perfect."

Their gazes fused, although despite her encouragement, John still went slowly. She was so tight it almost pained him—and he wanted this coupling to be all about pleasure, for them both.

Sliding to the hilt, he halted a moment, letting her adjust.

Neave continued to stare up at him, her lovely tits rising and falling fast, a flush rising blooming across her cheeks. And then when he rolled his hips, moving inside her, her lips parted and her eyelids fluttered closed. "Oh … do that again!"

He complied, watching as her flush deepened, traveling down her neck to her chest.

John's gaze devoured her. Watching Neave gradually unravel was the most erotic sight of his life. He wanted to send her over the edge, wanted her to lose control completely.

Careful not to knock his bandaged wound, he hooked his right arm under her left knee. He then pulled the knee up, drawing her thighs even wider apart. Withdrawing almost to the tip of his rod, he slid deep once more with exquisite slowness, before reaching down and finding the exquisitely sensitive spot between her thighs with the pad of his thumb.

Neave's eyes snapped open, and her hips bucked against him. Her voice caught as she gasped his name.

"Aye," he murmured, sliding into her harder this time as his thumb stroked her. "That's right, lass."

She gave a loud, sensual moan, and John's self-restraint snapped. Moving over Neave, he thrust into her now with such vigor that the head of the bed slapped against the wall. Again and again, he took her, aware that they were both making a good deal of noise, their cries drifting up to the canopy above the bed.

It was fortunate that Castle Varrich had thick stone walls, yet John didn't care about the din they were making.

He had to lose himself in this woman. He had to make her his.

Hunger twisted in Neave's belly. The feel of his long, hard body against hers, the fullness of each plunge as he buried himself inside her, made it hard to think about anything else.

Leaning in, John kissed her once more. His tongue tangled with hers, the sensual slide setting every nerve in Neave's body alight.

His mouth was so hot, each thrust of his tongue moving in time with the glide of his shaft. Aching pleasure now pulsed through her lower belly, making her writhe against him.

She couldn't believe this was finally happening, that they had finally crossed the bridge from friends to lovers. After this, there would be no going back.

Gasping his name, Neave shattered.

She arched up, her body shuddering and her thighs trembling. And when John spent himself within her a moment later, his raw cry joining hers, she clung to him.

Sweat-slicked and panting, they lay entwined in each other's arms, letting the storm pass.

Neave's eyes fluttered shut, while her racing pulse gradually settled.

That had been better than her wildest dreams. No wonder Beth had blushed and given her a coy look whenever Neave had questioned her on what it was like to couple with a man. No wonder Beth and Niel spent hours entwined in each other's arms.

She'd found heaven on earth.

John propped himself up on his elbows then so that he didn't crush her, his lean, finely muscled body gleaming with sweat in the aftermath of their loving. He was still buried deep within her, and she had wrapped her legs around his hips, determined to keep him there for a while yet.

Neave glanced down at his bandaged forearm and was relieved to see it hadn't bled. Their lovemaking had gotten so passionate, she'd forgotten that he was injured.

She'd forgotten everything except John.

Having him buried inside her felt right.

She hadn't exaggerated earlier. It was perfect. And so was he.

The way he'd loved her, touched her: he'd made her body sing as if he were a minstrel and she his harp. Every stroke, every caress and kiss, had made wild need roar within her.

She felt boneless and utterly destroyed in the aftermath.

And when John's gaze eventually found hers, it gleamed with emotion. Swallowing hard, he reached up and brushed her hair away from where it had stuck to her sweat-damp cheek. "Neave Munro," he spoke her name huskily. "Where have ye been all my life?"

31

FEASTING AND DANCING

NIEL MACKAY BOUND his cousin and his sister-by-marriage in wedlock before one of the hearths in the great hall of Castle Varrich. Many couples chose to wed in the doorway of a kirk or chapel, but John had asked the clan-chief to perform the ceremony instead—a request Niel was happy to honor.

Outdoors, the stormy weather had arrived. Rain lashed the walls of the keep and hammered against the shutters. But no one paid the howling wind any notice, for all gazes were upon the man and woman who faced each other, their wrists bound by a strip of Mackay plaid.

John stared into Neave's eyes as he spoke the words that would bind them together. "I, take ye to be my wedded wife, to have and to hold from this day forward," he said, his voice carrying across the hall. "For better for worse, for richer for poorer, for fairer or fouler, in sickness, and in health, to love and to cherish, till death we part." He paused then, his fingers tightening around Neave's. "I plight ye my troth."

Gazing back at him, Neave swallowed the lump that had risen in her throat. Like all her sisters, she was prone to weeping at weddings. For that reason, she'd deliberately not looked their way as the ceremony had begun.

This was her own wedding, and she didn't want to dissolve into floods of tears.

Her chest ached with the force of the love she felt for the man standing before her, and when she spoke her vows, her voice kept catching. Likewise, his uncovered blue eye gleamed with emotion. Once they had both finished their parts, she and John turned their attention to their clan-chief.

Niel Mackay, resplendent in a black velvet lèine and chamois braies, with a sea-blue and emerald-green sash across his front, was smiling. Reaching out, he unwrapped the length of plaid that bound them.

"I now declare ye wed," he said, his smile widening into a grin before he favored his cousin with a wink. "Go ahead, and kiss yer bride, John."

Thunderous applause went up, shaking the walls and the heavy beams overhead, as John swept Neave into his arms, his mouth claiming hers. Neave clung to him, returning his embrace with equal fervor.

And when they drew apart, both breathless, Neave finally turned to look at the whooping, cheering crowd.

Her father's hazel eyes shone with tears, while next to him, Laila was delicately dabbing at her wet cheeks with the sleeve of her kirtle. However, Beth, Jean, and Eilidh were not so restrained. Nor was Greta, who stood with them. They were all smiling, yet tears ran unabashedly down their faces. Jean and Eilidh were clutching at each other, laughing as they wept.

Neave grinned back at them, even as her vision blurred.

This day was special, for it didn't just mark her union with John Mackay of Aberach, but a new chapter in her and her sisters' lives. Beth had brought them north with her to Castle Varrich, and they'd been relieved to be able to continue living under the same roof—but they'd always known this day would come. The day one of them would break their circle.

It was the way of life, and yet Neave's chest knotted at the thought of leaving them.

She knew then that, as much as she loved John, being parted from her sisters was going to break her heart.

The lilt of a harp and the soft strains of a woman's voice drifted across the great hall. The musicians and singer sat in the gallery on the far side of the wide space, providing entertainment for the rows of feasters who lined the long trestle tables within the hall. There were so many people packed in that there was barely space for servants to pass by, bearing ewers of wine, jugs of ale, and platters of food.

Seated next to her husband upon the dais, Neave watched as John served them both a selection of roasted meats, and vegetables braised in butter and garlic, onto the trencher they would share.

Glancing down the table then, Neave caught Janneth's eye. She and Breac had made the journey from Balnakeil. The chieftain's wife flashed Neave a warm smile, and Neave grinned back. Like Neave, Janneth was probably reflecting on how different their situations had been a month earlier.

Yet things had worked out for them all in the end.

Neave was also pleased to see that Hugh had attended the wedding. He sat next to Connor Mackay of Farr, regaling him with a long-winded story, a horn of mead in hand.

Iver Mackay of Dun Ugadale sat farther down the table, opposite Eilidh. The handsome young laird was clearly flirting with her sister, and Eilidh laughed at something he'd just said. Next to Eilidh, Jean and Robin Mackay were deep in conversation, and for once, the laird of Melness's face wasn't set in hard lines. Instead, he listened to Jean, his expression thoughtful.

Neave's smile lingered upon her lips as she watched her younger sisters. Aye, nothing in life ever stood still. Both Jean and Eilidh were comely and of marriageable age. It wouldn't be long before one of them received a proposal of marriage.

Neave's smile turned wistful. A few months earlier, she'd have stuck her nose in, would have questioned Jean and Eilidh about their feelings for Robin and Iver. She might have even tried to help nudge them in the right direction. But she now resisted the urge.

She would be there if they ever needed her—but she didn't need to take responsibility for their happiness.

Turning back to her husband, she watched while servants poured rich plum wine into their silver goblets. They then drank from each other's cup, their gazes fusing as they did so.

"I can't believe this day has finally come," John murmured before leaning in for a kiss, his lips brushing across hers. "The past days have crawled by."

"And if Roy Gunn had gotten his way, it wouldn't have come," Neave reminded him. She reached out, placing a hand over his forearm, bandaged under the sleeve of his lèine.

Captain Reay and his men were still out hunting the fugitive, but Neave sensed that, once again, he'd eluded them.

"Gunn was never going to keep me from ye, Neave," John murmured back, and although his voice was soft, the iron underneath and the glint in his eye that accompanied it made his feelings clear. "Nothing would."

The feasting and drinking lasted a long while. Although Beth hadn't been able to oversee the cooks' preparations for the wedding banquet, she'd ensured that Jean was her proxy. As such, course after course of delicacies were brought out, and the banquet concluded with a selection of cheeses accompanied by sweet bramble wine.

And once the wedding guests had savored their last mouthful, and sat sipping their wine, those seated below the dais rose to their feet and helped the servants push back the trestle tables and bench seats, creating a space for dancing.

Neave and John were the first to take to the floor.

He led her through dance after dance—without missing a step—and by the time they retired to their seats upon the dais, they were both flushed and out of breath.

Niel held his goblet up to them as they rejoined him and Beth. "That was a fine display," he said, his mouth curving.

"Aye," Beth added with a wistful sigh. "I've always wished I could dance like ye and Eilidh."

Neave smiled back at her elder sister. Beth and Jean were built differently to her and Eilidh—although small, they had curvier builds and ample bosoms that Neave had always secretly envied. "I can't compare with Eilidh," she admitted, nodding to where their youngest sister now glided around the dance floor like a swan. The music had gentled to a melancholy *basse danse*. Not surprisingly, Iver Mackay was her partner. The laird of Dun Ugadale danced well. He was tall and muscular, yet moved with a grace that belied his size, and his mane of ice-blond hair tied back at the nape of his neck gave him a striking appearance. It was clear the man was descended from the Norse who'd settled Scotland centuries earlier.

"Have ye noticed how Jean has taken a shine to Robin of late?" Beth asked then, drawing Neave's attention from the dancing.

Letting her attention travel down the table, Neave noted once again that Jean was chatting away to the laird of Melness. Robin said little, although he seemed the most relaxed Neave had seen him.

"I'm pleased to see that," John replied, as he too looked Robin Mackay's way. "I've hardly recognized Rob of late."

"Aye," Niel murmured. "He's a changed man ... but it'll take more than the company of a comely lass to heal what ails him."

A groove etched between Beth's eyebrows. "Yet it's a start. At least he doesn't look miserable today."

As they watched Robin and Jean interact, one of Niel's warriors approached the table. The music and the rise and fall of the surrounding conversation and laughter drowned out the man's words—yet it was clear he was asking Jean to dance.

The lass flushed before murmuring something to Robin.

Neave noted how he shrugged, a mask of indifference settling upon his face. She wanted to take Beth's view on things, to believe that Robin MacKay would find his way out of the darkness that shrouded him these days—but Niel was right. His wife's betrayal was a wound that festered still.

His reaction wasn't lost on Jean either, for her pretty face tensed.

Nonetheless, she recovered swiftly, squared her shoulders, and nodded to the warrior who had asked her to dance. A moment later, she rose from the bench seat and joined him upon the floor below.

Watching Jean join the dancing, Neave became aware of Beth's gaze upon her. She glanced back at her sister, catching the shrewd light in her eyes. Beth then leaned close. "Ye and John disappeared for a while yesterday," she murmured. "Where did ye get to?"

Neave was already flushed from the dancing, and as such, the warmth that rose to her cheeks didn't bother her. "I was tending his arm," she replied, feigning innocence.

"Aye?" Beth raised an eyebrow, not fooled for a moment. "A task that made ye both miss supper?"

This time, Neave merely smiled.

32

YE ARE MINE

NEAVE WATCHED AS Father Lucas exited the bed-chamber before she exchanged a look with John. Although the chaplain hadn't wed them today, he'd insisted on blessing the bed and the newlyweds before they consummated their vows.

And when the door whispered shut, her husband's mouth quirked into a boyish grin. He then rose from the bed, drawing Neave to her feet as well so that she faced him. "I thought he was never going to leave," he said, his gaze fusing with hers. "And all that feasting and dancing went on for an eternity as well."

"We could have left earlier if ye had wished," Neave pointed out with an arch look.

He stepped close to her before leaning down, his lips brushing across her cheek to the shell of her ear. "I wanted to leave after the cheese course," he whispered.

Neave's breathing hitched. It was hard to concentrate when he was standing so near, when his lips branded her skin. "And what stopped ye?"

"It seemed rude to not linger awhile," he murmured. His left hand was now trailing down her neck to the low-cut bodice of her gown, the back of his hand brushing the soft swell of her cleavage. "And Niel would have been merciless."

Neave huffed a laugh. "What ... are ye afraid of being teased by yer cousin?"

"Not about most things," he admitted. "But when it comes to my marriage, I find I'm a man who values his privacy."

Neave took this in. Aye, John was a private man. He also had a shy side to him—one that Niel sometimes enjoyed exploiting.

"This gown is lovely, Neave," he said, his fingers tracing the embroidered bodice. "But all I've been able to think about all day is peeling it off ye."

Her pulse quickened, and she drew in a shuddering breath. "Ye'll have to unlace my back," she said, her voice husky now. "It takes me an age to get in and out of this gown … usually, one of my sisters, or Greta, helps me."

Moving behind her, John started to loosen her stays. As he did so, he swept her hair out the way and placed a gentle kiss on the nape of her neck. "I like the crown of wildflowers in yer hair too," he said, a smile in his voice. "I have a bonny wife indeed."

His words made her heart race, made sweat bead her skin. The blend of gentleness and raw male sensuality in his voice caused her limbs to turn boneless. Weakness flooded over her, and she resisted the urge to sink down upon the bed. However, John hadn't yet finished unlacing the back of her gown.

He slid it down off her shoulders, and the golden damask pooled at her feet, leaving her clad in nothing but a thin shift.

"I want to see ye naked," he whispered in her ear, tickling her skin.

Heart pounding now, she turned to him. Neave then stepped out of the gown, nudging it to one side with her foot. Holding his eye, she reached down and grabbed the hem of her shift, pulling it over her head so that she stood before him, nude.

His gaze devoured her, sweeping down from the crown of her head, to her toes and back up again, and Neave's skin prickled in awareness. Aye, he'd seen her naked the day before, but everything still felt so new.

Not taking his gaze from her, John unstrapped his wooden hand, tossed it aside, and shrugged out of the fine dark-green lèine he'd worn for their wedding.

"It never ceases to amaze me," Neave said, watching him, "how well ye manage with just one hand."

He flashed her a wry smile. "I didn't in the beginning. I swear I turned the air blue with all my cursing and snarled at servants when they tried to help me. I was determined to be able to cope on my own."

"And ye have."

"Aye." His hand went to the tie of his braies, and he loosened it, his gaze still never wavering from hers. "I'm a stubborn one, Neave … as ye might have already noted."

Her lips curved, even if her mouth had gone dry. The sight of him undressing was sensual indeed. She longed to step closer and help him disrobe faster. But she restrained herself.

Moments later, he stood before her, as naked as she was. And, just as he'd done to her, Neave drank him in. The welt on his forehead had gone down considerably after she'd used a comfrey salve on it the eve before, and the bandage upon his forearm still looked fresh; the wound hadn't bled, even with all the dancing. Whorls of black hair covered his chest. The scars upon his torso gleamed silver in the candlelight. Her gaze then slid down his hard-muscled torso, to where his shaft strained against his belly.

"Ye are quite a sight, John Mackay," she breathed.

His gaze burned into her, his expression serious now. "As are ye, wife."

Shivering with pleasure, Neave rode her husband.

She slid herself up and down his length, with agonizing slowness at first, and then with increasing wildness. Tension coiled in her lower belly, seeking release. Her breathing came in ragged gasps, her skin now slick with sweat. She was lost.

Lost in John. Lost in spiraling, consuming pleasure.

In the end, they were both gasping and clutching at each other. John's grip on her hip held her fast, and he pulled her hard against him, each time she slid down his shaft. When he was buried deep inside her, he touched her in a place that made her dissolve.

John's face was feral with lust now, his jaw tight. And then he gave a hoarse shout, his body going rigid against hers. The heat of his seed rushed up, deep inside her. An instant later, Neave climaxed, a sob ripping from her. She arched back, tremors seizing her. Tension exploded deep in her womb, and delicious pleasure twisted within her.

Gasping, she collapsed in his arms, and for a while, the rasp of their exhausted breathing filled the chamber.

John was breathing hard, weakness flooding through his body, as he cradled his wife against his sweat-slicked chest.

He'd never experienced a joining like that one before—it wasn't just physical pleasure Neave gave him, but something far deeper: a completeness, a feeling of safety, of coming home.

When he was buried inside her, everything in this world was right. And all the hardships of the past faded into the mist. He'd felt capable of anything.

And now in the aftermath, a wave of tenderness swept over him, the sensation so strong that his throat thickened and his vision misted. Pulling Neave closer, he kissed the crown of her head, burying his face in her lavender-scented hair.

"Mo ghràdh," he whispered. "Ye are mine."

Neave raised her head, meeting his eye. Her own luminous hazel-green gaze glistened with emotion. "I am," she whispered huskily. Her small hand slid up then, from where it had been resting upon his belly, her fingertips tracing the whorls of dark hair upon his chest. Reaching up, she gently pulled up his eyepatch.

He stiffened. "What are ye doing?"

"Ye don't need to wear this at night, my love," she said, her voice low and sure. "Not when we're alone together. Don't hide from me, John."

She removed his eyepatch then and leaned forward, placing a feather-light kiss upon the hollow of his eye socket. She then set his eyepatch down on the table next to the bed.

Swallowing, John met her gaze again, even as discomfort tightened his chest. "Am I not unpleasant to look upon without my eye-covering?"

She shook her head, her elfin features firming. "Ye are a wonderful man, John Mackay … never forget that. Any woman would be honored to have ye."

John stared back at her, the pressure on his chest increasing. He hadn't wept in years, yet he was on the verge of doing so now. The way Neave was looking at him, the love in her eyes, made him feel *seen* in a way he never had before.

Her fingers trailed a tender path down his cheek as she favored him with a soft smile. "All I see when I look at ye is yer strength and courage. I'm proud to be yer wife."

They lay there together in drowsy silence for a while. Yet even sated and on the verge of falling asleep on his chest—Neave wanted John again. Her loins still ached, still throbbed, and without being able to stop herself, she wriggled against him.

John's eye opened, and a teasing smile stretched across his face, causing his cheek to dimple.

"A temptress ye are indeed, Neave," he said huskily. "Only, ye shall have to wait a wee while longer before I can give ye more of what ye crave." His eye glinted. "But fear not … I shall."

Neave grinned back. She then reached up, running her fingertips over his chest once more, following the course of that long scar that ran just under one of his nipples. "I'm glad to hear it," she murmured.

Laughter rumbled through his chest. "Christ's bones, woman … I should have offered for ye the moment ye arrived at Varrich last year. We could have been doing this for months now."

Neave gave a soft laugh, her hands now exploring the breadth of his shoulders. She adored his body, the lean iron strength of it. "Aye," she murmured. "But we weren't ready then, were we?"

"No," he agreed.

Nestling her head in the hollow of his right shoulder, Neave continued to explore the contours, planes, and hollows of his torso. She wanted to commit every inch of him to memory.

They lay in silence for a short spell, and when John spoke once more, the teasing, playful edge had gone from his voice. "So ... are ye now cured of yer need to solve other folk's problems, my love?"

Neave raised her head, meeting his eye. The directness of his question unbalanced her. "Of course."

He arched an eyebrow. "I'm not sure ye are ... some habits are difficult to break."

Neave gnawed at her bottom lip. "I suppose I'll always look out for my sisters. There's no harm in that, is there?"

"No ... but all the same, it's best to let them find their own way in life." He'd started to stroke her back now, and the feel of his fingertips sliding down the indentation of her spine was distracting.

"Of course," she murmured, before flashing him an impish smile. "Although ... sometimes people do need a little push in the right direction."

He snorted. "Ye, my love, are incorrigible."

33

LEAVE-TAKING

ONE WEEK AFTER Neave and John's wedding, Beth Mackay gave birth to a healthy baby boy. They called him Angus, after his grandfather.

Neave looked on as Niel Mackay took his son in his arms and stared down at the bairn. Raw emotion rippled across the clan-chief's face, and to Neave's surprise, a tear trickled down his cheek. "Good morning, lad," he murmured, his voice roughening. "Welcome to the clan."

"Angus is a fine choice of name," Beth replied. Her voice was weak, tired, for the birth had been a long one, yet happiness suffused her face as she leaned back against a nest of pillows. "May he inherit yer iron-will."

Niel snorted before glancing across at his wife, his eyes glinting. "Hopefully, he'll have *yer* character, my love."

"Aye," John piped up from next to Neave. Glancing his way, she saw he was grinning. "We don't want him growing up to be a prickly bastard, like his da." He'd slung an arm around Neave's shoulders, and squeezed gently.

Niel's mouth quirked at this comment. "I agree ... one of me under this roof is enough."

Laughter rippled through the chamber, and even though she was now wiping away tears of her own, Neave joined them. She and John weren't the only ones visiting the newborn. Jean and Eilidh were both hovering near the bed, clearly anxious to get a closer look at the bairn.

"His eyes are dark-blue, like yers, Niel," Eilidh breathed.

"All bairns' eyes are that color when they're born," Jean replied, only to receive an irritated look from her younger sister. "It's true," Jean persisted. "Ye shall have to wait a few weeks before the true hue reveals itself."

The bairn gave a squawk then, his mouth opening. A wail carried through the chamber, and a grin stretched across Niel's face. "Aye, well, he's certainly got a good set of lungs upon him." He perched on the edge of the bed, passing Angus back to Beth.

Watching the three of them together, the joy on Beth and Niel's faces as they stared down at their newborn son, Neave smiled through her tears. It was such a tender scene, and something tugged deep within her chest at the thought that she wouldn't be here to watch wee Angus day-to-day.

Aye, she'd visit a few times a year, but it wouldn't be the same. She wouldn't be here to look out for him, or her sisters.

Her throat constricted then, as her vision misted once more.

Suddenly, she felt torn. How she wished she could live at *both* Varrich and Achness.

Neave had known that she and John would depart Castle Varrich once Beth gave birth. Her father and Laila left two days after Angus's arrival, although Neave and John lingered for another week.

Yet the day of leaving-taking loomed all too quickly.

They couldn't stay on at Varrich any longer, for although the Sutherlands had been dealt with for the present, John was keen to return to Achness and rebuild the villages they'd razed. Over the past days, she'd noted the sadness that shadowed John's gaze whenever he mentioned the devastation the Sutherlands had brought to his lands and people. She couldn't blame him for wanting to rebuild what they'd destroyed.

A crowd of well-wishers, Beth and wee Angus among them, gathered in the bailey to see them off.

John and Neave traveled with an escort of his men, and Greta. The maid had asked to join Neave at Achness, a request that John had happily agreed to. Greta's cheeks were flushed with excitement this morning, as one of John's warriors helped adjust her stirrups before she mounted her sturdy garron. The maid had wept earlier when she'd bid Beth, Jean, and Eilidh goodbye. However, she appeared to have recovered now and was keen to be off.

Neave wasn't feeling quite so stoic.

She couldn't wait to start a new life with John, yet she felt as if something were twisting tight inside her chest. It was difficult to breathe as she hugged each of her sisters. Grief clamped around her throat.

"Don't look so bereft," Beth admonished her, even as her hazel eyes glittered with fresh tears. Angus, swaddled across her front in a sling, let out a soft wail as if sensing his mother's distress. "Ye aren't going that far … we shall see each other often." The tremor in her voice gave Beth away. Even though she was doing a fine job of keeping her composure, a storm raged within—as it did in Neave.

"Aye, but it won't be the same," Eilidh sobbed. The youngest of the sisters sagged against Jean, weeping noisily. "We've always been together until now."

"I know, lass." Neave stepped forward and pulled Eilidh into her arms. Her throat now ached, as if she'd tried to swallow a plum whole. "But this was never going to last forever … we knew that." They were brave words— ones that weren't just meant to reassure Eilidh, but herself.

Eilidh drew back, her oaken-colored eyes red-rimmed. "I thought it would."

The vulnerability and pain in her sister's voice nearly made Neave crumble. Thankfully, the lass had Jean at her side. Strong, sensible Jean, who even though her cheeks were wet with tears, clung to her self-control.

"I shall miss ye, Neave," Jean admitted huskily. "Aye, ye are insufferably bossy at times … but what shall I do without ye?"

"Ye shall have to be the bossy one in my stead," Neave replied, knuckling away the tears that now flooded down her own cheeks. "Someone has to make sure Eilidh behaves herself."

Their youngest sister gave an unladylike snort, but all three of them were now smiling, the mood lightening.

Neave glanced then over her shoulder at where John stood with their horses. He'd said little since they'd gone outside to ready themselves for their departure. His expression was veiled, although she spied the shadow in his clear blue gaze. He'd known this would be an emotional scene—there had been no way around it.

John had kept himself busy of late. He'd joined the hunt for Roy Gunn, but the man had disappeared once more. Niel had even sent a party to Inverness, but there was no sign of him there either.

The clan-chief had also joined them this morning. He stood behind Beth and shifted awkwardly at the outpouring of feminine emotion. Like John, he too remained silent, not rushing their goodbyes.

Neave appreciated that John and Niel didn't try to brush aside the sadness this farewell brought. Aye, she would be living just two days' ride away, but the bond between the four Munro sisters had always been something special, and after their mother's death, it had grown stronger still.

And as much as Neave wanted to go to Achness, as much as she wanted to be the mistress of her own home, she wished bidding farewell to her sisters didn't feel as if she was leaving part of herself behind.

"We shall be back before ye know it," she promised Eilidh, pulling her sister into another hard hug. "Samhuinn will be here soon."

"Aye … we won't miss that," John assured them, speaking up finally. "And we will be back for Yule, as well."

"Can we visit ye at Achness?" Jean asked, casting John a hopeful, if shy, look.

He favored her with a wide smile, one that dimpled his cheeks. "Of course, lass ... ye are all welcome in my hall."

Warmth spread through Neave's chest at these words, easing the twisting pain under her breastbone. Aye, this wasn't the end, just another chapter of their lives. Tears and discomfort were part of it—just as much as excitement and joy.

"I can hear the river," Greta called out, her excited voice cutting through the twitter of birdsong and the whisper of the wind. "We must be close."

John twisted in the saddle, flashing Neave's maid a grin. "Ye have fine hearing ... ye shall see the falls shortly, to yer right." He then cast a look in Neave's direction. "I hope ye are as excited about seeing yer new home?"

Neave smiled back. "Of course."

Nonetheless, she saw the concern in his gaze. Although she'd tried her best to cheer up, a subdued mood settled over Neave when they'd set out south. For the first day of their journey, she'd found herself lapsing into long periods of silence—unusual indeed for a woman who loved nothing more than to talk.

John had marked her low spirits, yet he'd let her be. But she'd noted the question in his voice. He was worried she was regretting her decision to come away with him.

Urging her mare up close to him so that their knees brushed, Neave reached out, placing her hand upon his thigh. "I can't wait to see it, John."

The tension on his face eased a little, although he still looked unconvinced. "The broch isn't as fine as Varrich ... or Foulis."

Neave harrumphed. "I care not about that."

The tall pines to their right parted then, and Neave caught sight of the rushing River Cassley. They had left the wild open glens and hills south of the Kyle of Tongue behind and were in the midst of Rosehall Forest—a dark press of scented pine, nestled amongst birch, alder, and oaks. The air was cool and crisp, and laced with the smell of moss, damp peaty earth, and conifers. It was fine hunting territory, and they'd spied a number of fallow deer darting across their path during the journey. It was a largely uninhabited area, although they'd just passed through the hamlet of Rosehall.

And then a moment later, the Falls of Achness themselves hove into view. Water foamed over rough rocks, cutting through a craggy, wooded gorge. There were a series of falls, descending into dark pools.

Neave breathed the fresh air deep into her chest, a wide smile flowering across her face. "It's spectacular," she breathed.

"And deadly," John replied. His voice was quiet, although there was no missing the edge. "Ye must be careful where ye bathe here."

A shadow fell over them then, as Neave recalled this was the spot where his parents had been swept to their deaths. Indeed, one glance at the river and she could see that one would have to be attentive. The pools themselves were tranquil enough, but the river was a raging torrent. Even a strong swimmer wouldn't be able to break free of the current.

They rode on, eventually reaching the village of Achness. Children rushed out to greet them, squealing when they spied their laird. Men and women emerged from their thatched cottages shortly after. It was getting late in the day, and the sky was now darkening. The laird of Achness's arrival had interrupted their supper.

They called out to John, smiles creasing their tanned faces, and he waved back, greeting some of them by name.

Neave's mouth curved. Of course, this was a tight-knit community; John would likely know everyone here.

They passed through arable fields then, farmland that had been cut out of the surrounding forest, the road hugging the path of the river. And there, rising above the trees, Neave spied her new home for the first time.

Achness broch appeared an ancient construction, its stacked-stone bulk encrusted with mildew and moss of the centuries. A new tower rose from what appeared to be a much older original building. A high wall, where fires had just been lit with the coming of dusk, encircled the broch. Firelight illuminated the craggy stone.

Neave's breathing caught. She wasn't sure what she'd been expecting, but Achness broch surpassed all her expectations. It was a part of the landscape, built of the same rough dark stone as the nearby waterfalls.

"What do ye think, Neave?" John's voice intruded then, and she caught the edge to it. He was worried she'd find it too humble for her tastes. She swung her gaze to him, grinning. "I love it."

His mouth quirked. "Ye do?"

"Aye … don't sound so surprised." She glanced back at the tower that now loomed over them. "How old is it?"

"No one really knows," he replied. "My grandfather said the original round tower is over a thousand years old." He paused then. "And locals say that the broch was built upon a fairy mound … and that the Mackays of Aberach have Aos Sí blood running through their veins."

Neave smiled, casting him a veiled look. "And do ye believe such tales?"

He inclined his head. "I did once … I used to go hunting for brownies as a lad."

Her smile widened. "And did ye find any?"

"No." His gaze turned intense. "But I did find my own fairy maid one day."

They stared at each other a moment, while ahead, the rumble of the gates opening greeted them.

"Ye aren't grieving too deeply about leaving yer sisters, are ye?" he asked then, clearing his throat as if embarrassed by his words. "I never wanted our union to bring ye pain."

"No," she answered honestly. Aye, her heart had been heavy upon leaving Castle Varrich, but with each furlong south, it had gradually lightened. She'd needed time to ponder things, to accept this parting. Saying goodbye to her sisters had been hard, but as she rode toward her new life, excitement had quickened in her belly, and the pressure on her chest eased. An adventure lay before her, one she wouldn't shy from.

"Goodbyes are never easy," Neave admitted then, her mouth lifting at the corners, "but without change, life would be dull indeed." She urged her mount up the causeway toward the open gates, before glancing her husband's way, her smile widening. "And how can I be sad for long ... when I wed my best friend?"

EPILOGUE

I CHOOSE YE

Three months later ...

"NEAVE ... WILL YE come with me? I have a surprise in store."

Glancing up from where she was sorting through a basket of wool, Neave raised her eyebrows. "A surprise?"

"Aye, my love. Will ye allow me to lead ye to it?" John walked into the solar and held out his hand.

Next to the Lady of Achness, Greta let out a giggle. Looking at her maid, Neave spied a knowing glint in the lass's eye. It seemed that Greta knew what was awaiting her.

Neave's breathing quickened, curiosity blooming. Over the past three months, John never failed to surprise her. Of course, he was as loving as she'd expected, and the ease of their relationship, which had grown from a deep friendship, came as no shock.

However, the little things he did for her—the meadow flowers he'd bring, the long massages after a busy day, the rides alone together, and the spontaneous hunting expeditions—were an unexpected delight. John was more playful and romantic than she could have ever hoped for. Neave was his world—and he never missed the opportunity to prove it to her.

Sometimes, Neave would stand at the window of the solar and gaze out at the dark-green carpet of pines, with the purple outline of the surrounding mountains forming a protective cradle around them, and a sense of contentment so profound that her eyes would sting with tears would settle upon her.

She hadn't seen her sisters since her arrival at Achness, although she wrote to them regularly, and received frequent missives from the trio. Samhuinn was approaching—the nights were drawing in, and the morning and evening air held a bite. Soon she would be reunited with her siblings once more.

However, it had surprised her how quickly the ache of loss under her breastbone had eased. Aye, she missed Beth, Jean, and Eilidh, yet with each passing day, she worried less about how they were faring.

Somehow, over the past months, she'd learned to let go.

Rising to her feet, she flashed Greta a smile, before stepping toward John. "Where are we going?"

"Ye'll see soon enough," he replied cryptically. "Although, ye'll need a shawl, love ... the air's a bit chilly out."

Neave's curiosity deepened as she retrieved her favorite woolen wrap, took her husband's hand, and let him lead her from the solar, and down the narrow stone steps to the hall below. Servants were readying the space for the noon meal, which wasn't far off, and the rich smell of braising mutton wafted in from the kitchens.

They didn't linger in the hall. Instead, John led her down the steps from the broch into the barmkin—a defensive enclosure around the base of the tower— below. A chill breeze gusted down from the mountains this morning, and Neave shivered, drawing her shawl tightly about her. Dressed in a quilted gambeson and heavy braies, her husband didn't appear to notice the cold. Instead, John wore an enigmatic smile as he turned left and lead her past the stables.

On the way, they passed Murtagh, John's steward. He was giving instructions to a servant before the entrance to the granary, although he looked up as the laird and lady of Achness approached.

The older man's weathered face creased into a grin at the sight of them. "So, today's the day, is it, Laird?"

John smiled back. "Aye."

"It seems everyone here knows about this ... except me," Neave observed.

John cast her an arch look. "Well, it wouldn't be a surprise if ye did, would it?"

At the western edge of the barmkin sat a postern gate.

Neave's brow furrowed at the sight of it, for although she'd explored most of the broch, the tower, and its barmkin and out-buildings, John had told her that he kept his hunting dogs in the western enclosure, and she wasn't to venture there. A few of the dogs were dangerous, he'd explained, and he didn't want any of them attacking her.

"Are ye going to gift me a pup?" Neave asked with a coy smile. She liked the thought of having her own faithful hound, trailing her heels.

He shook his head. "That isn't yer surprise, mo chridhe ... although if ye wish for a wolfhound or collie of yer own, it can be arranged."

Pushing open the gate, he led her through—into a wide, walled space.

Neave's breathing caught, and she halted, her gaze sweeping over the symmetrical lines of empty plant beds, intersected by pebble-strewn paths.

"John," she breathed, squeezing his hand. "Ye have built me a garden?"

"Aye," he replied. "I know how much ye loved that terrace garden at Varrich ... and I thought it was time ye had one of yer own." She glanced his way to see that he was watching her face, marking her reaction. "Do ye like it?"

A wide smile bloomed over Neave's face. "I adore it!" She flung herself at him, wrapping her arms around his neck and drawing him down for a kiss. As often, her husband smelled of leather, mixed with the scent of wood smoke and the spicy musk of his skin that was uniquely him. The kiss drew out, and for a few instants, Neave forgot the garden.

She eventually broke away, her hands sliding down to his chest, where they splayed.

"At the moment, all our food is grown in the fields beyond these walls, yet a garden this size will feed every resident in this broch ... with a surplus for the villagers as well," she told him, as she struggled to catch her breath. "Ye wait ... ye won't recognize it in a year."

"It does look barren at present," he admitted, pulling a face. "However, it's getting late in the year ... and I knew ye would want to choose what to sow."

Neave nodded. Indeed, planning out which vegetables and herbs to plant was part of the joy of gardening. "There are a few vegetables I can sow for the winter," she replied. She'd brought cabbage, turnip, and kale seeds—tightly wrapped in oiled leather—with her from Varrich, hoping that one day she'd have use for them.

Stepping away from John, she walked the paths that crisscrossed the garden, while she mentally planned out what she would plant and where. Finally, she swiveled upon her heel and flashed him another smile. "I should like to espalier apples and pears against the walls ... to make every inch of this garden useful."

"And so ye shall," he replied, meeting her eye. "And whenever I lose my wife over the coming months, I will know where to find her."

Neave favored him with another playful smile. "Aye, ye have made certain that I will never grow bored with a garden like this to tend."

He smiled back. "I know that yer garden at Varrich was yer sanctuary ... and so can this one be."

Neave's expression sobered. "I no longer need to seek refuge from the world," she said softly. "Not now. Not with ye by my side."

John approached her, halting when they were almost touching. Then, reaching up, he cupped her cheek. "Are ye truly happy here, Neave?"

Staring up at him, Neave was surprised to see a flicker of insecurity in his clear blue eye. Even after three blissful months, her husband worried she wished she were back in Varrich, watching over her sisters and wee nephew.

Neave's throat constricted. She couldn't let him doubt her. She'd have to put him right on this and ensure he never worried about such things again. Lifting her own hand, she placed it over his. "If I were any happier, my heart would burst," she murmured. "Aye, I miss my sisters ... but I chose to leave them, to be here at Achness ... I choose ye, John Mackay of Aberach."

And then, not awaiting his response, she stood up on tip-toe, leaned into her husband, and kissed him once more.

The End

FROM THE AUTHOR

I hope you enjoyed the second installment in the COURAGEOUS HIGHLAND HEARTS series.

Neave and John's story was so heart-warming to write. I love the idea of falling in love with your best friend—in fact, it happens often in 'real life' too … it happened to me! As such, I had a lot of fun developing Neave and John's friendship, before they realize they have deeper feelings for each other. I loved their banter and the respect they have for each other. They are both adorable!

Neave is such an irrepressible character, and John is a swoon-worthy blend of warrior strength and gentleness. I love what a gentleman he is, and how Neave helps him overcome his insecurities about his battle injuries.

Get ready for Jean and Robin's emotional story, up next!

Jayne x

HISTORICAL NOTES

As with all my novels, I've based HIGHLANDER TEMPTED around real historical figures and events.

Just like Niel Mackay (who was actually John's half-brother rather than his cousin), John Mackay of Aberach is a real historical figure. In reality, John Mackay didn't wed Neave Munro (he married a daughter of the chief of Clan Mackintosh instead), but for our story, I have altered history a little!

John famously led the forces of Angus Mackay against the Neilson Mackays in the Battle of Drumnacoub, which took place in 1433. This conflict was between the Mackays, whereby Neil Neilson Mackay and Morgan Neilson Mackay challenged Angus Mackay's rule (with assistance from the Sutherlands). Although the battle ended in victory for the Mackays, John suffered grave injuries. Some records mention him possibly losing an arm, but I decided on the loss of a hand and an eye instead. It was a bloody battle—very few from around 3,000 men (around 1,500 on either side by some estimates) were left standing.

After the battle, a despairing Angus Mackay asked to be carried to the battlefield to search for John, but an opportunistic Sutherland archer spotted him and killed him with a well-aimed arrow.

John headed the Mackay clan after the battle, but when Niel Mackay escaped from imprisonment at Bass Rock and made his way back north (it turned out the governor was married to a Mackay, and she possibly helped him break out), John deferred to the legitimate heir. In thanks for his loyalty, Niel gifted John the land around Lochnaver.

The skirmish with the Sutherlands at the end of this novel is entirely fictionalized. However, there are accounts that Robert Sutherland—the Sutherland clan-chief at the time—carried resentment toward John Mackay after Drumnacoub. Indeed, Sutherland had promised his two daughters to the Neilson Mackays as part of their alliance, but both men fell in battle. Some historical sources mention that he tried to kill John in the months following the battle.

Castle Varrich was the seat of the Mackays. Built out of sandstone, the castle perches upon a high point of rock, overlooking both the Kyle of Tongue and the village of Tongue. The castle's precise origins and age are unknown, although some historians believe it is over a thousand years old, and the medieval castle may have been built atop a Norse fort. The original castle had two floors, plus an attic. The ruin is located around one hour's walk away from the village of Tongue. It has views of the mountains Ben Hope and Ben Loyal.

The Mackays of Aberach did indeed reside at Achness. I couldn't find any reference to their broch, so I created my own. However, the Achness Falls and River Cassley are real locations. I imagine John Mackay's stronghold lay nearby.

I hope you have enjoyed my notes. I really enjoyed researching the history and landscape of this wild and beautiful corner of Scotland.

COURAGEOUS HIGHLAND HEARTS CHARACTER GLOSSARY

The Mackay clan

The Mackays of Varrich
Beth Mackay (neè Munro—Niel's wife)
Niel Mackay (Mackay clan-chief)

The Mackays of Farr
Connor Mackay (Mackay chieftain—laird of Farr Castle), married to Keira (they have three children: Rose, Rory, and Quinn)
Morgan Mackay (Connor's brother), married to Maggie (they have one daughter, Tara)
Jaimee Mackay (Connor's sister), married to Alexander Gunn (they have two children, Anice and Aodhan)
Kennan Mackay (Connor Mackay's cousin), married to Cait (they have two sons, Blake and Logan)

The Mackays of Loch Stach
Hugh Mackay (Mackay chieftain—laird of Loch Stach)
Janneth Mackay (Hugh Mackay's daughter)

The Mackays of Aberach
John Mackay (Mackay chieftain—laird of Achness—Mackay clan-chief's cousin)

The Mackays of Melness
Robin Mackay (Mackay chieftain—laird of Melness broch)

The Mackays of Balnakeil
Breac Mackay (Mackay chieftain—laird of Balnakeil broch)

The Mackays of Dun Ugadale
Iver Mackay (Mackay chieftain—laird of Dun Ugadale)

The Gunn clan
Tavish Gunn (clan-chief)
Roy, Blair, Evan, and William Gunn (Tavish's younger
brothers)

The Munro clan
George Munro (Munro clan-chief)
Laila Munro (the clan-chief's wife)
Fionn Munro (the clan-chief's son)
Neave Munro (the clan-chief's daughter)
Jean Munro (the clan-chief's daughter)
Eilidh Munro (the clan-chief's daughter)

Other characters
Greta (maid to the Munro sisters)
Father Lucas (chaplain at Castle Varrich)
Cullodina (healer at Farr)
Tess (healer at Varrich)
Ewan Reay (captain of the Varrich Guard)
Murtagh (steward of Achness)
Mòrag (seamstress in Tongue)

ABOUT THE AUTHOR

Award-winning author Jayne Castel writes epic Historical and Fantasy Romance. Her vibrant characters, richly researched historical settings, and action-packed adventure romance transport readers to forgotten times and imaginary worlds.

Jayne is the author of a number of best-selling series. In love with all things Scottish, she writes romances set in both Dark Ages and Medieval Scotland.

When she's not writing, Jayne is reading (and re-reading) her favorite authors, cooking Italian feasts, and going on long walks with her husband. She lives in New Zealand's beautiful South Island.

Connect with Jayne online:
www.jaynecastel.com
www.facebook.com/JayneCastelRomance
https://www.instagram.com/jaynecastelauthor/
Email: contact@jaynecastel.com

www.ingramcontent.com/pod-product-compliance
Lightning Source LLC
Chambersburg PA
CBHW021115110726
47900CB00007B/2195